CL

PRAISE FOR THE ANIM███████████████.ES:

Catwalk:

"Smart characters and intricate plotting.

—*Booklist*

"For a story that wins a blue ribbon for entertaining readability, *Catwalk* is purr-fect."

—*The Free Lance-Star*

"Janet MacPhail's latest adventure will delight dog lovers, cat lovers, and mystery lovers … Five stars for *Catwalk*!"

—Susan Conant, author of the *Dog Lover's Mystery* series

The Money Bird:

"Equal parts mystery and dog appreciation, with a dash of romance thrown in for good measure, this second case for Janet and her pals … is accessible to fans of all three."

—*Kirkus Reviews*

Drop Dead on Recall:

"Boneham packs a punch in her series debut."

—*RT Book Reviews*

"A smart first mystery. Fans of Laurien Berenson or Susan Conant will especially enjoy this pet-centered mystery."

—*Booklist*

"Boneham's debut will delight dog fanciers."

—*Kirkus Reviews*

"[A] delightful debut. Right up there with the likes of Sue Grafton (Kinsey Millhone novels) and Janet Evanovich (Stephanie Plum novels), without the profanity. An intriguing whodunit."

—*The Australian Shepherd Journal*

"With a sense of humor, a light touch of romance and a solid base of dog training experience under her collar, Sheila Boneham's first novel is worthy of honorable mention."

—*The Free-Lance Star*

"Sheila Webster Boneham's mystery, *Drop Dead on Recall*, is drop dead good. The writing sparkles and the dog-obedience competition setting unleashes a surprising hotbed of motives and opportunities for multiple murder. Animal photographer Janet MacPhail makes a, yes, dogged amateur investigator, dealing with her mother's Alzheimer's and maybe a new midlife beau between finding a vicious killer. The dogs, Labs and Aussies, and cat, Leo, are of course key players in the proceedings. Five enthusiastic arfs."

—Carole Nelson Douglas,
bestselling author of the *Midnight Louie* mysteries

"Sheila Webster Boneham's delightful debut mystery combines a likeable sleuth, a keep-'em-guessing plot, and wonderfully authentic portrayals of the human and canine denizens of dogdom. First place with a perfect score!"

—Susan Conant, author of the *Dog Lover's Mystery* series

Shepherd's Crook

OTHER BOOKS BY SHEILA WEBSTER BONEHAM

Shepherd's Crook

SHEILA WEBSTER BONEHAM

3 1336 09849 6871

MIDNIGHT INK
WOODBURY, MINNESOTA

Shepherd's Crook: An Animals in Focus Mystery © 2015 by Sheila Webster Boneham. All rights reserved. No part of this book may be used or reproduced in any manner whatsoever, including Internet usage, without written permission from Midnight Ink, except in the case of brief quotations embodied in critical articles and reviews.

FIRST EDITION
First Printing, 2015

Book format by Teresa Pojar
Cover design by Lisa Novak
Cover Illustration by Gary Hanna
Editing by Rosemary Wallner

Midnight Ink, an imprint of Llewellyn Worldwide Ltd.

This is a work of fiction. Names, characters, places, and incidents are either the product of the author's imagination or are used fictitiously, and any resemblance to actual persons, living or dead, business establishments, events, or locales is entirely coincidental.

Library of Congress Cataloging-in-Publication Data

Boneham, Sheila Webster, 1952

  Shepherd's crook / Sheila Webster Boneham.—First edition.

    pages ; cm.—(An Animals in Focus Mystery ; #4)

  ISBN 978-0-7387-4487-2

  I. Title.

  PS3602.O657155S34 2015

  813'.6—dc23

                                      2015020894

Midnight Ink
Llewellyn Worldwide Ltd.
2143 Wooddale Drive
Woodbury, MN 55125-2989
www.midnightinkbooks.com
Printed in the United States of America

For Roger

ACKNOWLEDGMENTS

Writing a book can be a lonely endeavor, and I am fortunate to have a supportive community of people and animals who keep me connected. I can't possibly thank everyone by name, but if you have ever talked to me about books or animals, please know that you're part of my journey as a wrtier and a reader. Still, a few people deserve special mention.

Corey Norman and April Bruce shared hilarious herding-dog stories, some of which I've adapted for the book. The Aussie Rescue & Placement Helpline (ARPH) raffled off a guest part in the book, and Crystal Anne Aguilar went above and beyond to promote the event. Thanks to everyone who played to support Aussie Rescue, and especially to the winner, Lilly, and her human, Jean Becker Inman—it's been great fun interacting with you ladies. Brenna Spencer and Rhonda Calhoun Mullenix of Lumos PhoDOGraphy graciously provided reference photos for the cover. They also talked Donald Schwartz, VDM, into volunteering his legs—much appreciate, as not everyone is willing to be hanged for a book cover. Thanks to all of you!

My critique partners Nancy Gadzuk, Charlene Pollano, Georgia Mullen, and Mike Connolly gave helpful feedback on parts of the book, and my sharp-eyed friend Linda Wagner read the full manuscript and, as always, helped me see what did and didn't work. The folks who turned the manuscript into the book deserve special tail wags—Lisa Novak for designing the beautiful cover, illustrator Gary Hanna for turning my cover concept into art, Teresa Pojar for designing the interior of the book, and copyeditor Rosemary Wallner for making the book better. Remaining booboos are, as always, mine.

My agent Josh Getzler has championed the Animals in Focus series since the beginning. Plus he's a funny guy, which never hurts. Thanks, Josh!

As always, my deepest gratitude goes to the animals who enrich my life and inspire me in so many ways.

"Here lies the body of Thomas Kemp, lived by wool died by hemp."

(at the grave of a man hanged for sheep stealing, Larne, County Antrim, Northern Ireland)

ONE

THE DOG SHOULDERED THE gate open and dove into the pen, intent on driving the sheep into the open. Five of the animals bolted through the gap while seven more huddled in a back corner and eyed the little predator as she stalked them along the back fence. The sheep edged deeper into the corner, seemingly unable to think themselves out of their self-made trap.

A series of sharp yaps shattered the silence, and the dog, a black-and-white Shetland Sheepdog, catapulted her twenty-five pounds toward the tail end of the nearest ewe. The rest of the flock scooted out of the corner and through the gate, but the one closest to the dog turned to face her tormenter, head low, ears forward. The standoff seemed to go on and on, but judging by the number of pictures I clicked off, it all happened in about four seconds.

Did I mention that I'm a professional photographer? Janet MacPhail, at your service. Technically I wasn't working. I was spending the weekend at the Northeast Indiana Herding Club's Dogs of Spring event with my Australian Shepherd, Jay, to try for a herding instinct certificate. Jay's the one with the instinct. I just hoped to stay out of his way and on my feet.

As always, I had my camera with me and I hoped to get some nice shots during the two-day event. Besides Saturday's instinct test and herding clinic, the club had a full agenda planned for Sunday. To draw spectators, there would be a herding demonstration with experienced dogs; a parade of the herding breeds; an all-breed disc-dog competition; and displays by a dozen or so vendors, breed clubs, and rescue groups. There would also be a dog-and-owner lookalike contest. I was still trying to talk Tom Saunders into entering with his Lab, Drake.

Tom's my, uh … Someone should invent an alternate term for "the approaching-sixty friend, lover, occasionally irritating male companion with whom a woman in her fifties might or might not want to spend the rest of her life." Boyfriend seems silly, lover too crass. We're not engaged, although Tom would like to be. More to the point, Tom would like to be married. To me. I still have my doubts about that venerable institution, though, based on brief and ancient experience. But I digress.

A quick scroll through the images on my camera showed that, working officially or not, I had a nice jump on the weekend thanks to the Sheltie and the sheep, especially the ewe who was still holding her ground. The dog's owner watched in silence from another open gate at the far end of the arena. It led to an adjacent pen where the woollies would be held when they weren't testing some dog's mettle.

I looked through my viewfinder and zoomed on a partial profile of the ewe and a clear view of the Sheltie's face. Nothing moved but the rim of the ewe's nostril and the dog's long white ruff, lifted and dropped by the breeze. I stopped breathing, camera poised. A shard of wood bit into my forearm where it rested on the wooden fence, but I held my camera still. A chickadee sang in a white pine off to my right, and human voices droned in the distance, but there at ringside there was nothing to hear but the faint huffhuffing of the ewe's breath.

The man by the gate finally spoke, his voice soft but clear on the morning air. "Bonnie, git 'er!"

The Sheltie let loose a stream of high-pitched threats and abuse. The ewe shook her head and took two steps toward the little dog. Bonnie jumped at the bigger animal's face, then spun around and got behind her. The ewe turned and snorted, and if I can read emotions at all, I would say she had murder on her mind. She might have done something about it, but she just couldn't find the pesky little dog; if she turned one way, Bonnie was somewhere else.

The ewe stopped and stood for a heartbeat as if deciding, then sprang out the gate to join the rest of the flock. Bonnie galloped after her, but slowed to a satisfied trot as she fell in behind the sheep. All ten had merged into one woolly intention, and they made a bee-line for the holding pen at the far end of the arena. Bonnie followed, and once the sheep were in the pen, she stationed herself in front of the gate, waiting for her master to close it.

The Sheltie's owner was a short, wiry switchblade of a man with a big belt buckle, down-at-the-heels cowboy boots, and a big-brimmed cattleman hat. He was so burnished by wind and weather that his age was hard to guess. If pressed, I would have put him in his early forties. I'd met him before and knew his name was Ray Turnbull. I thought that a good surname for a stock handler, even if there were no cattle in sight. Ray and Bonnie would be working the arena today, starting with this early morning roundup to relocate the sheep from their nighttime quarters. Truth be told, I liked Bonnie, but her owner unsettled me. He kept it sheathed in politeness, but he had a dangerous edge.

Like Bonnie, I expected Ray to close the gate, but he had turned his back on the activity in the arena. He was bent slightly forward, one hand to his ear, the other punched knuckles-first against his belt. I looked at the little dog, but she seemed content to stand where she was. When I looked back at Ray, he was pushing his phone into his pocket and walking toward his dog. If I weren't used to photographing predators from a safe distance, I might have retreated when I zoomed in on his face. His jaw muscles were clenched and although I couldn't see the look in his eyes, something about his brows spoke of violence. He spat into the dirt and pushed the gate shut, and Bonnie scooted under it to join him.

I lowered the camera and watched man and dog for another moment. Bonnie leaned against Ray's leg, and Ray seemed to relax a notch. He bent and patted his dog's shoulder, and she grinned and waved her tail. As the official stock handler for the weekend's sheep-dog events, it was Ray's responsibility to ensure that none of the sheep were worked by dogs more than four times during the day, with half-hour breaks in between. These sheep were all accustomed dogs, but Ray would still monitor their stress levels and remove any animal that seemed unduly vexed. We humans were on our own in that department.

The sheep were gathered across the arena from me, still watching the dog and man but reasonably relaxed. I took a few more photos of them before turning my camera on Ray and Bonnie. Ray was on the phone again, his dog sitting beside him with one paw on her master's left boot. I started to raise my camera to capture the tender-ness of that gesture, but Ray shifted his feet and swore into his phone, and the moment was lost. He made a few loud aspersions on someone's maternal parentage, then lowered his voice. As I scrolled through the photos I had just taken and tried to appear uninterested in the conversation, Ray came through the gate two fence panels to my right and walked away, still talking into his phone, Bonnie at his heels. I was struck by the joy in the dog's jaunty trot and the fury embodied in the few words I could make out—"no idea … why in the hell would I … threaten me." That last two came out like a warning snarl.

The conversation had nothing to do with me, but as I watched Ray flip his phone shut and spit to the side as he walked away, I felt a tiny electric thrill of apprehension lift the hairs on my arms. I shook it off and, knowing that nothing else would happen in the arena for another half hour, started across an open field toward the shady fence line where I had parked my van. I wondered what kind of early morning phone call makes a man that angry, but my inner fuddy-duddy whispered "mind your own beeswax, Janet."

I wish it had been that easy.

TWO

THE SUN HAD NOT yet lifted the dew from the grass, and my socks wicked the moisture through the vents in my running shoes, turning the knit cotton cold and rough. Wild roses festooned the woven wire fence, alive with bright leaves, but they wouldn't bloom for at least another month. Mid-April is risky for all but the bravest wildflowers in northern Indiana, and the only scent I could find on the breeze was the musk of moist spring earth and greening grass.

Mine was still the only vehicle in the exhibitor parking area, but a shiny black SUV was turning in through the gate, followed by a green pickup hauling a pop-up camper. People were arriving. I stepped to the open back of my van and grabbed my cooler in one hand, slung my folding canvas chair over my other shoulder, and picked up the lightweight folding canvas crate I use for shows and other events. Whoever invented these things has my back's undying gratitude—I remember well the days of lugging heavy plastic and metal crates around. These days, the heavy one stays in the van, and that's where Jay stood, giving me a full-on Aussie wiggle.

"Down, Bub," I said. "Let me set this stuff up, okay? I'll be back to get you." He lay down and crossed his front paws, panting softly. I pulled his favorite chew bone out of my tote and slipped it between the bars of the crate, but Jay wasn't interested. He tasted sheep on the breeze, and knew there was better fun afoot.

By the time I reached the near end of the long pole building designated for crating, my left heel was sending out the barest whisper of a blister. *Should have worn my waterproof mocs,* I thought, adjusting my gait to minimize the friction and thanking my pesky inner fussbudget for making me throw an extra pair of socks into my tote. Hopefully I had a few plastic bandages in there, too.

I had skipped breakfast, and my stomach issued a loud reminder. Louder yet was the voice that rose into the sweet spring air just as I pulled on my second dry sock. I couldn't make out the words, but knew the voice. It was Summer Winslow, a farmer from DeKalb County who raised wool sheep, gave herding and weaving lessons, and often supplied the livestock for local herding events. I bit into a gluten-and-sugar-free cashew-and-cranberry breakfast bar I'd bought at my friend Goldie's favorite health food store, slid the heavy door open, and hurried out of the building to see what was wrong. *Uck.* I dropped the rest of the bar into a garbage can. *They forgot to list Styrofoam on the ingredients list.*

The rich fragrance of lanolin and fresh sheep droppings hit me as I rounded the building. Summer was still shouting. "Where in the hell are they?" was the first full sentence I could make out.

"What are you yelling about?" Summer's husband, Evan, arrived at a long-legged lope. "I'm getting the feed. Just give me a mi…" He slowed to a walk and stared at the pen behind Summer. "You moved them already?"

Summer threw her arms around like a demented windmill and let out a verbal stream that would have made a black sheep blanch.

"What's going on?" I asked, wondering how so much anger could be floating around on such a gorgeous morning. Maybe the call that ticked Ray off came from Summer? That would make sense, since he worked for her.

Summer ignored my question and patted her pocket. "Do you have your cell?" *Okay then, Summer didn't call Ray.*

I worked my phone out of my jeans, glad they weren't any tighter.

"Call the sheriff."

"What am I calling about?"

"There were a dozen ewes and wethers in here last night," she said, pounding the gatepost with the bottom of her fist. "And now they're gone!"

THREE

When Summer said that a dozen sheep were AWOL, I was sure it must be a misunderstanding. "They're down there," I said, waving a hand toward the pen where I had watched Ray and Bonnie do their jobs.

Before anyone could respond, the Sheltie burst into sight, barking and spinning and doing her best to speed Ray along. He wasn't far behind her, and when he turned the corner, Summer shouted, "Ray! Did you move the sheep from this pen?"

"No ma'am, I did not." His voice was borderline surly, but that seemed normal for Ray, at least from my limited exposure to him.

Summer flung her arms out and turned her gaze to the pen, as if she might have overlooked the flock somehow. "Then where the hell are they?"

Ray showed Bonnie the palm of his hand. The barking and spinning stopped and the dog fell into a trot beside him, but the wag never left her tail. Ray fixed a hard gaze on Summer and said, "You have a problem." His intonation made it a statement, but Summer replied in the affirmative as if he were asking. Ray pulled a bandana from his pocket, took off his hat, mopped his shaved head, and replaced his hat in what looked like a well-practiced sequence.

"If you didn't move them, where in the hell are the sheep that were in this pen!" Summer's voice had a rough edge, as if it might turn to a scream with the tiniest push. I'd been around Summer and Evan enough to know they loved their animals, and although they used the sheep for herding lessons and harvested their wool, for the most part they treated them like pets. I had been to their farm and knew how well they cared for everyone in their charge. They even had one elderly ewe named Rosie who slept in their screened-in porch.

Evan was bent toward the metal latch, his head cocked and his fingers pulling something from the latch handle. "Summer, did you open this gate last night? After we—"

"No, of course not," Summer said. She reached for my phone, poked it three times with her finger, and turned toward Evan. "You know I always... What's that?"

Evan held whatever it was toward Summer. From where I stood, he seemed to be holding thin air. Summer took a step toward Evan's hand, then turned away and spoke into the phone, so I took up the slack.

"What is it?" I asked, and moved closer. A clump of wavy dark hair fluttered between Evan's thumb and forefinger. "Hunh." I wasn't sure what I was supposed to make of the find. *So someone got a strand of hair caught in the latch. So what?*

Evan grasped the waving end of the hairs and stretched them to their full six or seven inches. "Weird," he said.

Summer was still talking into the phone, and getting louder. "Ewes and wethers. You know, girl sheep and boy sheep... No, not rams. They're castrated... Very funny, but no, I don't think that's why they ran away." She looked at me and rolled her eyes.

I spoke to Evan. "You brought the sheep last evening, right? So—"

He cut me off, held the hair toward me and stated the obvious. "It didn't come from any of us." Evan had dark blonde hair pulled back in a ponytail, and Summer's fiery braid hung past her waist.

Ray stepped up beside me and, when we both looked at him, he lifted his hat and said, "Ain't mine."

"I'm sure it wasn't there last night," said Evan. "I checked all the latches to be sure they were all sound. I would have noticed that."

Summer handed me the phone and said, "Sheriff's on the way. I'm going to get Nell and take a look around." She started away at a trot, and I thought I heard her say "catch whoever" and "hang rustlers." She stopped and turned around. "Maybe someone should stay with the rest of the flock until we figure this out." And then she was gone, her long braid spilling down her back like a stream of molten copper.

Ray mumbled something that sounded like, "Right," and spat. I was starting to wonder how often he had to refill his reserves to keep from dehydrating. He turned back the way he had come and whistled for Bonnie, who was sniffing the gateposts and the ground between them, but Evan said, "I'll go. You have a long day ahead. There's hot coffee and some donuts at our trailer. Help yourself."

Ray left without another word, and I walked to the gate for a closer look. A voice in my head whispered *stop that right now*, and I knew she was right, "she" being my pesky voice of reason. Truth be told, she does occasionally keep me out of trouble, but she's not nearly as much fun as that *other* little voice. You know, the one who counters, *Go ahead*, followed by those five little words that have come to make the back of my neck tingle. *How bad can it be?*

FOUR

EVAN WENT TO CHECK the other sheep, Ray and Bonnie went for donuts and coffee, and Summer went to search for the missing sheep with her dog, Nell. Curiosity had me well in hand, and I studied the latch where Evan had discovered the wavy dark hairs. When I found everything normal there, I slowly scanned the area outside the pen. Nothing screamed "out of place," so I turned to look down the dirt drive that ran alongside the long red pole building where I had set up my crate.

Neither the other sheep nor the large arena were visible from where I stood, but I knew they were thirty or so yards beyond the building and off to the right. I also figured that, unless they were beamed up by aliens, the missing sheep must have gone that way. The heavy hanging door to the pole barn had been closed tight and latched from the inside until I slid it open, so they couldn't have gone through there unless someone shut and latched the door behind them. Summer and Evan were camped in the middle of the only other way out, and it was hard to imagine they had slept through a sheep drive. Even if they had, their English Shepherd, Nell, wouldn't have. Neither would Bonnie, but I had no idea where she and Ray had spent the night.

I was walking down the roadway toward the main part of the property, still thinking about ovine escape routes, when Summer yelled, "Get out!" My first thought was that she was talking to Nell, since "get out" tells a working dog to back off the stock. Then I heard more people yelling. I recognized Evan's voice and picked up my pace when he said, "The Sheriff's on his way. You're trespassing." Then another voice, gaining volume, tossing out fragments. "... public property ... cruel ... liberate ..."

Even before I cleared the end of the building, I knew what was happening. A half-dozen protesters, some of them sporting leashes and chains around their necks, waved cardboard platitudes at Summer and Evan. *What the heck is going on?* screamed a little voice in my head. *First stock rustlers, now a flock of wackos?*

"This is not public property. It's privately owned," said Evan, his voice strong and steady. "And we are asking you politely to leave. Now."

Over the previous few weeks, there had been several incidents of animal rights extremists "liberating" animals around the state. Could this group have let the sheep loose during the night or early morning? Based on the reports I had heard, they focused mostly on dogs, often showing up at events, opening crates, and shooing the animals out. Two dogs had been lost and not yet found, and at least one other had been hit by a car. We all live in terror that it could happen to the dogs we love.

Dogs we love! My heart skipped and I broke into a run. *Jay!* I had left him crated in the back of the van with the tailgate open. Had I padlocked his crate? I couldn't remember. I usually did if I had to leave him alone at a public event, but this early in the morning, at a

14

stockdog event on private property ... I didn't think I had. My legs seemed to sprout lead shackles.

A handful of vehicles snuggled up under the trees along the fence line where I had parked, and a couple dozen more were now parked closer to the arena. It was a typical dog-event assortment—lots of minivans, two RVs, the pop-up camper I had seen earlier, one or two tents. People were busy setting up portable canopies, folding chairs, exercise pens, and dog crates. Most of the dogs were herding breeds, although I spotted a Jack Russell Terrier walking beside a Border Collie at the far end of the field. There would be more variety, I knew, the next day. A couple of people waved at me, and my panic subsided a notch. There's safety in numbers and I knew that no one who knew me would let anyone mess with my dog.

I could see the front and side of my van, and someone walking across the parking area from that direction with two Aussies racing ahead, a flying disc shared between them. *Dog person.* Someone stepped out from behind my van and looked both ways before turning away from me and breaking into a run. Away from my van. *Running away, or just running?* If you followed the fence line to the back of property, you would hit the new Rivergreenway extension, a popular place for walkers and joggers. It could be someone out for a morning run. *Or it could be someone up to no good.* I boosted my speed and yelled "Hey!" but got no response. I ran faster, panic pulling its knot tighter around me. I tripped over something, or nothing, in the grass and almost fell, but momentum and fear kept me upright. I ran on, my heart thick in my throat and my eardrums threatening to explode from the pressure building up behind them. A frail voice whispered *he's fine, he's fine,* but when I finally rounded the back end of my van, the voice died.

Jay's crate door hung open. He was gone.

FIVE

I AM TOLD THAT I screamed. It may be true. I'm not much of a screamer, but as I stared at the empty crate in the back of my van, my world went black. If I did scream, it had to be my dog's name, because that was the word I clung to.

Jay.

Jay Jay Jay.

What I do remember is a woman I didn't know. She and her dog, a small black-and-tan mixed-breed with a bobbed tail and upright ears, had just entered my peripheral vision from behind me, and I half-registered their presence.

"Is something wrong?" The stranger was taller than I am, maybe five seven, and her face was a mask of concern framed by short silvery hair. Her dog whined and sank into a sphinx position. "Are you hurt?"

I spun around and looked up and down the field, unable to get anything out of my mouth beyond "no, no, no, no."

"What is it? Can I help?"

I forced myself to focus on her face. "I ... my dog."

She looked past me at the empty crate and blanched. "Oh my God." Her dog jumped up and barked twice, looking back and forth between us. "Edith Ann, down!" The dog lay back down, but kept her dark eyes riveted onto the woman in front of her. "What's she look like? She? He?"

"He. Blue merle Aussie, white and copper trim." I walked to the other side of the van and looked up and down the fence line, but there was no sign of Jay, so I returned to the open field and walked a few yards out to scan the growing line of vehicles. I yelled, "Jay!"

"Like that one?" she asked, gazing at something behind me.

Hope spun me around. Disappointment nearly laid me flat. Billie Smithson, an Aussie breeder from Indianapolis, was walking toward the arena with her blue merle bitch Maggie. She smiled and waved and walked on.

"You go that way," said my new friend, waving the back of her hand down the field behind me. "And I'm Kathy, in case you need to get my attention." She turned and walked the other way, looking between vehicles as she went.

"I'm Janet," I called as I turned the other way. My end of the field was shorter, and held only another van and a pickup truck hauling a camper. Beyond them was the unobstructed field hemmed by a shrub-dense tree line, an old farm fence still standing in parts of it. I called for Jay and told everyone I saw to be on the lookout for a loose dog. I also pointed out the demonstrators by the arena and warned them not to leave their dogs unattended.

In the distance, I could see Summer waving her arms and, apparently, yelling, but the protesters had dispersed and her target had shifted. Ray Turnbull stood in front of her, arms crossed over his chest. I looked away to check between vehicles, and when I glanced back their way, Ray seemed to be shaking Summer by the arm. Her hand came up and pushed him away.

At the time, the whole scene barely registered beyond the oddity of the interaction between employer and employee, but it did seem to shake something loose in my mind. By the time I got back to my van, my fear and panic had merged with a rational thread, and I was able to focus a little. I pulled my phone out of my pocket.

The list of "people to call when a pet goes missing" rolled through my head, and I decided to start with Giselle Swann. She knew Jay, and she was computer savvy. I hadn't seen her for a while, but I knew she would put the word out on the Internet for me so I could focus on the search. Her quick-dial number was six. I pushed it and waited, still walking and looking around.

A man answered. Giselle is single, lives alone, has no brothers, and as far as I knew, no boyfriend. "I told you, it's not going to work now, not after … Just leave me out of it, will you?" The voice had a slobbery quality that made me think of Daffy Duck.

I apologized for the wrong number, and tried again.

"What's the matter with you? I told you—"

I disconnected and looked at the phone. It was similar to mine, one of the few remaining flip phones in use, but it wasn't mine. Had Summer given me the wrong phone? Had she had hers with her and missed it in the confusion?

That could wait. As my fingers punched in Giselle's full number, my brain scrolled through the list of other calls to make, and I knew I would need my own phone for most of them. First, my vet's office in case someone called them because of Jay's rabies tag. And then—

And then someone goosed me.

SIX

I took two jerky steps forward and spun around. Jay was behind me, his back end wiggling like a Tahitian dancer and his front feet doing a tap dance. Tom's black Lab, Drake, stood beside him, whapping Tom's leg with his beater of a tail and grinning at me. The next thing I knew, I was on my knees, my arms around Jay and my face buried in the thick silky fur of his neck. Drake shoved his cold nose into my neck and I pulled him into a group hug.

"Some guys have all the luck."

At the sound of the voice, I took a deep breath, squeezed Jay a tiny bit tighter, stroked Drake's velvety cheek, and disengaged. Jay got me with one good cheek slurp before I got to my feet and turned on the man at the far end of the dogs' leashes.

"You scared me to death!"

Tom Saunders is the last person in the world likely to hurt anyone's animals, and the first person I want at my side if there's trouble. During the year I had known him, I'd seen him shine in the worst of times, as well as the best. Besides, gray highlights in his beard and yummy brown eyes aside, he had a way of wearing his jeans that made my insides go gooey. But not at that moment.

"What were you thinking?"

Tom looked as if I'd slapped him. He leaned slightly back and said, "He had to pee. What's wrong wi—"

"Where *were* you? I looked … Oh my God. I think I'm going to barf." *Or cry.* I didn't want to do either.

"We went for a little walk," said Tom. "I left you a note. I thought—"

"You didn't think!" My mouth was set on anger blurt, and I regretted the words as soon as they were out. Adjusting my volume and tone a bit, I said, "A note?"

Tom pointed at the bottom of the crate. A green index card lay on the green rug I used as a crate pad. A note.

"I didn't see it." *I was blinded by terror.* Part of me wanted to slug Tom for not using a large poster board and Day-Glo paint to let me know he'd taken my dog. The other part wanted to slap *me* for missing a perfectly thoughtful note, although green on green *had* made it hard to spot. I knew I should apologize, but decided he could go first. "If I'd known you were coming I might have … What are you doing here, anyway?"

Tom didn't say anything and I couldn't tell whether he was hurt or angry or surprised. All of the above, I decided. We stared at each other for a few seconds before we both said some version of, "Sorry, I should have—"

"I didn't think you were coming today," I said. "I thought you had papers to grade."

"The realtor called. Drake and I had to clear out for a showing, so we came to see what's happening in herding-dog land." Then he asked me why I had gone into a meltdown over something we did with each other's dogs all the time.

"You hear those wackos over there?" The little nag in my head whispered *you're a bit of a wacko yourself, Janet,* but I ignored her. "I thought someone … They're over there … Someone took …" As I struggled to speak a complete sentence, I stepped out from behind the van and spotted Edith Ann and Kathy coming our way.

"I don't see him down that way."

"He's here!" I smiled as she reached us, and Edith Ann squirmed her way to Jay and Drake and rolled belly-up at their feet. When Jay snuffled her neck, she jumped up and all three started the requisite canine sniffing routine, twisting their leashes into a tangled mess. I held my hand out to the woman and introduced myself, Tom, Jay, and Drake.

"Kathy Glaes," she said. "We're on our way to Chicago and stopped by for the disc event." We talked a bit more, and she led a reluctant Edith Ann back toward the disc practice area.

Jay sat in front of me and cocked his head to the left. Tom stood beside him and cocked his head to the right. Drake stood behind Tom, watching Edith Ann's departure and slowly waving his tail. I sat back against the van's bumper. As if they had choreographed the move, Jay put a paw on my foot and Tom laid a hand on my shoulder. My adrenaline level was tapering off and my inner crybaby had crawled back to her crib, so I signaled Jay to pop his front end into my lap, massaged behind both his ears, and looked at Tom.

"You didn't hear the ruckus over by the sheep pens?" I asked.

Tom looked toward the structures on the far side of the field. "I heard voices, but figured they were just getting organized." When he looked at me again, a line had formed between his eyebrows. "Why? What's going on?"

"Wackos were going on," I said. "And on and on. Animal rights nuts. They were over there waving signs, you know, 'liberate the enslaved animals' and that stuff."

"So that's why the Sheriff is here?"

I shook my head and eased Jay back to the ground. "No, but it's good timing." My butt was protesting the sharp edge of the tailgate, so I stood up and took Jay's leash from Tom. "Summer actually called the Sheriff about the sheep."

Tom raised an eyebrow and said, "The sheep did something illegal?"

"Part of the flock disappeared during the night."

We had talked a few times about incidents of livestock rustling around the area. Several recent cases had been reported in the news, but they had all involved cattle. Ten head of Black Angus had been stolen from a pasture near Auburn, and some Herefords from a farm east of Fort Wayne, near the Ohio line. The newspaper said there was evidence the animals had been hauled off in stock trucks. I was just thinking that there was no way anyone pulled a semi-trailer onto the property without being seen when Tom spoke again.

"So the rustlers are branching out," said Tom. "That's disturbing."

Just what we need. Thieves and wackos.

SEVEN

THE FOUR OF US walked to the pole barn and Tom put Drake in the canvas crate I had set up earlier. He gave him a chew toy, which Drake would probably not touch, and filled the water dish. A man—a contestant's husband, I surmised—was sitting next to a matched pair of crates a few feet from mine. He had headphones and a very fat book, and looked like he'd be there for a while, which was reassuring. Still, I slipped a padlock through the zipper pulls on my crate and reminded Tom that the combination was my address. "Just in case."

When we got back to the arena, everything seemed normal. The protesters were gone and people were arriving with chairs and coolers to stake out good spectating spots. Jay whined softly when he spotted the sheep huddled in a tight cluster at one side of the arena, as if they knew they might be next. In fact they might, but they'd face well-monitored herding dogs, not stock rustlers.

Ray and Evan stood near the arena gate, their dogs lying at their feet, calm but alert. The men weren't talking, and although they stood not more than two feet apart, they were turned slightly away from one another. As I watched, Evan said something, and Ray spat in the dirt. I was beginning to think his spitting was in lieu of speech. Evan wheeled toward Ray and the hand hanging at his side curled into a fist, then relaxed.

Tom apparently hadn't noticed the hostile body language. He said, "I'm going to say hello," and veered toward the two men, whom he knew from tagging along to a couple of my herding lessons at Evan and Summer's place. My first thought was that he might learn something juicy if the obvious trouble between the two men had anything to do with the missing sheep. I considered tagging along, but thought better of it. I walked on past the corner of the building, Jay trotting beside me, and reminded myself that I wasn't going to get involved in any kind of sleuthing. Nightmares from the previous year's misadventures still disrupted my sleep. I didn't need any new ones.

Three people formed a loose circle halfway up the dirt roadway that paralleled the side of the pole building and led to the empty sheep pen. One was Summer Winslow, talking fast and pointing this way and that. An Allen County sheriff's deputy stood side-on to me, sunlight glinting off the spit-polished holster at his hip. The third person was a big man in tan chinos and a corduroy jacket. He had his back to me, but there was no mistaking detective Homer "Hutch" Hutchinson of the Fort Wayne Police Department. I'd gotten to know the man pretty well over the previous year, and I felt oddly comforted to see him there.

As if he had heard me thinking, Hutch turned around. He nodded at me and broke into a big grin when he saw Jay. Judging by the furry butt wiggling against my leg, the feeling was mutual.

Summer stopped talking and stared at me, and the deputy—Deputy Johnson, according to his name tag—turned as well.

"Sorry," I said. "I didn't mean to interrupt."

"No problem," said Summer. "The problem is between these gentlemen." She reached both hands behind her head, twisted her long penny-colored braid, and knotted it at her nape. She glared at the deputy, then at Hutch, and said, "You have my number. Call me when you get your act together." She walked past me toward the stock arena.

Hutch hunkered down and called Jay, so I dropped the leash and they had a major bonding moment, complete with Hutchinson cooing, "Ooh a good boy, ess ooh are." It was hard to believe the man had been afraid of dogs when we met a year earlier.

The deputy watched them blank-faced for a moment, cleared his throat, and nodded at me. "Ma'am."

"What's going on?"

"Little matter of jurisdiction," he said.

Hutchinson stood up and brushed a pound or so of Aussie fur off his pants. "The city limits line runs right though here." He indicated an imaginary line transecting the little road at a forty-five degree angle. "So we're not sure who has jurisdiction."

And meanwhile, whoever has the sheep gets farther away. I could see why Summer was upset, but I managed for once to keep my opinion to myself. I asked Hutchinson if he could stick around to watch some of the action, and he said he'd like to if he didn't get called away. The deputy answered his phone, told the caller to hang on, and looked like he wanted to talk to Hutch, so I picked up Jay's leash and excused myself.

As I walked back the way I had come, my eyes skimmed the dusty surface of the road. The sun was at just the right angle to make the footprints stand out. Hundreds of footprints. Or, more to the point, a few prints from boots and shoes, scores from canine paws, hundreds from hooves. I slowed myself until I was taking baby steps, telling Jay to heel to keep him at my knee. The marks in the dirt were, of course, a jumbled mess of partial prints overlaid by others, but still, it was clear that several people and several dogs, and a bunch more sheep, had passed this way recently. There were no tire marks that I could see.

Tom left the other two men and joined me where I was creeping along the roadway. Tom teaches anthropology at the Indiana University's Fort Wayne campus, and as a trained observer of human behavior, he knew that I wasn't just being eccentric. He stayed to the edge of the road and, as he approached, he asked, "Tracks?"

"Gazillions of tracks," I said. "Just what you'd expect—people, dogs, sheep."

He stepped in beside me and we crept on, both of us looking at the ground. "Interesting," Tom said, describing a circle over a section of road with his hand.

I stepped closer and looked. "What?"

"The prints travel both directions."

"Wouldn't you expect that?"

"I'm not sure." Tom looked at me, then back at the tracks. "The people and dogs, of course, but the sheep? If they moved them in from that direction yesterday," he said, pointing down the roadway toward the arena, "and if they didn't officially move any back out this morning, why do the hoof prints go both ways?"

Good question. I filled Tom in on the jurisdiction issue and said, "I guess we should let them know."

Tom agreed. "And soon, before the tracks are obliterated."

We turned back toward Hutch and the deputy, inching along the edge of the roadway for ten feet or so. I was just about to pick up the pace when Tom stretched his arm in front of me and said, "That's from a big dog." He pointed at a paw print near the edge of the roadway, almost under the bottom fence board, where the jumble of impressions was less confusing. In fact, most of the area was clear of marks. There were a few partial prints, clearly canine, but it was hard to tell much about them. And that one pristine paw print in a mound of soft dusty earth. Tom was right. It was made by a very big dog.

EIGHT

By the time I had alerted Hutch and the deputy to the possible significance of the tracks on the roadway and helped them block it off to further traffic pending a closer look, I had about half an hour to get ready for the instinct test. Not that there was much to do at that point, other than breathe deeply and review what little I knew about handling my dog while he handled the sheep.

At my van, I switched out Jay's everyday collar for the one he wore in competition, the one with no tags dangling. We walked past the handful of vehicles parked along the fence row and into a rolling, close-mown stretch at the back of the property. New fence posts marched across part of the area and more were stacked in scattered piles, along with tight rolls of welded wire fencing.

Jay stopped to test the wind, which was blowing from the direction of the arena where we would be taking our test. I turned that way. Ray and Bonnie were moving three sheep into the pickup pen for the first dog. I looked at Jay, and he looked at me, eyes bright and tail nub wagging. "Pretty soon, Bubby," I said, and Jay went into full body wiggle and let out a squeal. "Come on, let's finish our walk."

Walking helped me gather my thoughts and burn off a little pre-performance adrenaline, and it was something I tried to do any time we competed. The instinct test isn't competitive, but it *feels* a lot like competition when dog owners talk afterward about whose dog passed and whose did not, and which handler made what ridiculous mistake. Twenty minutes later, I decided it was time to grab a folding chair and head over to the arena.

When I opened the back hatch of my van, a huge sheet of brown paper, formerly a grocery bag, stared back at me. It was bungeed against the two crates that live back there, and its message was neatly printed in giant black caps: YOUR CHAIRS AND I ARE AT THE ARENA. TOM.

I was still smiling as I passed the disc dog practice ring and waved at Kathy and Edith Ann. Jay bounced with excitement, shifting his gaze every few seconds from me to the arena and back and tipping his twitching nose up and into the wind. I stroked his cheek and followed his gaze to the arena. The remaining dozen sheep were gathered into a loose off-center knot. They didn't look overly concerned about what was coming.

Ray Turnbull stood outside the far right end of the arena talking to a heavy-set man in a dirt-beige suit that was out of place in this land of animal-friendly jeans and sweatshirts. As always, Bonnie sat at his feet. I couldn't see the stranger's face, but judging by Ray's expression, he was involved in yet another unfriendly conversation. He took a step back from the fat man and shook his head. The other man stepped toward Ray, his right hand raised and index finger pointing at Ray's face. Bonnie let loose a high-pitched series of warnings and the stranger stepped back. Bonnie stopped barking when Ray held his palm toward her, but she kept a close eye on the man. Ray said something to the man, then turned and walked toward the arena, his dog beside him.

What the heck was that? Not for the first time I wished I had one of those gadgets that let you pick up conversations from far away. I pulled Summer's phone out of my pocket and checked the time. "We'd better get over there, Bubby," I said, and Jay let out a soft *boof* of agreement. I found Tom sitting by the arena, kissed his cheek, and said, "Thanks for the note." Jay hopped his front end onto Tom's lap and one-upped me with a full-face flurry of kisses.

Tom lowered Jay gently to the ground and was still laughing when he asked, "When are you up?"

I handed Tom the leash and said, "No idea. I'll check the board."

Summer stood in front of a white board displayed on an easel near the gate to the arena, apparently checking the list on the board against the paper in her hand. When she finished, I asked her whether there was any news, and how she was doing.

She shook her head and said, "Just dandy." She looked me in the eye and said, "No, not dandy at all." Her eyes narrowed and her voice went flat and low. "I'd like to find whoever's responsible, truss him up tight, and let the whole flock trample him into the dust."

Summer's urge to hurt whoever had stolen her sheep was understandable, but I'd seen enough violence in the previous twelve months to keep me from commenting directly. Instead I said, "Hopefully the police will find them." I almost asked whether area slaughterhouses had been given a heads up, but I couldn't get the question out of my mouth.

"Do you need something?"

"No, thanks, I just came to see when Jay and I go." I smiled at Summer, then turned to the white board with the list of dogs in the instinct test. *Please don't let us be first.* I read the six names. Jay and I were second. I breathed again.

Summer patted my arm and said, "You'll do fine." She tried for a smile and added, "Well, Jay will. Just stay out of his way and do what the tester tells you."

Way to bolster my self-confidence at my first herding event, I thought, but I knew she was right. Even without much training, Jay knew a lot more about handling sheep than I did. I started to walk away, but turned back, pulling the cell phone out of my pocket. "You gave me the wrong phone," I said.

Summer stared at the phone in my hand, looking confused. She reached into her right pocket and when she came up empty, checked the left. She looked at the phone in her hand—my phone—and said, "Oh, wow. Sorry."

I rejoined Tom and Jay, but was too jumpy to sit down. As usual, my dog was fully in the moment, and as I watched him, my scared-o-meter dropped a degree or two. Jay sat beside Tom's chair, his whole being focused on the three sheep that Ray and Bonnie had just moved from the holding pen to the main arena. The Aussie breed standard described Jay's ears perfectly—the base of each lifted away from his head, with the remaining three-fourths of the soft triangular flaps falling slightly to the side. That, and the look of eagles in his eyes, gave back whatever confidence Summer's comment had taken from me.

NINE

THE FIRST DOG INTO the arena for the instinct test was a very young blue merle Border Collie named Spring. April Bruce, her owner, had told me that she was seven months old and had never seen sheep before. Spring entered the ring calmly enough, and the tester told April to walk her closer to the sheep. As they approached, one of the ewes raised her head and turned to stare at the puppy. My heart was beginning to pound as I watched, but Spring stood still, one front foot a few inches in front of the other, shoulders slightly crouched, head thrust forward.

"Have her down," the tester said. Spring lay down on April's command, and the tester said, "Take her leash and send her."

As soon as she was released, Spring got to work. She ran a wide circle to get behind the three woollies and pushed them forward with her quiet presence.

Tom touched my arm and asked, "Did you say she's never seen sheep before?"

"That's what April told me."

"Wow."

Wow indeed. As her owner walked a serpentine path across the ring, Spring moved back and forth behind the trio to keep them moving. She stopped and backed up on command, working like a dog that had some training.

"She's a hard act to follow," I said.

"You'll do fine." Tom ran his hand over the top of Jay's skull and down the back of his neck. "Both of you."

I took my attention off the action to smile at Tom. He grinned back, and then his gaze shifted to the arena and he gestured toward it with his chin.

Spring stood frozen, still focused on the three sheep. April walked backward a few more steps, and Spring glanced at her and back at the sheep. The dog's whole expression softened and she bowed at the sheep, inviting them to play. She sprang back up and bounced toward the lead ewe, who looked as confused by her well-spoken canine body language as an American tourist trying to make out a thick Highland brogue. Who could watch that and not laugh? I glanced at the tester, and she was practically doubled over. I looked back at the dog. She bowed once more, looked around as if to see who everyone found so funny, and went back to work until the judge signaled the end of the test.

My stomach went a bit gurgly as I took Jay's leash from Tom, but I sucked in a long breath and walked to the gate. Jay and I waited while Ray and Bonnie moved the first three sheep into a holding pen and brought three fresh ones out. Hutchinson stood about twenty feet away, talking to Summer. Her arms were crossed tight across her body, and even from that distance, I could see the rage that played across her face. She turned her head toward the arena, but I couldn't tell whether she was looking at something or away from Hutch.

"Come on in."

The tester's voice brought me back to the task at hand and, as I stepped into the arena, all my saliva turned to dust. Jay pulled against the leash, but let up when I said, "Easy." Like many Aussies, Jay can be quite the comedian, and I couldn't help wondering whether Spring's performance had inspired him to try something funny.

He didn't try anything funny, at least not on purpose, but he clearly thought his job was to keep the sheep very close to me. Two feet, max. And the sheep, a trio of Rambouillets, looked gigantic. And nervous. I was sure each one outweighed me, and that they wouldn't hesitate to throw that weight around to get away from a dog. Monty Python's famous "killer sheep" skit popped into my mind.

At the tester's direction, I released Jay and he sprinted around the little flock. Before he could get behind them, though, they took off toward the far end of the arena. Jay raced away on a parallel track, clearly planning to outrun them and turn them back. Which he did. The ewes turned away from him and came at me, shoulder to shoulder, full speed ahead. I ran to my left, trying to get out of the way, but the sheep adjusted their course. The one in the middle butted me in the belly, and I flew up and back and fell flat. I shut my eyes as they passed over me, landing a couple of good hoof strikes but missing vital organs.

"Get up!" I heard the words, but for a moment, my body wouldn't cooperate. More words filtered into my brain. The tester yelled at me. "Get up! Now!"

I picked myself up and turned around, expecting to see the sheep galloping away with Jay on their funny little tails. *Oh, shit.* They were coming straight at me again, my delighted dog right behind with a look on his face that seemed to say, "I got 'em, Mom! Here they are!"

And they knocked me flat again. I scrambled up, half expecting them to take another crack at me, but the sheep apparently had given up the notion that they could escape. They were coming toward me, but at a fast shuffling walk, and I managed to back away, follow instructions, and complete the test.

"Call your dog," the tester said, and when I had him beside me and on leash, she put her hand on my shoulder. "Those were tough sheep for an instinct test." She chuckled. "Flighty." I was still trying to catch my breath, so I just nodded. "Your dog could use a bit more training, but he passed."

Jay grinned at me, butt wiggling, and as soon as we left the arena, I knelt on the ground and hugged him. "You did great, Bubby." He answered by leaning into me and sliding his body against mine until he was on the ground, paws in the air, for a belly rub, which, of course, he got.

I grinned at Tom, who gave me a thumbs-up. Still grinning, I walked Jay up the little roadway where we had found the tracks so that we could both unwind a bit. Thirty yards along, we veered onto a narrow lane—a narrow dirt track through grass, really—that ran between the back of the arena's holding pen and a field of corn stubble. We went only a short distance, but the lane ran on, apparently, to the back of the property, which I guesstimated to be a hundred acres or more. I stroked Jay's head and said, "Maybe we can take a longer walk later, Bub."

As we turned around, the light caught a disturbed stretch of ground at the edge of the cornfield. I stopped for a closer look. Paw prints. *Big* paw prints, like the one we'd found earlier. There were only four of them, as if the dog had hopped off the grass momentarily as he headed for the pole barn at the end of the lane. I made a mental note to tell Hutchinson, but my attempts to think through what the prints might mean were cut short by the sound of a woman's voice. It was Summer Winslow, and although she was not yelling, her words slashed through the distance between us like a machete.

"How could he do that?"

I tried not to stare, or to draw her attention, but I couldn't resist a quick glance as I turned away from her toward the arena, aiming to rejoin Tom. She was talking into her phone, her whole body radiating emotion, but for a few seconds I could no longer hear what she was saying. Then her voice rose again and she made another threat. It hit me in the gut like the stampeding ewes.

"He'll pay for this."

TEN

THOSE HUGE PAW PRINTS Tom and I had found came back to me six hours later as I stood in a hot shower and studied a hoof-shaped bruise above my knee. The paw prints were at least four and a half inches from heel to toenail. They were made by a humongous dog. Not only that, but they were oddly placed. Why would a dog be that close to the fence? Something must have forced him, or her, off the roadway. The print I saw later was just as big, and its placement also suggested that the dog had been nudged off the grassy edge of the lane, but only for a few steps. Maybe the dog was dodging a vehicle? Or a stampede? Could someone have used one of the bigger herding breeds to drive the sheep? Then again, maybe whoever owned the property had a big dog. Who *did* own the property? I had no sooner thought *I'll have to find out* when my inner Voice of Caution screamed *No you don't! No more snooping around!*

Despite the questions whirling around my brain, I was enjoying my little bit of time alone in the house. Not really alone, but the cats were napping. Tom had left the event after Jay's instinct test, and he'd taken Jay and Drake to free me up to take photos. The upshot was several hundred images of dogs and sheep. I had also photographed those tracks we'd found, all the while reminding myself that I was not getting involved in any sort of investigation. I knew where that could lead. I also knew it was already too late.

When the clinic had wrapped up, I helped Evan secure the sheep in the larger holding pen. Evan said Summer was busy elsewhere, and Ray and Bonnie were nowhere to be seen. I wondered whether it was Ray who had prompted Summer's hissy fit on the phone earlier in the day. If so, had she fired him? Was that why he wasn't around to help wrap things up? Evan had been uncharacteristically silent, so I hadn't asked. I'd just pitched in and moved sheep. I had minimal contact with them, but sheep are a smelly lot, and by the time we finished, my hair and skin and clothes reeked of lanolin. I went straight for the shower when I got home and let water, steam, and speculation swirl around me for a good long time.

The paw prints had looked fresh, and they were much too big for any of the dogs at the instinct test or clinic. We often see Bouviers and Briards and other large breeds at herding events, but not today. I was stumped. I was also worried about the missing sheep. The thought of rustlers taking those sheep to slaughter made me ill, but who steals sheep for their wool? Then again, Summer had bought a half dozen new animals a few months earlier, and I thought I remembered that she paid four hundred a head, so they did have some monetary value.

Tom and the dogs rolled in around six, but I had my hair dryer on and didn't know they were back until I emerged from the bathroom with my arms full of towels and dirty clothes. Jay and Drake escorted me to the bedroom, where I piled my load into the clothes basket before lugging it through the kitchen to the laundry room.

"Pizza on the way," said Tom, saluting me with a bottle of local brew. "Lie down, boys."

I smiled, poured a hard lemonade, added a slosh of vodka, stepped over the dogs, and gave Tom a big smacker on the cheek. "No wonder I love you."

"Are you sore?"

"A bit," I said. "I think it will be worse tomorrow, but at least sheep are fairly light on their pointy little feet." As an animal photographer, I'd been bitten and trampled, though never seriously injured. As a herding student, I'd been jostled and knocked flat more than a few times, but again, the bumps and bruises were all superficial.

The alcohol was just beginning to ooze through me when the pain center in my calf lit up. I jolted straight up and screeched as I reached for my leg. My hands found soft fur over adolescent lankiness, and once I made sure all needleclaws were out of my flesh, I lifted Pixel onto my lap. "You little demon." I snuggled the kitten under my arm and gently pressed a paw until her stilettos poked out of their sheaths. I looked into her big green eyes. "Time for a trim." She made an O of her mouth and wiggled as I opened my grooming drawer, snagged the nail clippers and my ratty old rooster towel, and sat back down. My handsome orange tabby Leo lets me trim his claws without fuss, but at five months old, Pixel is not so complacent. I swaddled her in the towel and got to work, one paw at a time.

My phone rang as I nipped off the last nail point, so I handed the kitten to Tom and checked caller ID. My brother Bill. It was his day to visit my mother at Shadetree Retirement Home, so a panicky little bird fluttered around my head, chirping questions. *Has something happened? Is she sick? Has she blown the place up?*

Mom's health, physical and mental, had been relatively good for several months, but that could change in the time it took to throw a trowel at another resident, which she had done a few weeks earlier. Granted, she had cause. He had uprooted a row of coleus she had just planted in the nursing home's therapy garden. Luckily her aim was off, but the whole thing had upset her, and for two weeks she couldn't remember anyone except her new love, Anthony "Tony" Marconi. Then again, with Bill, a hangnail can be a medical emergency.

As I finished my phone call with Bill, Leo strolled into the kitchen and Pixel froze, then squirmed out of Tom's arms and leaped to the floor. She arched her skinny back, pointed her tail at the ceiling, and bounced sideways across Leo's path. He glared for two seconds, and the two of them raced down the hall toward the bedrooms. Jay cocked his head as he watched. He liked playing with kittens and puppies. Drake just wrinkled his brow as if he wasn't sure he wanted such an uncivilized creature disrupting his life. *Just wait, old man,* I thought, *just wait.*

"Everything okay with your mom?" Tom asked.

"She asked Bill to buy her a pair of size thirteen slippers." I sighed. "My dad's size."

Daddy's been gone for years.

ELEVEN

SUNDAY MORNING FOUND ME wishing I had drunk one fewer vodka lemonades the night before. If I hadn't needed to get to the trial grounds by eight o'clock, I would have wrapped my throbbing head in an ice pack for an hour or two. As it was, Tom had snuck out early for a field training session with Drake, and I had slept through the alarm clock. I barely had time to get dressed, grab my dog and my camera, and hit the road. Thank the caffeine gods that my favorite java drive-through was on the way.

I parked my van just about where I had the day before, but there was no way Jay was staying there unattended. He trotted beside me as I crossed the part of the field roped off for parking, which was filling up with vans and trucks and other dogmobiles. In the distance, several people tossed discs for leaping dogs, including Kathy, the woman I had met the day before with Edith Ann. I made a mental note to try to get some good shots to send her as a thank you.

The arena and adjacent pens were still empty, so Jay and I headed up the well-traveled roadway toward the big corral. Evan was loading the hayrack with breakfast for the woollies, and the sweet scent of fresh hay wound around me as I approached. Jay stopped to sniff at a door in the side of the building, whining softly, but he came to me when I called.

"Good morning."

Evan turned, brushing the front of his sweatshirt with his fingers. "Hi, Janet."

"Any news?"

He shook his head.

"I'm sorry."

He nodded, sniffed, and rubbed his cheek against his sleeve. "Damn hay dust gets me."

Right. The mental version of a photo I had taken of Evan holding a newborn lamb, still steaming, came to me. In the picture, he sat on the ground, his thigh pressed into the ewe's hip, the lamb cradled in his arms. The expression on his face would have done St. Francis proud.

"Ray usually does this." He glanced around and added, "Usually beats me by an hour."

Evan had no sooner stopped speaking than Summer's voice crackled behind me. "He's nowhere to be found. We'll have to make do." *Okay, so she didn't fire him.* She stopped beside me, her mouth smiling with no collaboration from her eyes, and said, "Maybe Janet can help for a bit."

My hand massaged the big killer-sheep bruise on my hip, but my mouth said, "Sure, happy to."

Summer turned back the way she had come, and Evan picked up a galvanized bucket and said, "Be right back. I'll switch this out for a wheelbarrow."

I stood close to the fence and breathed in the almost tangible fragrance of sheep and half-chewed hay. I like to watch animals eating. Unlike too many people, our nonhuman kin nearly always look

42

deeply satisfied, no matter the fare. The sheep nearest the fence eyed Jay as she—or perhaps it was a wether—chewed, and I would be hard pressed to say whether the look was thoughtful or indifferent.

Something clanked behind me and the whole flock jumped away from the fence, snorting and baaing. Jay spun around; I flinched and turned. Evan stood just outside the door Jay had sniffed, not the big sliding door, but what looked to be the way into a storage room. He folded at the waist and stumbled away from the building. The bucket rocked back and forth on the narrow concrete apron. I crossed the roadway, my heart racing even before I looked into the room and wished I had not.

Ray Turnbull hung from a crossbeam, a length of rope knotted around his neck.

TWELVE

IF I NEVER SEE another hanged body, I will still have seen one too many. I had seen several murder victims in the past year, but this was the worst. The last thing I wanted to do was enter that room, and I doubted there was any chance Ray was alive, but someone had to be sure. Evan was busy upchucking on the far side of the roadway, so someone was me. I put Jay in a down-stay and, without looking again at Ray's horrifying face, I stepped over a beat-up boot and started to reach for his wrist but hesitated. Three of his fingers were twisted in crazy directions, and swollen. I was sure they were broken. I forced my own fingers to grip his wrist.

Cold. No pulse.

I spun around and staggered out of the room, pulled my phone out, leaned against the side of the building, and slid to the ground. *Deep breath, Janet, deep breath.* Jay scooched up close beside me and placed a paw over the crook of my elbow as if to say, "It's okay, I'm right here." My hand seemed to be soldered to my phone at first, but I finally managed to punch in 9-1-1. It took a couple of tries before the dispatcher deciphered the message. She offered to stay on the line with me until the first responders arrived, but I declined, and dialed again. I wanted a cop I knew. I called Homer Hutchinson.

Once he recovered from the initial shock, Evan was so fidgety I thought my head might explode, so I sent him for coffee for both of us, preferably with a big shot of something very strong, early morning be damned. He was ten yards down the roadway when I called after him. "Evan, wait!"

He stopped and turned around.

"What about Bonnie?"

"What?"

"Ray's dog. Bonnie. Where is she?"

"Oh, God." He looked like he might lose it again.

I knew I should stay put to deflect lookie-loos and wait for the police or sheriff or whoever would have jurisdiction. But if Bonnie was missing, the sooner we started looking for her, the better. Ray might have left her in his truck or wherever he was staying, but that seemed unlikely. I couldn't remember ever seeing Ray without the little black-and-white dog. If she witnessed Ray's death, she might have run off, terrified. Then I remembered how she had barked at the fat guy in defense of her master, and my insides contracted. Whoever killed Ray might have hurt her—or worse. Especially if she had tried to protect him.

"I'll look." Evan's voice brought me back to the moment. "I'll get your coffee first." I told him to forget the coffee, and he took off.

I called after him, "I'll help as soon as the police are done with me."

Although I couldn't see him, knowing that Ray was hanging dead a few yards from where I stood gave me the shakes. There was no one nearby, so I scurried through the big sliding door, put Jay in his crate with a cheese-stuffed chewy toy, and grabbed my folding chair. When I re-emerged from the building, the sound of approaching sirens took me back to the first murder investigation I'd been near, almost a year earlier. *What happened to my quiet, boring life?*

And what makes you think this is murder? The more I thought about that, the more the answer slipped from my grasp. Ray wasn't a big man, but he had lived a life of physical labor and he appeared to be healthy and strong. It was hard to imagine anyone bettering him without a struggle, and other than his boot on the floor, nothing in the storage room suggested a struggle, at least not in the brief look I'd had. I remembered thinking that Ray seemed angry on Saturday, although he was always a bit sullen. Then again, several people had seemed angry on Saturday—Summer certainly, and Evan, and the fat guy I'd seen with Ray.

I got to my feet and paced back and forth across the roadway a few times, trying to force other images to replace my vision of Ray's dead face. It was going to take a long time to bury that one, I knew.

The next part of the morning was a blur of police officers, EMTs, the coroner, and I don't know who else. It seemed as if dozens of people were milling around, although I was in such a state of semi-detachment that I can't really say. About twenty minutes in, Hutch arrived and disappeared into the storage room. If you had told me a year earlier that I'd ever be happy to see Detective Hutchinson, I'd have said you were delusional. He had been one of the detectives assigned to the first murder investigation I was party to, and we had not hit it off at first. Not even close. I had been reminded in the interval that first impressions may be way off. Evan hadn't come back, and one of the police officers went to find him. He was, after all, the first person to find Ray.

I was in something of a daze when Hutchinson re-emerged from the storage room, calling back to whoever was in there, "Go ahead and take him down." He stood in front of me, shoved his notebook into his breast pocket, and said, "That was rough." I nodded. "Stay here, okay? I'll be back." And he walked away.

The coroner, a tall, gray man with gray hair and a rumpled gray suit, stepped out of the room, followed by two EMTs guiding a gurney. Ray's body was covered with a white sheet, but I still turned away as they loaded him into the ambulance. A police officer followed, a large plastic bag with writing on it dangling from one hand. It held a single cowboy boot. I have no idea how much time passed before I looked around and realized that everyone had cleared out and I was alone again.

I told myself at first that I had to stay there, had to wait for Hutchinson, but a voice whispered, *he's a detective—he'll find you.* I walked around the end of the long building in time to see the ambulance turn out of the gate and onto the county road. A city police car and a sheriff's department car were parked near the arena, and I could see men and women in uniforms talking to people in the spectator area. Some of the spectators were, of course, also competitors, and many had dogs by their sides. The general public was well represented, too, and all sorts of people, young and old, were exploring the vendor and information booths and watching the action.

I caught sight of Evan talking to two men in dark suits behind one of the booths. As I watched, I wished I had my camera so that I could zoom in on them. The taller guy was so thin he seemed to swim in his jacket as he edged back and around, positioning himself slightly behind Evan. The heavier man was speaking, and I wondered whether the strain across his suit coat would pop the button that held the fabric over his belly. It was the same fat man I'd seen with Ray on Saturday. He raised his hand and poked Evan in the chest, and Evan stumbled back and raised his hands, palms out, toward the man. *Don't watch, Janet,* whispered my prissier angel. *Too bad you don't have your camera,* said my inner troublemaker. As the men walked toward the parking area, Evan pulled his baseball cap off and threw it on the ground. He bent over, hands on his knees, and stood that way for a few seconds before he picked up his cap and worked his way along the backs of the booths, away from the parking area.

THIRTEEN

I GOT JAY FROM his crate and set out to look for Bonnie. I called Giselle Swann, thinking she would help put the word out on the Internet, but had to leave a message. For once I wished I had a smartphone so I could post to social media myself. Who else could I count on? Sylvia Eckhorn, mother of twins and most energetic woman in the world, answered her phone from the cereal aisle of Costco. She promised to put the news on Facebook, Twitter, and a few other places. Someone somewhere would eventually see a black-and-white Sheltie on the loose. At least I hoped so.

The morning events were delayed by a couple of hours, but aside from the ones trying to cop a view of the murder scene, people mostly went with the flow. Other than taping off the area around the room where Ray died and questioning me and Evan and a few other people, even the police saw the value in letting the day's events continue. By early afternoon things were almost back on schedule, and between laps around the property, I got to watch a bit. It gave me a good chance to ask everyone I saw to be on the lookout for Bonnie. The parade of herding breeds was lovely, and the dogs got plenty of applause. The group was well represented, too—Shetland Sheepdogs, Australian Shepherds, Pembroke and Cardigan Welsh Corgis, Australian Cattle Dogs, Summer's English Shepherd, and more. Border Collies, of course, and a Pyrenean Shepherd.

Judging by upright ears and sharp gazes, the spectating dogs seemed to enjoy the event as much as their owners, and I turned my camera on them from time to time. The result was several stunning head shots plus a couple of fifty-pound lap dogs squeezed into folding chairs with their people and a Corgi sacked out belly-up in a stroller with a toddler. I hadn't planned to shoot a photo essay, but as I panned the audience for interesting shots, Kali, a red-merle Aussie I knew from Illinois, opened a cooler, finagled a soda bottle out of it, and handed it to her owner, Kim Johnson. I got the whole hilarious sequence and decided to surprise Kim with the best shots. There was also a cute black tri-color Australian Shepherd sitting in a folding chair and wearing sunglasses and a pink floppy hat with "Lilly" embroidered across the front. I took several shots of her and made a note to track her owner down after the parade.

The herding demonstration, featuring a Corgi, a Border Collie, and an Aussie, was popular, but the real crowd pleaser was the disc-dog competition. My little friend Edith Ann was spectacular— she flew as if she had sprouted wings, and missed only one disc, which Kathy, her partner-in-sport, later attributed to her own "crappy toss." Edith Ann left the field bouncing and wagging and grinning. Kathy came out panting. I smiled to myself as I checked my photos and caught up with her to get her email address. She'd get a surprise in a week or so.

By late afternoon, Evan seemed to have gone to ground, but Summer was standing in the shadow of a big pin oak, watching as things began to wind down. I walked over and told her I needed to go home and regroup, but would be back later to help search for Bonnie, and the next day, too, if necessary. She nodded at me.

"It was a lovely weekend," I said, realizing how dumb that sounded even as the words came out. At least I didn't add, *aside from the hanged man and missing animals.* "Well, you know ..."

Summer barely answered. She was very pale, her eyes rimmed in crimson, and I could see that she wasn't as impervious as I had thought. She put her hand on my arm and started to say, "I appre ...," but her gaze slipped to something behind me and she froze. By the time she said, "Talk to you later," her body was already turning away, and in the next heartbeat, she was gone.

Maybe if I had looked right away, I'd have known what startled her, but I was a bit startled myself and I watched her for a few seconds before I turned around. Nothing and nobody stood out at first. Then I noticed two men standing near Dogs-on-Wheels. The fat one tossed a wadded-up hotdog wrapper on the ground and unbuttoned his straining jacket. The tall, skinny one was stuffing what looked like a Coney dog into his mouth. They were the same two I had seen talking to Evan earlier. *Who are they, and what the heck is going on?* That was, of course, the Janet Devil voice, the one that gets me into trouble. The other one was trying to drown her out. *Who cares? Not your beeswax.* I hadn't chosen a side in that argument yet.

It was past four-thirty by the time I made another tour of the grounds, picked up a bit of trash, packed up my stuff, and finally slid behind the wheel. As I reached for the key, the emotional weight of the weekend fell over me, heavy and black.

I could barely breathe. I had plenty to deal with running my photography business, planning a wedding, and merging my household with Tom's. The last thing I needed was to get dragged into another murder investigation. *But here you are again, Janet.* I forced myself to take some nice, long, healing breaths. *In, one, two, three.*

My neighbor and best friend, Goldie, had taught me to do this. *Out, one, two, three, four.* Count to ten … *eight, nine, ten.*

Twelve missing sheep.

One missing dog.

And a dead man.

FOURTEEN

ONE OF THESE DAYS I'll learn to see household chores through to the end. It will be part of the "get organized, stop procrastinating" self-improvement project I've been putting off for a while. *Okay, for decades.* Saturday had not been the day, though, and when I pulled the shower curtain back and reached for a towel, my arm on autopilot, I came up empty. My bath towels, all three of them, were still in the laundry room. *I told you to set a timer to remind yourself,* said that know-it-all in my head. I shushed her and looked around. For once I had not dropped my dirty duds on the bathroom floor. No, I had deposited them in the hampers in my bedroom, colors to the left, whites to the right. Besides, they stank of sheep and I no longer did, so I would have been reluctant to use them even if they were handy. The only bit of fabric in the bathroom was a navy blue washcloth. It wouldn't cover much, and besides, navy is just not my color.

I said some of those words I've been trying not to say and dripped my way across the three steps to the door. I listened carefully, then opened the door a crack and listened again. The house was still. Tom and the dogs weren't back yet, and the feline contingent must have been asleep in some secret lair. I tried to remember whether the kitchen blinds were wide open or down with the louvers at a modest-making tilt. Either way, the light was so much brighter outside than in that I figured a peeper would have to press his nose against the glass to see anything. I ran for it.

Maybe it was the day's stress that set me off, but by the time I left the hallway and scampered around the tote bag I'd left at the end of the hallway, I was flapping my bare-naked arms and laughing like a nutcase. Eight tippy-toes and a pirouette later I was in the kitchen, face to face with Leo, my lovely orange tabby. I stopped, still laughing, and reached out to stroke his cheek in greeting. His eyes went wide and his fur went wider as he flattened his ears against his neck, hissed, and backed away.

"Aww, Leo *mio*, it's just me."

Leo relaxed slightly, gathered himself, and levitated onto the counter. He stared at me for a moment, then stepped closer and sniffed, as if confirming that it was in fact me, not some otherworldly demon that sounded but didn't act like the woman he knew. Once he was convinced, he sat down and squinted at me, and I leaned in to bump noses. I didn't linger, though, as goose bumps were beginning to rise on my arms and who knows where else.

I flipped the light switch in the laundry room, visions of nice fluffy clean towels flapping in my head. Until I opened the dryer. Empty, but for a used dryer sheet and the well-worn kitchen towel I had used for Pixel's pedicure. For half a moment I was confused. Then I opened the washing machine and said *Aww, crap.* I said a few other things, too, before I started yanking the damp towels and clothes out of one machine and throwing them into the other. *Why can't they invent a machine that does it all?*

A car door closed somewhere nearby. I froze and listened. Tom's voice filtered faintly into the room. I figured I had enough time to race back to the bedroom and grab some clothes because he usually took the dogs through the gate and into the backyard. I heard Tom's voice again. "Here. Go on in." *Who's he talking to?* Leo dropped off the counter across from me with a muted thud and trotted out of the kitchen. I held my breath and listened. A knock followed by the clink of keys, the noisy front-door hinge, and another voice. My neighbor Goldie.

"Janet? Where are you? Oh, hello, Mr. Leo. How's my little man?"

With one hand I grabbed the laundry basket that held the laundry room door open and half slid, half lifted it out of the way. With my other hand I pushed the door closed, turning the knob to soften the sound of latching. *Okay, now what?* As I raised the laundry basket, meaning to set it on top of the dryer, its edge caught the open flap of the giant box of detergent that I'd neglected to stow against the wall. The tilt of the box traveled through the plastic basket, up my arm, and into my brain, but not in time for me to stop its momentum. *Whup.* The front of the box hit the floor and white powder with magic blue sparkly bits whooshed across the vinyl.

I grabbed the rooster towel from the top of the dryer and backed up against the wall, straddling the detergent box and trying to figure out how to use the terrycloth rectangle to best effect. It didn't offer much. I held my breath and listened.

The back door opened and Tom's voice came into my hiding place, loud and clear and much closer. "Mmmm. What's that?"

"Tomato basil bread. I baked an extra loaf for you two." Goldie, much as I loved her, was the bane of my weight-loss efforts.

Tom said something I couldn't make out, and then, "Where's Janet?"

She's trapped nekkid in the laundry room, I thought, wishing for two things. First, that Tom would leave the dogs outside for a bit so they wouldn't give me away. And next, that something would make Tom and Goldie go out with them for any crazy reason so that I could scamper back to the bedroom. If either of them had been alone, I would have braved the run back to my bedroom *au naturel*, but the two of them together ratcheted up the embarrassment factor. I wondered whether this was how the sheep felt when a dog had them cornered in a pen.

"Janet? Where aaaaare you? I have fresh bread!"

"I didn't see her outside. She must be changing or something," said Tom. The refrigerator opened, and Tom asked, "Beer?"

For the briefest moment I still hoped he would leave the dogs outdoors. If Tom and Goldie moved out of the kitchen, I might be able to grab a big wet towel from the dryer and sneak past them. But my hopes were dashed when something *thump thump thumped* hard against the outside of the laundry room wall and snuffling sounds filtered up from under the door, followed by a soft little whine, which anyone who hears dog spoken as much as I do would understand to mean, "In here! She's in here!" *Traitor!*

Goldie wasn't fluent enough in dog to have gotten the message, but Tom was. I grabbed the doorknob just as it began to turn, and heard Tom say, "What the … Janet? Are you in there?"

I leaned in and pulled the door open a crack. "Yes, but, umm …"

Tom pushed the door a little farther. "What are you …" His eyes traveled from my face to the arm I held across my breasts to my red rooster loin cloth and he broke into the biggest grin I've seen since my brother got his Corvette. "Nice outfit!"

"Could you please get me some jeans and a top? And stop laughing."

"Who's laughing?" He did a Groucho Marx with his eyebrows.

Jay wedged his head and shoulders past Tom and sniffed my knee.

"That tickles," I said, stroking his chin and easing him back out the door. "Come on, Tom, *please* get me some clothes."

"Okay, but only because Goldie's here."

He was still laughing when he got back from the bedroom.

FIFTEEN

Tom brought me sweatpants and a T-shirt, so I pulled them on and scampered off to the bedroom to get properly dressed. When I returned to the kitchen, Goldie was in full snit about something, but she got up and gave me a hug. "Congratulations! I understand Mr. Jay did you proud at the roundup." She seems to envision herding events as something akin to John Ford films, albeit heavier on sheep and dogs than cattle and horses.

"He did that," I said. *We'll ignore the part where he ran a flock of sheep over me. Twice.* The message light on my phone was blinking, but I ignored it and peered into the fridge. "I'm starving," I said, half hoping Goldie would invite us over for one of the fantastic concoctions she's so good at whipping up.

I turned to her. "What are you so sore about?"

Goldie snorted. "Your new neighbor." The last word came out in a tone I'm not used to hearing from Goldie. Pure sarcasm.

"They've moved in?" I glanced at Tom and he shrugged.

"He. Just one, and believe me, he'll be more than enough if today was any indication." Goldie rocked the bottom of her Ol' Woody pale ale at Jay and Drake where they sprawled on the floor. "He's not happy about them."

Pixel sauntered into the room, jumped onto Goldie's lap, and relaxed into her arms. "Totem is such a wiggleworm, the only time he does this is late afternoon. He's too wound up the rest of the time." Totem was Pixel's litter-brother. Goldie and I, and Detective Hutchinson, had adopted the three-kitten litter after a friend took in their feral mama and her brood, and we loved to compare notes as they grew. Goldie sat back and sighed. "We had just a quick encounter this morning, but it was enough. He's a jerk."

Tom and I exchanged a glance, and Tom asked, "Totem is a jerk?"

"Heavens, no! The new neighbor, what's his name. Martin. Yes, that's it. Martin."

"So what makes you say this Martin is a jerk?" I asked.

"First of all, I never trust a man who hides behind reflective sunglasses. They seem sneaky to me, and they give me flashbacks."

Goldie marched for civil rights and against the war back in the sixties, and she had spent more than a few nights "in the pokey," as she put it. I wish I'd known her then, but I knew my mother, and that was pretty close. Mom hadn't been doing so well for a couple of years, but Goldie still burned with a soft and steady flame. She took the name Golden Sunshine back in the day, and as I watched the light from the window dance in her silver hair, I thought again that she chose the right name, especially back when her hair was still blonde.

"He asked me how many pets you have, and when I told him two dogs, two cats, and a new puppy coming, he said something like, 'We'll see about that.'"

"What the heck does that mean?" I asked, and thought about the protesters at the herding clinic. Is there no end to people wanting to keep us from having animals in our lives?

"Maybe he's talking about that bill that's rumored to be coming up in the city council," said Tom. "Wait a minute—is Martin the guy's first name, or last? That bill is the brainchild of Phil Martin."

"What bill?" Goldie hadn't heard the rumors.

"If what we're hearing is true, and the bill passes, it will limit the number of pets in any one household. We haven't heard a solid number, but probably three to five."

"But if they pass that ..." Goldie didn't finish the thought, but we all knew where she was going. If they passed a number on the low end of the range, Tom and I would be in violation once his house sold and he moved in with me. And now we'd have a neighbor who, based on what Goldie said, would probably report us. The number chosen was, of course, entirely arbitrary. Our three dogs and two cats would be zero nuisance to the neighbors, unlike the single Dalmatian at the other end of the block who barked for hours on end, or the little terrierpoo on the next street who ran loose several times a week and used the neighbors' yards as his personal relief stations.

Tom patted my hand and said, "We'll figure out a solution if we need to."

Goldie sat up straight and said, "You know, it could be Phil Martin. He said he was in insurance, and I think the councilman works for Farm Bureau or State Farm or one of those. I didn't recognize him in the shades and baseball cap, but as I think about it ..." She paused, and her mouth twisted into a wicked little smile. "He's not going to be very happy here," said Goldie. "He's surrounded."

She was right. The Washingtons two doors down had three vocal little spaniel mixes named Flo, Mary, and Ross because, as Bill Washington liked to say, "they're the supremes!" Mr. Hostetler across the street had Paco the Chihuahua, and the Machados behind Martin's house had an enormous Golden Retriever x Newfoundland cross named ChaCha. There were cats in the neighborhood, too, but most were indoor pets who stared out their windows at the dogs and people walking by.

"I thought he had one of those beautiful old mansions on Old Mill Road?"

"His wife does. I mean, she inherited it. Her family owned the Three Rivers Brewery." She looked at me. "You probably don't remember it."

I had a vague memory of several huge old brick buildings somewhere along the river, but they were long gone before I was old enough to pay attention.

No one said anything for a moment, until Goldie changed the subject again.

"We really should go find that dress soon, Janet." Goldie held her beer to her lips and peered at me over her readers. "Wedding day will be upon us before you know it."

There are few things I hate more than shopping for clothes, and I knew this particular quest promised to be fraught with stumbling blocks and hazards. I glanced at Tom. He shrugged and said, "You can't go nekkid."

"Okay, okay. Tomorrow afternoon." *I can hardly wait.*

SIXTEEN

STRESS MAKES ME HUNGRY for things I don't want most of the time, and although finding Ray's body had made me skip lunch, by the time Tom and Goldie finished their pale ales, I was ravenous. The problem was compounded because I'm not much of a cook, or shopper. Tom is, but he hadn't moved in yet, so there weren't many raw ingredients in the fridge or cupboards to assemble into a meal. If I had been alone, I might have settled for the stuff I did find—crackers with peanut butter, a freckled banana, some chocolate chips, and popcorn. Goldie's a great cook, and she offered to thaw some homemade soup from her freezer, but Tom nixed that idea.

"How about Indian?" he asked. "All three of us. My treat."

He didn't need to ask twice. I shut Pixel and Leo into my guest room, checked the litterbox, ran a brush through my hair, and we were out the door.

"Should I lock Totem up when I leave him?" Goldie asked as Tom cleared his backseat.

"Not if he can't get hurt," I said. "I just don't like to leave a baby loose with the dogs. They'd never hurt her on purpose, but play can get out of hand." *Face it, you're over-protective.* "I won't lock Pixel up once she's bigger."

"Jerk."

For half a second I thought she meant me, but Goldie was looking past me. I turned, and there he was, the new neighbor. He had a point-and-shoot camera hanging against his chest and a notebook and pen in his hand, and he seemed to be examining the exterior of his house inch by inch. That seemed a little tardy, since he'd already moved in. It also seemed an odd time for photos since it was almost dark out. Then again, he was an insurance agent. What do I know?

"No time like the present," I said.

Goldie clucked and got into Tom's van, and I crossed the stretch of lawn between me and Mr. Martin and said, "Hi there. I'm Janet MacPhail. Welcome to the neighborhood."

"You live right there," he said, gesturing toward my house with his chin. He didn't smile, and he didn't tell me his name.

And that pushed my pushy button. I held out my hand to force the issue, and said, "Yes, right there."

He was tall, close to six feet, and had a long, jowly face. He slowly shifted his writing tools to his left hand and offered me his limp right one. "Phil Martin," he said. His voice seemed familiar, but of course it would. He was in the news from time to time.

My skin was in contact with his for only a second, but that was enough. His hand was cold and clammy and shot me straight back to those god-awful square dancing sessions in fifth-grade gym class. With *boys*. And I always seemed to get matched with Herbie Mac-Fadden. He had limp, clammy hands like that.

"We're just on our way out, but I hope we'll have a chance to chat soon."

I was turning away when he said, "Understand you have a lot of pets."

"A dog and two indoor cats," I said.

Martin shoved his clammy hands into his pockets, rocked his shoulders back and his belt buckle forward, and narrowed his eyes at me. "I saw two dogs out there just a little bit ago."

I almost answered, but a little voice whispered that I didn't have to defend myself or our dogs to him. Actually, the little voice wasn't that polite, but I decided to keep what I really wanted to say to myself. I found a smile somewhere in my over-taxed resources, pasted it on, and said, "We'll talk soon." I rejoined Tom and Goldie.

Tom winked at me and drawled, "That looked right friendly, pardner."

"Nice crotch thrust." Goldie patted my shoulder. "Good for you not to engage."

I cranked my head around to look at Goldie and echoed her opinion of Phil Martin. "He's a jerk."

"Unfortunately," said Tom, backing out of the driveway, "he's a jerk with some juice, so proceed with caution."

SEVENTEEN

A COLD FRONT SWEPT in during the night, and Monday morning brought us a vicious wind and glowering sky. April is, as T.S. Eliot said, "the cruellest month," or at least it can be in northern Indiana when you think spring has sprung and suddenly there's ice on the birdbath and you need fleece and Gore-Tex. The eastern sky was bleeding a narrow slash of crimson light beneath a dark bank of clouds when I went out with Jay to police the backyard. I was wearing a long-sleeved T and the light jacket I'd worn over the weekend, and by the time I went back in I had my jaws clamped tight to silence my chattering teeth. Weather that made me want to crawl back into a warm bed turned Jay into a bouncing bundle of enthusiasm for, well, anything more fun than crawling back into bed, so we played an indoor game of "find the toy" to take the edge off. It warmed me up a bit, too.

Goldie was usually up early, but her windows were dark, so after I changed into warmer clothes I wrote a note to remind her about our shopping trip and stuck it on the window of her back door where I knew she'd see it. I found one leather glove and, after rifling through all my dresser drawers with no results, I gave up and took a pair of fleece mittens instead. They'd make handling Jay's longline more difficult, but I could always defy my own advice and wrap the nylon line around my hand for control. *Just don't break your hand for the wedding,* said that annoying voice of caution. I would have traded a broken hand, though, for finding Bonnie safe and sound.

The six-thirty news led off with a story about yet another insane cut to school funding, followed by one about a proposed new tax break for corporations choosing to set up shop in Indiana. *Because they'll want to come here for the uneducated work force.* I was about to turn the radio off when the next story made me turn the volume up instead.

"A Nevada man, Ray Turnbull, was found dead at a property belonging to Collin Lahmeyer of Fort Wayne on Sunday morning." I registered the owner's name even as I listened to the rest of the story. Collin was a member of Tom's retriever training club, and his family owned another property where the group trained frequently. It was also a property where a murder had occurred the previous August. Collin couldn't be happy about having another man die violently on his property.

The announcer's words brought my wandering thoughts to heel. *A Nevada man?* Until that moment, I'd had no idea where Ray was from, but that seemed odd since he had been working on and off for Evan and Summer for at least a couple of years. Surely he had a house or apartment or something near the Winslows' farm. Wouldn't that make him an Indiana man by now? "Police say that preliminary evidence suggests that Mr. Turnbull died of asphyxiation, and suicide is suspected." The reporter, who sounded very young, went on. "Some sheep also disappeared earlier from the same location, but police wouldn't say whether the two incidents were related."

I turned the radio off and thought about what I knew and didn't know. Ray was from Nevada. Some faint memory made me think that Summer was from somewhere out west, but I wasn't sure where, or even why I thought I knew that. I did know that she came to Indiana originally to go to Purdue, where she had earned a degree in animal sciences. Her diploma, issued four years earlier, hung in her office at the farm. Evan was a Hoosier, born and bred. He grew up on a farm near Bluffton, about thirty miles south of Fort Wayne. Had Ray and Summer known each other before they landed in the Midwest? And who were the two goons in the sloppy suits who were hanging around on Sunday? They didn't fit in at a dog event, and the encounters I saw between them and Evan and Ray didn't exactly smack of friendships.

My thoughts were spinning like circus Poodles by the time I pulled into the field and parked my van near the arena, now free of ropes and tents and dogmobiles. *So this is Collin Lahmeyer's property.* I wondered whether Tom knew that. Surely he would have told me if he did. A black sedan and small red Honda sat side by side at the end of the arena, but no one seemed to be around. I got Jay out and attached the longline we use for tracking to his collar. No point using his tracking harness, which is designed to allow the dog to pull when he's following a scent. We would be searching, not tracking, because I had nothing with Bonnie's scent to get Jay started. If Drake or Leo or Pixel went missing, I could tell him to find them by name and he would track the familiar scent, but he knew Bonnie only for quick doggy hellos. I would have to trust that if he sensed her where I couldn't see her, he'd let me know, as he would with any animal. I shut the van, buttoned the top button on my jacket, and wished I'd brought a hat or earmuffs to cut the wind.

"Okay, Bub, let's see if we have any better luck today." Jay bounced up and down a couple of times, and then trotted about twenty feet ahead of me, keeping the line loose. He had his nose to the ground and began weaving left and right and back again across the roadway, pausing to check occasional clumps of grass before moving on. He took his time with a large rock, hiked his leg on it, and moved on.

As we proceeded, I watched for places where a smallish dog might hide, but I didn't see any likely spots. If Bonnie were injured, she would probably try to hole up somewhere. If she were frightened, there was no telling how far she might have run. She could be in the next county by now. And if someone had picked her up, she could be anywhere. Jay rounded the end of the long pole building several strides ahead of me. He stopped, hair poofed away from his neck as his hackles rose, and scared me back to the moment with a loud *woof*.

EIGHTEEN

JAY STOPPED BARKING AND his whole body started to vibrate. About halfway down, outside the fatal storage room, Hutch was talking to a woman. At her side stood a dog wearing a harness over a blue-and-gold vest that said Marion Co. Search & Rescue K9. The dog's shoulder came to the woman's knee, and his medium-length coat was a bright yellow-gold, but unlike a Golden Retriever, he had four white stockings and a collar of white fur. He was angled away from me so I couldn't see it, but I knew he had a white muzzle and heavy white ruff as well. It was Hutch's former partner, Jo Stevens, and her young search-and-rescue dog, a Golden Retriever x Australian Shepherd cross named Shamus.

"What are *you* doing here?" I asked when I reached them.

Jo hugged me and Shamus poked me with his nose, wagging and grinning, while Jay shared his joy with all three of them. When she let go, Jo said, "I was here for the weekend, visiting family. Hutch called and told me what happened."

When I first met him, Hutchinson hadn't cared a bit about animals in peril. Now, a year later, he said, "I thought Shamus might track the missing dog."

Even if they had a way to give Shamus the scent, tracking Bonnie in the sea of olfactory input around this place was going to be challenging, to say the least. Judging by the look on Jo's face, she knew it, too. I said, "I wish we had something with Bonnie's scent." I thought for a moment, and an image came to mind of Ray's rattletrap old pickup pulling into the Winslows' place, Bonnie riding shotgun. "Hutch, is Ray's truck still here? Bonnie always rode beside him on the front seat."

"It's parked at the far end of the building," he said. "I don't think it's locked. It wasn't yesterday."

"Let's do it," said Jo as she gathered Shamus's leash.

As she and Hutch turned away, I asked, "How long are you going to be in town?" Jo had moved to Indianapolis to join an inter-agency canine search team. It was a great opportunity, but I missed her.

"I work tonight," she said, shrugging at me. "I've got about an hour, then I need to hit the road."

I thought about taking Jay to the truck to get the scent, but decided a general search would probably be as effective. If Jay sensed Bonnie hiding somewhere or ... I wouldn't let my thoughts go there. In any case, Jay would let me know if Bonnie was nearby.

We began with the overgrown lane I had found on Saturday. Jay ranged back and forth across the grassy stretch and into the corn stubble, tangling the longline twice on the remains of last year's crop. I unclipped him and let him move freely, knowing he'd be at my side in a snap if I called. About halfway along the lane, he veered into the field and ran between the rows, not chasing, but determined to reach something. My heart took a little leap and I jogged to where he had entered the cornfield, hoping to see Bonnie hiding there. The field rolled just enough that all I could see was Jay's back, but I could tell that he was sniffing something. I walked into the stubble, afraid to breathe.

Fur. I let my breath go. Gray fur, and a few bones. The remains of a rabbit dinner, and they had been there awhile.

"Jay, come." He took one last sniff and followed me out of the corn. We spent another forty minutes or so, walking to the end of the lane before cutting across the back edge of the big field and returning to the buildings by way of the tree and fence line. There was no sign of the dog, at least nothing I could see. I would swing by to check the animal shelter when I went to see my mom. *And go shopping*, whispered that nag in my head. *You need a dress for the wedding.*

Yeah, yeah.

The red Honda—Jo's car—was gone when we got back to the arena. Hutch's car was still there, but he was nowhere in sight. I grabbed a bottle of water from my van and poured some into a stainless steel bowl. Jay drank enough to be polite, and I took a swig from the bottle.

"Okay, Bub, let's think about this a little," I said, pulling my phone out to check the time. "We'll give it half an hour, and then we'll have to go home." Jay cocked his head, letting his tongue dangle out the side of his mouth, and looked at me as if to say, "Sure! Whatever you say!"

We strolled to a stump and I sat on it. The charcoal clouds had thickened, and the place felt spooky. I glanced at the door to the storage room and flashed on the way Ray had looked. I closed my eyes, forced myself to breathe, forced other images to the top. A blue jay was screeching somewhere behind me, and a pair of mourning doves cooed from the corner of the building.

There are no ghosts here. I shivered. *You're alone with your dog, and safe.*

And then I wasn't.

NINETEEN

An almost slim young woman in pressed jeans, blue cowgirl boots, and a fitted denim jacket over a red sweater was coming my way from the far end of the pole barn. I could hardly believe how much she had changed in the past year. Apparently trauma can have positive effects on some people.

She bent to pet Jay and said, "Hi, Janet. How are you?"

"Giselle! What are you doing here?"

Giselle Swann trains at Dog Dayz, as do Tom and I, but since Precious, her Maltese, weighs about six pounds, collar and all, Giselle wasn't one of the sheep-herding crowd. Not that Precious wouldn't have been willing—he's a gung-ho agility and obedience dog, and Giselle had recently started tracking with him. He might control the sheep by sheer will.

"I heard about the missing dog, the Sheltie, and I had a little time between classes, so ..." She smiled at me, and I realized that she was wearing lipstick and eye makeup, all very subtle and becoming. And I would bet a morning's photo shoot that she weighed at least eighty pounds less than she had a year earlier.

"Giselle, you look fantastic."

Color rose in her cheeks and I expected her to deflect the compliment, which had always been typical Giselle, but she fooled me.

"Thanks, Janet." The smile expanded. "I'm pretty excited to be able to wear jeans that don't have an elastic waist."

I resisted the urge to pull my comfort-waist pants a little higher.

Giselle leaned in and lowered her voice. "What's going on? I heard that some sheep went missing on Saturday, and a man committed suicide?"

"I don't think we know that it's suicide."

"That's what the radio said." Giselle looked thoughtful. "I'm not really sure which is better."

She had a point. In case she had heard a different newscast than I had, I asked, "What did the news story say about the sheep?"

"Just that they were missing and police were investigating. They said it might just be a case of negligence, that maybe someone didn't latch the gate."

"I really don't think so. Summer and Evan are obsessively careful about their animals."

Giselle narrowed her eyes at me. "Maybe you should do some sleuthing. You're pretty good at it."

I was about to decline when Hutch came around the far end of the long building. I pointed with my chin and said, "I think I'll let him take care of it."

Giselle turned around and gasped. "Is that …?" Her voice drifted off, and I wondered whether Hutchinson made Giselle nervous. He had interrogated her during a murder investigation a year earlier, and he may have been in on her arrest for vandalism last November, although I couldn't remember for sure. But when she spoke again, it wasn't fear I heard in her voice. "It is. It's that handsome cop."

Handsome? Hutchinson?

Giselle seemed to stand a little straighter and I could swear she thrust her breasts out and sucked in her belly. She smiled and cocked her head the tiniest bit as Hutchinson closed in on us.

Hutch handed me a bottle of water. "I thought you could use this." He turned to Giselle and froze for a heartbeat or two before he said, "Miss ... Miss Swann?"

I was amazed that he recognized her, she had changed so much. Then again, he was a trained observer.

Giselle held out her hand, the picture of poise. "Officer Hutchinson. It's lovely to see you again. And please, it's Giselle." He took her hand and they looked at one another and I swear I felt the tiniest shift in ... I don't know what. I half expected sparks to fly into the air. *Holy jumpin' agility cats.*

Giselle broke the spell. "Are you the investigator on these cases?"

"Uh, yeah." Hutchinson retrieved his hand and looked at me, then back at Giselle. "I'm, uh, just starting ..." His voice trailed off as he stared at her.

I decided to help him. I didn't have a bucket of cold water handy, so I asked, "What happens now?"

Before he could reply, Giselle said, "If you'll excuse me, I just came to see if I could help look for the missing dog. Bonnie, right?"

"Right," I said.

"You seem to have things covered here, so I'm going to drive around the back roads and alert the neighbors. Then I have to get to class." Giselle barely glanced at me, but she threw Hutchinson another big smile and said, "I hope I'll see you again."

My jaw felt a bit slack as I watched her walk away. Hutchinson watched as well, and didn't turn back to me until Giselle disappeared around the end of the building. When he did look at me, his cheeks went as red as a police cruiser's turret lights.

TWENTY

HUTCHINSON SEEMED FLUSTERED, BUT he finally grinned and said, "Giselle's not, you know, involved with this investigation, is she?"

"Not yet." I waited, but Hutchinson didn't seem to know what to say, so I tried again. "She wasn't around yesterday, and doesn't do any herding, if that's what you mean. And I don't think she knew Ray, or Summer and Evan for that matter."

He grinned but said nothing.

"Go for it," I said, play punching his arm. My own feelings made me pretty goofy when I was first getting to know Tom. To be honest, I still feel gooey-kneed when he looks at me a certain way.

Hutchinson nodded and cleared his throat, and then pulled a Moleskine notebook from his pocket and flipped through to about the middle. He was forty-four going on fourteen when it came to girls, apparently, and I decided to give him a break and follow his change of direction.

"Finally got rid of the spiral bound?" I knew he was forever snagging his cheap notebook wire on his pockets.

"Oh, yeah." He held the notebook out and looked at it. "Jo got me one of these awhile back. I like 'em." I agreed, and he moved on.

"So, we're waiting for the autopsy, and forensics, and we're doing backgrounds on people, you know, the sheep owners, the dead guy." He glanced at me. "You know them very well?"

"Not really. I've known Summer and Evan for a couple of years, and I've been out to their place quite a few times. Jay and I take herding lessons from Summer. They wouldn't ..." I hesitated, remembering Summer's angry phone conversation and the obvious nastiness between Evan and Ray. Those memories in turn brought back an argument I had overheard a few months earlier. They apparently had money problems. Summer had wanted to sell some of their livestock and Evan hadn't.

Hutchinson looked up. I wanted to let my memory clear before I said anything more, so I changed directions again. "I don't, uh, didn't really know Ray. I've seen him at the Winslows' farm and a few events, but that's it. He was good with the animals, but not big on conversation." *Just say it—he gave you the creeps.* Then again, the animals liked him, and that said something. "So are you thinking Ray's murder is connected to the missing sheep?"

"Murder?" Hutchinson eyed me, but he didn't seem too surprised. "Who says it was murder?"

"No one, but suicide? And here, at a herding event? It just doesn't make sense."

Hutchinson pressed his lips together, closed the notebook, and stuck it back in his pocket. "Why don't we see what the coroner says before we jump to any crazy conclusions? Unless you know something you should tell me."

I shook my head and reminded myself that he was a friend, but still a cop. "Have you and the Sheriff's department sorted out the jurisdiction question?" Summer Winslow had been furious about the city police versus county sheriff question, and I couldn't blame her. With her sheep's lives on the line, who cared about a technicality?

And even with Ray's death thrown into the mix, they still needed to find those sheep. Or try. *And if this turns into a homicide investigation, they'll really have to figure out whose it is.*

"We're teaming up. They've formed a 'joint task force.'" Hutchinson snorted. "We'll see how *that* goes." He pointed toward the eve under the building behind me. A camera I hadn't noticed before looked back at us. "In the meantime, we've got people looking at the videos."

"Videos?"

"They used to store boats in the building, and they had four cameras around the grounds, set on motion sensors at night. They're still working. We're hoping they picked something up." He grinned at me. "You know how helpful pictures can be." Hutchinson paused, his cheeks reddening again. "Say, Janet, you wouldn't happen to have Giselle's phone number, would you?"

TWENTY-ONE

MY MOTHER RECOGNIZED ME only about sixty percent of the time, but she was always happy to see Jay. Granted, she often called him Laddie, and maybe she thought he *was* Laddie, a Collie who died before I was born. Jay doesn't mind, and his presence both perks her up and calms her down, so I take him with me to Shadetree Retirement Home as often as possible. He's a certified therapy dog, and as patient as I am antsy around the residents.

It's not that I don't want to be compassionate. I'm just clumsy about it, and the stress of wondering whether I'll be spending any given visit with my mother or a stranger inhabiting her body just makes me worse. Clumsy or not, I'd been visiting several times a week since we moved her to Shadetree a year earlier, and I was happy to see how Mom had regained some of her faculties since she started seeing Tony Marconi. As I parked across from the front door, I whispered a request to the universe that this would be a good day for Mom.

I had bathed Jay the night before—I always do after close encounters of the woolly kind—so he was clean aside from some dry plant matter stuck in his britches. I gave him a quick going over with his brush, then used it to touch up my own wild hair. *Too bad Bill isn't here*, whispered Janet Devil. Seeing me use my dog's grooming supplies on myself makes my brother crazier than usual, so naturally I do it in his presence whenever possible. Fifty years of siblinghood and we're still pushing each other's buttons. Oddly, dealing with our mother's problems over the past months has brought us closer than we've been since grade school. I was smiling about that as I checked my murky reflection in the van's window. Between the wind and the dampness of impending rain, I was a curly mess. I did what I could, tossed the brush back into the van, and went to find my mother.

Jade Templeton, Shadetree's manager and reigning angel, smiled at me from the far side of the main lounge. She was holding Percy, her Toy Poodle, for a resident to pet. Seeing Percy always twists my emotions in confusing ways. I'm glad he landed with someone who loves him, and if a dog can have a vocation, Percy seems to have one for spending time with lonely old people. The twist comes from the reason he's here at all. Jade adopted Percy when his owners were murdered. Now, a year later, another man was dead, another dog homeless. I just hoped that Bonnie was alive and uninjured, and that someone would find her soon. I'd had enough of murder. I'd had enough of it months earlier, and yet the specter of violent death was back. *Don't jump the gun, Janet. Ray Turnbull really might have committed suicide.*

As if sensing my thoughts, Jay bumped my knee, and I shook off the dark thoughts in favor of a cheery visit. We can usually find my mother in the atrium, soaking up the sun surrounded by the raised beds of the therapy garden. Mom is the self-appointed head gardener, and the way she runs the operation, you'd think she was overseeing work at Kew Gardens. Bossy as she is, everyone seems to acknowledge that she deserves the job. Whatever else she may forget, the names and needs of all the plants are at her memory's every beck and call. Today, though, the only person in the atrium was a man I had seen but never met because he was usually sound asleep. He was tucked into a wing chair with a blanket across his lap, a book in his hand, and a walker by his side. I left him to his nap.

Jay and I struck out for the smaller lounge at the back of the building, and halfway there, Jay started to pull. He always knew where Mom was before I did. And there she was, tucked into a recliner facing the picture window. She was focused on the *Fine Gardening* magazine in her hands. I might have interrupted more gently, but Jay had no such compunction, and he shoved his nose up under the magazine, grinning and whining at her. She started to laugh, tossed the magazine onto the end table, and bent to kiss my goofy dog.

"Jay! How are you, sweetheart?" Jay popped his front end into her lap and leaned his head into the cradle of her arms.

A long breath of relief left me. *Mom's here.*

"Hi, Mom." I was pulling a red-flowered armchair around to face her when she reached for me. My mother has never been much of a hugger, but lately she's much more touchy-feely. I wondered if that came from Tony, too. We hugged each other as well as we could with a fifty-pound dog in the way, and I sat down across from her. "How are you doing?"

"I'm fine, Sweetie." She had a new softness about her, a calm and, odd as it sounds, a glow, as if a quiet fire were burning inside her. "And how are you? All set for the big day? It's only two weeks now."

"Do you want me to get him off you?" Jay was leaning into her lap. Gentle or not, he's a load even for me, and I'm not frail.

But she shook her head and kept stroking his cheeks and ears as he squinted in ecstasy. "Have you found a dress yet?"

Gaaaa. I haven't worried about dresses in longer than I care to say. My wardrobe is decidedly animal friendly, which means mostly pants of various lengths, stretchy, comfy tops, and running shoes.

Admit it, whispered my inner nag, *you're more frightened of dress shopping than you are of rustlers and murderers.* Encountering the missing sheep and Ray's death in a single thought sent my mind down a path that had nothing to do with clothes shopping.

Were the events connected? The police didn't seem to think so, but a link seemed more plausible now. Still, how exactly would the two crimes be connected? If Ray was involved in the theft, why take the sheep from the weekend event? As far as I knew, he had access to them all the time at the Winslows' farm. Then again, removing sheep in the daytime would be nearly impossible, I thought. Summer's weaving school and wool shop were on the property, so she was rarely gone. Evan was a graphic designer, and he also worked from home. Ray might have been able to steal the sheep at night since he knew the Winslows' dogs, but that too seemed foolhardy to me.

No one else would pull it off, though. I was sure of that. Nell, the Winslows' English Shepherd, had the run of the place, although I had no idea whether she was loose outside at night. Still, she would hear intruders even if she were inside. And then there was Luciano, Summer's hundred-pound Maremma. He'd been raised with the flock and was very protective, and although he loved Summer, he was none too fond of anyone else. Summer always secured Luciano in the barn before any dogs other than Nell were allowed near the sheep, but Summer had mentioned more than once that he was loose with the flock at night. Trying to get past him really would be suicidal. So it made sense that the theft took place away from their farm. The question now was whether Ray was involved, or whether he found out something and died for his trouble. And the bigger question—did he commit suicide, or did he have some help? His swollen, twisted fingers suggested a struggle, although I couldn't picture how fighting could cause that kind of damage. Had someone broken his fingers on purpose?

Hutchinson had mentioned security cameras, and by now the coroner might have an opinion about manner of death. I'd have to remember to call Hutch when I got home, although I knew he might not tell me much. I was pondering how I might wangle the information out of him when I noticed my mother watching me, a bemused smile on her lips and one eyebrow raised.

"Janet, dear," she said, leaning across Jay to pat my knee, "shopping for a dress won't kill you."

TWENTY-TWO

MI PUEBLO WAS NOT directly on our route, but they have the best *chili rellenos* in northeastern Indiana, and the drive gave me a chance to drop off flyers about Bonnie at some vet clinics on the southeast side of Fort Wayne. I didn't need the menu, but the picture of the *margarita grande* on the table display was calling me. I'm not much of a lunchtime drinker, but dress shopping seemed like a pretty good reason to make an exception.

"Don't you dare," said Goldie.

Stop reading my mind. "Wouldn't think of it."

"Right." She closed her menu and set it aside. "Any news about the missing sheep?"

"Not that I've heard," I said. "Nothing about Ray, either."

"Ray?"

Our server took our order, and then I answered Goldie. "Ray's the man who ..." I almost said "hanged himself," but changed it to "died."

"Do you think he had something to do with stealing the sheep?" Goldie shook about half a cup of Cholula green pepper hot sauce into her salsa, turning it brown and making my salivary glands go into overdrive. She dipped a corn chip, held it in front of her mouth, and went on. "Do you think that's why, you know, the suicide? Remorse, maybe?"

I waited, ready to slide my ice water her way, as she popped the hot salsa into her mouth. No reaction. Goldie scooped up another chipful and said, "Good salsa, once you jazz it up a bit."

"Let me try that," I said, dipping a chip into the brown mix. "I thought that green stuff was really hot."

Goldie spoke while I taste tested her salsa. "It's very sad, and it seems like an odd place to, you know . . ."

She seemed to be waiting for me to finish the thought, but I was busy trying to breathe, and the water I gulped just spread the fire down my throat and into my chest cavity. Goldie pushed the chip basket toward me and told me to eat a couple, plain. Our food arrived, and I forked up a mouthful of rice. It soaked up some of the heat, and the fire in my esophagus sputtered and died back to a warm glow. I excused myself and scurried off to splash cold water on my face.

When I got back, we picked up the conversation, and as usual, Goldie knew what I was going to say before I said it.

"You don't think it was suicide, do you?" She made it sound like more of a statement than question.

Don't I? "I'm just not sure it makes sense. But I don't know why I think that," I said, pausing to bunch the pieces of my thoughts into a usable bundle. "That's not true." I told her about Ray's injured hand, and added, "I didn't really know Ray, didn't know anything about his life."

"What does Hutch think?" Goldie and Detective Hutchinson had gotten to know each other over a box of kittens back in the fall. He had adopted Pixel's and Totem's sister, a little calico he called Amy.

I shrugged. "He's waiting for the autopsy, I suppose. I decided not to say too much until I knew more. "We haven't really talked about it."

Goldie patted her napkin against her mouth, folded it, and laid it on the table. "I hope someone finds his dog soon. Poor little thing."

We were waiting for our change when my phone vibrated in my pocket. Tom. I'm not big on taking calls in social situations, but he rarely calls me during the day, so I thought it might be important. Goldie excused herself and I answered.

"The realtor just called," Tom said. "The people who looked at the house on Saturday want a second look."

"And you're in a cleaning frenzy?"

"It's not too bad," he said. "I'll just shovel the bones and toys into a box and take the dog bed out to the van, and Drake and I will get out of here." No one said anything for a moment, and then Tom said, "So this is good. Maybe we'll get an offer."

We. My tummy did a little flip-flop. It was his house, not ours, but he had been speaking of us as a "we" for months. I was committed to Tom and I knew I could trust him in a pinch, but I'd been on my own so long, I wasn't sure I could share living quarters well with anyone who didn't walk on all fours.

"That's great. I guess we'll know soon."

"I hope so," he said. "I'm going to drive out to Collin's place and take another look around for Ray's dog. I'll drive around the area. There's an old barn about half a mile down the road, might be a place she'd hide."

"So you knew Collin Lahmeyer owns that place?"

"Well, yeah." He sounded a bit surprised at the question. "I told you he'd bought some property. He wants to put up a dog-training facility."

My complete inability to recall Tom telling me that gave me pause. Ever since Mom started having memory problems, I've worried about my own mental future. Then again, maybe he only thought he had told me, or maybe I hadn't heard him. I let it go, and told him that I had dropped off flyers at both shelters and several veterinary offices.

"You're still nervous about this, aren't you?"

"Not nervous. I just hope we find her soon," I said. "I found a coyote kill out there this morning. That's not a good thing for a little dog."

"Not Bonnie. Us."

Yes, I'm terrified. "No, I'm not."

"It will be great, Janet."

A quarter hour later, Goldie and I walked into Pamela's Bridal and Formal Wear. I had suggested Macy's or Kohl's, but Goldie insisted on something a bit classier. "You're only going to do this once, Janet. Get something special to wear."

Get something expensive, you mean. "I'll probably never wear it again."

A bubbly blonde was approaching from the back of the store, a big "what can I sell you" smile on her face. Goldie elbowed me and said, "Stop grumbling."

"Hello, ladies. I'm Candace. How may I help you?" The way she looked at my jeans and not-so-new sweater suggested that I might be beyond help.

"We're just looking," I said.

Goldie peered over her glasses at me and turned to Candace. "She needs a lovely, special dress."

Candace pressed her hands into prayer position and said, "Lovely! Mother of the bride?"

I tried not to look at Goldie, but couldn't help myself. She had her chin tucked toward her chest, her lips pursed, and the corners of her eyes crinkled. We both burst out laughing, and Candace took a step backward, a little wrinkle furrowed between her well-groomed brows.

"No, dear," I said. "I'm the daughter of the bride." *Could be worse,* I thought. *I could be the bride.*

85

TWENTY-THREE

TOM WAS ALMOST VIBRATING with excitement when he picked me up bright and early Tuesday morning. He had three dog crates in the back of his van—two big ones side by side for Jay and Drake, and a medium for his yet-unnamed puppy girl. Hers was snugged up to theirs at a right angle, just behind the front seats. I smiled at a plastic caddy full of cleaning supplies—a spray bottle of water, another of diluted Dawn, a third of no-rinse dog shampoo, several elderly hand towels, a roll of paper towels—resting on a clean crate pad next to the puppy crate. Leave it to Tom to be prepared for a carsick baby dog.

Jay hopped into his crate, wiggling his nubby tail, and Drake thumped back at him. I stuck my fingers between the bars of Drake's crate and he pushed his velvety muzzle against them. "Brace yourself, old man," I said. He cocked his head and lifted the base of his ears as if to say *Why would I do that?*

"There's coffee in the thermos." Tom leaned over and kissed me, handing me a travel mug in the same motion. "And breakfast in the cooler."

"You don't look like you need much more stimulant, Dr. Saunders." *You look like you might leap out of your skin.* As soon as I had the lid back on my mug, he backed out of the driveway, a big grin on his face. I glanced at the doggy boys, both of them panting happily. "The boys are in for a surprise," I said.

We beat the morning rush and were on I-69 headed south just as the sun prepared to clear the treetops. Tom slipped a Grupo Putumayo disc into the CD player, set it to background volume, and sang along to the beginning of "Madre Selva." I took my own advice to the dogs and tilted my seat back a tad, savoring the morning light and the pleasure of being cocooned in a small space with three of my favorite friends. The coffee was rich and warm and smooth, with no acid bite and just a suggestion of cinnamon. I reached for the cooler, hoping for a bear claw or at least a bagel with cream cheese.

"You call this breakfast?" I asked, pulling out a container of sugar-free low-fat Greek yogurt, a baggie of hard-boiled eggs, and an orange.

"You said you were cutting out sugar and bread."

"And you believed me?" I sighed, fished a spoon from the bottom of the cooler, and opened the yogurt. "At least it's key lime."

"If you start to feel faint, we'll stop at the first rest stop and get some junk food from the machines," said Tom, patting my knee and grinning sideways at me. "Shopping trip a success?"

"It was." We laughed about the sales clerk's confusion over my status as daughter, not mother, of the bride, and I changed topics. "Still no sign of Bonnie."

"No. I talked to most of the neighbors within about a mile last night. But there's a lot of land, and more than a little of it covered with woods and brush."

The idea of that lovely little dog lost or hiding alone out there made my stomach heave. "We have flyers out all over the place, and

Giselle has been posting to social media. Luckily, I had some pretty good photos of her from Saturday. Bonnie, not Giselle."

We rode in silence for a few minutes. Leo had been abducted once, and my eyes still burned when I thought of that time. As far as I knew, Tom had never had a pet go missing, but I'm sure he could imagine the pain and guilt, fear and second-guessing the experience brings on. Even if Bonnie wasn't our dog, her disappearance had spurred a lot of dog lovers to help with the search. I knew that if we found her, someone would give her a good home.

The sun cleared the tops of the trees and slammed into the side of my head. I pulled the visor to the side and down, but it didn't reach far enough, so I gave up on my semi-reclining position and re-adjusted my seat. Maybe it was my movements, maybe it was the brighter light, but the mood in the car shifted again.

"Guess what?" Tom's face was all grin.

"Let me guess ... You're getting a puppy?"

He laughed. "That too. But there's more."

"You have a new book contract?" That was true, too, but it was week-old news. Tom had signed a contract with Indiana University Press for a book on something to do with herbs and magic among New Agers in the desert southwest. He'd spent the previous summer doing fieldwork in Arizona and New Mexico, so much of our early relationship had developed over the phone and through emails.

Tom pulled me back to the moment. "More."

"I think you're going to have to tell me."

"The house is sold!" He was practically bouncing in his seat.

"Yeah? The second showing?"

He nodded. "I accepted the offer last night. The realtor called while I was out looking for Bonnie, and I signed the paperwork on my way home." He grinned at me.

"So now we wait to see if they get the loan approval? How long—"

"Nope." Another glance and grin my way. "It's a cash deal."

I couldn't imagine having enough cash to pay outright for a house. "No kidding?"

"They're moving back here after thirty-five years in the Bay area, so they came with big-time equity from their house," he said. "And they want to close and take possession as soon as I can get out."

Whoa, screeched both my little voices. I'd been counting on a leisurely adjustment period between offer and closing to let me ease all the way into this realignment of the earth's axis. I'd been living alone for decades. So had Tom. Neither of us was completely inflexible, but we had developed our own ways of living. *It'll be fine*, said Janet Devil, eager as always for adventure and risk. *Oh dear oh dear oh dear*, muttered Janet Angel. *He's tidy. You're not. He cooks. You don't. He's easy going. You're a hot head. He minds his own business. You snoop.* Not that I hadn't thought of all that many times already.

"Janet?" Tom's voice, still excited but stitched through with a slender thread of worry.

"That's great news!" I said, meaning it. "I was just thinking . . . . I'll have to speed up the reorganizing." I had promised to clear out my guest-cum-storage room to make an office space for Tom, and I hadn't made much progress. Plus we had to decide which pieces of whose furniture we wanted to keep. I might have to take Goldie up on her offer to lock me out and purge, as she put it, "all this crap." And then there was the little matter of Phil Martin's pet limit bill. "So, what are you thinking, time wise?"

"How does May Day sound?"

May Day! May Day! "Perfect," I said.

TWENTY-FOUR

AN HOUR AND A half into the drive, Tom took the Pendleton exit, turned west onto State Road 38, and engaged his GPS system. "They're just this side of Noblesville," he said. "I think we should take the boys out before we get there."

He was right. Most breeders with young puppies aren't keen on having strange dogs on their property. Even healthy dogs can bring in disease, and puppies who have been weaned but not yet fully vaccinated are vulnerable. We pulled into the parking lot beside a small branch bank and walked Drake and Jay across a side lawn to a gnarled redbud in its full glory. The sky overhead was clear and blue, but gray clouds rolled across the horizon and, judging by the prevailing wind, were headed our way.

Ten minutes later we turned onto a county road and found the mailbox we were told to look for. "Kurt and Karen Williams, Sycamore Labrador Retrievers" was stenciled under a pair of Lab faces, one black, one yellow. Tom parked in a gravel pull-off and grinned at me. "Wait 'til you meet the 'screening committee.'"

Karen Williams opened the door before we were up the steps, and five adult Labs surrounded us, shouldering each other out of the way to check us out. Tom scratched chests and tail-bases with both hands. One black boy with grizzled muzzle and eyebrows leaned against my leg, his paw on top of my foot, and gave me that woeful look that retrievers do so well. I pulled on the strap to position my camera in the middle of my back and leaned down, talking softly and scratching the old dog's chest while he made little groany sounds.

"Guys, guys, that's enough," said Karen, a laugh in her voice. The four younger dogs broke off their attentions and ran back into the house. "Tom." She nodded at him and turned to me and my new friend. "Fowler, that's quite enough, you old flirt." She guided the old dog toward the door with a gentle hand, held out the other, and said, "Karen Williams. You must be Janet." When I felt the confidence of her hand in mine, I couldn't help but think of Phil Martin's flaccid imitation of a handshake.

Karen ushered us through the door and said, "The screening committee seems to approve of you both!" She led us to a great room at the back of the house and sent the dogs out through a sliding door. Fowler hesitated, turning big eyes on me for help, but Karen laid a hand on his shoulder and said, "No you don't, you. 'Everybody out' includes old guys, too." The dog sighed and walked slowly onto the outside deck.

Karen positioned a baby gate across the end of the hallway we had come through and looked at us, a sparkle in her eyes. "Ready for the next wave?"

Tom sat down on the floor, his back to the couch, and grinned at me. Karen opened a door to another room off the kitchen. There was the sound of scrambling on the vinyl floor, a soft *whump!* against a something out of sight, and five roly-poly Lab puppies bounced and slid into the room followed by a yellow bitch with drooping boobies and a whirligig tail.

I may have squealed. I set my camera in a safe place and joined Tom on the floor. Lucy, the mama dog, inspected us both, switching between us as she confirmed that we were okay to be with her puppies. And the puppies! Three blacks, two yellows, and if you can find anything cuter than baby Labs, I'd like to see it. They were all over us, clambering onto our laps, untying our shoelaces, tugging on our clothes.

A few minutes in, Karen took Lucy, the three black pups, and the yellow boy back to their room, leaving the yellow girl. Tom threw a few toys, and the pup brought them right back. I stepped outside and took some photos of the big dogs, and when I came back in, Tom had the yellow girl cradled in his arms. She was relaxed and quiet as he rubbed her soft round tummy and they studied each other. Call me a sap, but my eyes stung and my throat tightened.

"Winnie," said Tom, and the puppy lunged at his face and licked his nose. "She looks like a Winnie."

"Perfect," I said.

It took another quarter hour to do the paperwork. When that was finished, Tom handed me the folder and scooped up his baby dog. Karen walked us to the car, where Tom set Winnie in her crate. She wagged her little tail with perfect Labrador enthusiasm, sniffed Drake and Jay through the bars of their crates, and let out one loud *yip*. The boys stood and sniffed back, Jay's rear end vibrating and Drake's tail waving slowly. Puppy girl bowed at Drake, jumped at his face, and bounced off the wires that separated them. Drake pulled his head away from the wires and gave Tom a look that seemed to say, "Really?" Winnie spun around and repeated the maneuver with Jay, and he pushed his nose against the bars, whining softly. Drake lay down facing away from the puppy and let out a low, grumbly moan.

"You'll adjust, old man," said Tom. To me he added, "Change is hard."

No kidding.

We stopped to eat in Anderson. Tom seemed to glow with happiness, and my doubts about our next move—his move—drifted away. Most of them, anyway. I knew we were great together, and that I could depend on him. He wasn't the problem at all. The problem—my problem—was the reality of giving up my long-standing autonomy. *But you've already made most of the adjustments,* whispered a voice. That was true. But hanging out at one house or the other knowing that the one who didn't actually live there would go home eventually offered a safety cushion that cohabitation did not. *Better get over it soon, MacPhail.*

After lunch, we found another stretch of grass behind another business—an auto parts store this time—where we could let the dogs out for a pee. It was also a good place to introduce each of the boys to the puppy, up close and extremely personal. We had just pulled in when my phone rang.

"Janet, have you heard the news?" It was Giselle, and she was talking faster than a terrier after a squirrel. She sounded angry.

"No, we left early to pick up the puppy." My lunch turned into a cannonball in my stomach. *What now?* "We're in Anderson, on our way back. What . . ." I started to ask, but a terrible thought stopped the question in my mouth. *Please, not bad news about Bonnie.*

"The city council. They released the details of the bill."

Tom cocked his head at me, a question all over his face, and I shrugged.

"The bill?" My heart was beating so loud in my ears that I wasn't sure I heard her.

"The pet limit bill?" Giselle must be upset, I thought. She's back to her old habit of speaking in interrogatives. "I thought of you and

Tom right away. It's going to affect so many people and pets. And they're being very hush hush about when the public hearing will be."

Tom pointed at the clouds to the northwest. They were bigger, darker, and closer than before, so I told Giselle I would have to call her later.

"But Janet," she said. "It's worse than expected."

I didn't want to spoil the fun of picking up the puppy, so I tried to keep my voice light. "Okay."

"They want to set the limit at four pets per house. Two dogs and two cats." Giselle paused. "Oh, you don't want to spoil the moment. I'm sorry. I guess I already did?"

"That's fine." I forced a lilt into my voice. "I'll call you later."

"Wait! One other thing?" Giselle spoke quickly.

"Okay," I said. Tom gave me a look and stepped out of the car.

"I thought you'd want to know. Hutch told me … they got the coroner's preliminary opinion, you know, pending the autopsy on that man Ray? You were right. It wasn't suicide."

TWENTY-FIVE

I SHOVED GISELLE'S DOUBLE whammy as far back in my mind as I could and walked Jay onto the grass. Tom was already there with Winnie. Jay whined softly and I could almost hear him say *Aww, a puppy!* Winnie ran right to him, licked his chin and lips, rolled on her back, spun in a circle, and jumped on his head. Jay stood still but for his wiggling tail.

"Well, this is promising," said Tom.

Jay flopped on his side and rolled onto his back, and Winnie crawled over his throat and straddled his head. He squirmed, and the pup ran around him in goofy loops until their leashes were a twisted mess.

"Okay, little girl, that's enough of that." Tom was laughing as he picked her up and snuggled her under his chin while I unwound the leashes. When I looked up, Winnie was pasting kisses all over Tom's grinning face. She stopped, sniffed his beard, and grabbed it. Tom gently lifted her away with both hands, then set her on the ground and led her away. Deprived of her boy toy, she squatted on the grass. "Hurry up," he said, and when she'd finished peeing, Tom gave her a tiny treat from his pocket. He wasn't trying to rush her, he was beginning her "go on cue" training right from the start. Having a dog who does her business when you say so can be very handy.

"Trade," said Tom, holding the puppy's leash toward me. "I'll bring Drake out. He seemed a little grumpy."

I wouldn't say he was grumpy, but he didn't seem thrilled, either, about the bouncing bundle of joy on the leash I held. If anything, Drake seemed incompetent, like some people I've seen who freeze in close proximity to human toddlers. When Winnie jumped at his face, Drake backed away. Tom hunkered down beside him and draped an arm over the big dog's shoulder. With his other hand he scooped the puppy onto his knee and held her. Drake seemed more comfortable with her restrained, and he sniffed her face and neck and paw. She licked his face. Drake shifted on his front feet and looked at Tom, then back at the pup. He heaved a big sigh as if to say, "Okay, if this is what you really want." Drake drew his big tongue up Winnie's cheek, then leaned into Tom's side. Something in my chest tightened as I watched Tom hug the black dog and, laying his cheek against Drake's glossy head, murmur, "Don't worry. You'll always be my best Labby boy."

The first raindrops hit the windshield as we pulled out of the parking lot, and by the time we were back to the concrete hum of the interstate, it was raining in earnest. The wipers tapped out a steady rhythm, and Tom hummed along. It was something he did when he cooked, and when we walked hand-in-hand some evenings. I don't think he even knew he was doing it. At first I couldn't make out the tune, and then I got it. "Singing in the Rain."

I shifted in my seat and looked at the dogs. "All sacked out," I said. "Jay and Winnie are nose to nose."

"Aww," said Tom, and winked at me. "So what was Giselle upset about?"

96

"Did I say she was upset?"

He glanced sideways at me.

"Nothing."

"Janet, you're tapping a hole in the armrest. Just tell me."

"The city council released the details of the pet limit bill."

"Stupid," he said.

"Worse," I said. "If Giselle had the details right, the limit is four. Two dogs, two cats." *And you've sold your house* and we now have five pets. We could have moved out of the city limits to escape the ruling, but I didn't want to move. I loved my little house. Sharing it was going to be adjustment enough—I didn't want to sell it.

The only sounds in the car for the next few minutes were Winnie's paws dream-racing against the floor of her crate, Drake's soft snoring, and the rhythm of the windshield wipers. Inside my head, though, all sorts of thoughts were banging around. The stupid new law and the dilemma it created for us. Bonnie lost on this wet, chilly day. A killer on the loose. Finally Tom took my hand in his and said, "We'll figure it out."

I hoped he meant our living arrangements, because I was still reluctant to get involved any more deeply in a criminal investigation, especially murder. Either way, Tom was right. We'd figure it out. We always did. I just couldn't imagine how.

TWENTY-SIX

TOM BROKE THE SILENCE as he slowed into the curve to exit onto Coldwater Road. "What else did Giselle say?"

"The coroner has ruled that Ray's death was not suicide."

"But you already thought that."

"I didn't know him well, but," I paused, trying to assemble the pieces into a hint of a picture, "suicide just didn't seem to fit. But neither does murder. It seems like his death must be connected to the theft of the sheep, but that seems a bit extreme."

"Do we know for sure they were stolen?"

"What do you mean? You think they ran away?"

"You said Summer and Evan were having money problems, yes?"

I considered the conversation I had overhead. "I think so. Summer wanted to sell some of the sheep a few months ago, and I got the impression it was to pay some bills. But she called the police and reported the missing animals stolen..." I let my voice trail off as I considered the possibilities.

"What if she sold them but didn't want to tell Evan?"

That possibility hadn't even been on my radar. Then again, if no one came forward, maybe it would be Summer's little secret. Hers and the buyer's. Still, it didn't make sense to me. "Why would she do it at an event, though, with lots of people around? And, come on, he's her husband."

"Stranger things have happened."

"But that would be pretty stupid. I mean, they must have been insured, so the insurance company will investigate, right? And the police." At least I thought they would be insured. Tom must have felt me staring at him because he turned toward me and our eyes met and I knew that we were thinking the same thing.

"Maybe she staged a theft and Ray found out," said Tom.

"But hanging?" It wasn't a typically feminine way of killing, and even if she wanted to, how would she manage it? He would have fought back, and how would she pull him off his feet?

I was pretty sure I didn't ask the question out loud, but Tom said, "Summer's strong. I saw one of the sheep lie down in the arena, and she lifted it back onto its feet. What do those babies weigh? Must be over a hundred pounds, right?"

"The ewes are one-fifty to two hundred. More sometimes." They felt like more when they ran me down in the instinct test. Thank goodness they're light on their feet.

"Ray wasn't a big man. Maybe one-forty? I think Summer could hoist a guy his size a few feet off the ground, especially with leverage."

I thought about the rope over the cross beam in the storage room and knew Tom was right. "But he wouldn't just stand there while she slipped a noose over his head and pulled him up."

Tom shrugged. "Maybe she conked him over the head with something."

That was certainly possible. There were plenty of potential head-conkers in that storage room—at least one shovel, a rake, several buckets. I thought I remembered seeing a toolbox, but I couldn't be sure. And Ray's attacker could have brought a weapon with her. Or him.

"You know, Evan acted shocked when he opened that room and found Ray, but what if that was all an act?"

"But you said he got sick. How would he stage that?"

Good point. "I don't know. Maybe the realization of what he'd done?" I thought about Ray's swollen, discolored face. "Ray wasn't very pretty after hanging there for … I don't know how long. Maybe the sight of him made Evan sick. Maybe coming face to face with what he'd done." I thought of Evan and Ray standing by the arena gate. "Tom, remember when you went to say hi to Evan and Ray on Saturday? Did you notice any, I don't know, hostility between them?"

"Now that you mention it, there did seem to be something going on," said Tom. "They were fine with me, but it felt awkward. I didn't stay long." We had turned onto East State, and Tom asked, "You coming home with me?"

"Drop me at my house and go bond with your puppy," I said. "I want to have another look for Bonnie." Then I turned the conversation back to potential suspects.

"What about those two goons I saw? They seemed to be hassling both Ray and Evan, but I think they scared Summer as well."

"Maybe something to do with the theft of the sheep?"

"Like cops, you mean?"

Tom shrugged.

I thought for a moment before I said, "I don't think they were cops. Or insurance investigators." I didn't want to sound overly dramatic so I kept my next thought to myself. *Maybe Ray or Evan—or both of them—were involved in something more deadly than insurance fraud or sheep rustling.*

TWENTY-SEVEN

THE AFTER-WORK RUSH WAS just revving up when I pulled onto Coliseum and headed east to look for Bonnie. I debated whether to walk the property, or cruise the surrounding roads and talk to the neighbors again. Volunteers had already canvassed the neighboring farms and subdivisions, but someone may have seen Bonnie since then, or taken her in. I wasn't sure I had decided until I pulled up along the west side of the arena and shut the engine off. I let Jay out and picked up his leash, but there was no one else around so I clipped the clasp to the loop end and slung it over my shoulder like a bandolier.

If I hadn't been looking for a lost dog, it would have been a perfect April evening. It was cool enough to invite a long walk, and tender bits of green were showing everywhere. Even the long-established grass under our feet had a freshness that comes only in that narrow space between winter's cold and summer's heat. We crossed to the roadway alongside the pole building and walked toward the scene of the crimes.

The yellow tape the police had put up to warn people off the storage room had been pulled down and tossed to the side of the concrete apron in front of the door. I don't know why I thought I'd find Bonnie in there if the detective and crime-scene techs hadn't, but I tried to picture the interior of the room, and whether there were any places for a frightened smallish dog to hide. Had there been bags of feed leaning against the wall, or was my memory mixing this room with another somewhere?

I should have realized that if the police had released the scene they wouldn't just drop their trash on the ground, but at the time I was in the throes of a decision. *To snoop or not to snoop.* I grasped the cool metal knob and turned. I expected it to be locked, but I didn't expect it to bite me.

I jerked my hand away and looked at the long bubbling scratch along the outer edge of my palm. A couple of expletives shot out of my mouth and I shoved my wounded flesh between my lips and licked the blood away before I looked at it again. The scratch didn't seem to be deep, but it bisected some enthusiastic capillaries. I found a scrunched-up tissue in my pocket and dabbed at the blood. It kept coming, so I flattened the tissue, pressed it hard against my palm, and bent to look at the doorknob.

A tiny bit of metal jutted from the bottom edge of the key slot. Several scratches marred the surrounding surfaces, and they were too bright and clean to have been there long. Jay tilted his nose toward the knob and sniff sniff sniffed. "Interesting, huh, Bub?" Not for the first time I wished he could speak. I didn't need my dog to tell me someone had jimmied the lock. Who would do that? And why?

I turned the knob. The door swung out with a long, low moan and Jay growled behind me. I shushed him and peered into the storage room. The gloom made it hard to see, especially after the bright light outside, so I felt cautiously along the wall for a switch. A bare bulb responded, but there still wasn't much to see. Other than a broom in the corner, the tools I remembered from Sunday morning were gone, and I assumed the police had taken them. One thought led to another, and I pulled my phone out, dialed Hutchinson's number, and left a message on his voice mail. After I ended the call, I called back. "Hutch, I, uh, I opened the door and cut myself on the knob where it was jimmied, so, um, my fingerprints and blood are on it. Just so you know." *Right. Just so you know I'm a big dope.*

I stepped onto the concrete stoop and elbowed the door shut. I wondered whether I should re-rig the crime-scene tape until Hutch had a chance to check it out but decided I had tampered with enough evidence for one day. Jay was looking toward the far end of the building, ears forward and nose working. "Come on, Bubby, you're good at finding lost souls," I said. "Let's find Bonnie." He trotted a few steps, then stopped and let out a short, soft *boofff.* Something moved just past the far end of the building, about where Ray's truck was parked, assuming it was still there.

Bonnie? Had she come back to Ray's truck?

Almost as soon as I thought of Bonnie, I knew it wasn't her. It was too big. And it was brown. Jay growled, and I laid a hand on his neck and whispered, "Quiet." We crept a few steps farther, and I realized I was looking at the back of a person. A large person in a shapeless brown suit. It was the heavy half of goon and gooner. I told Jay to sit, pulled his leash over my head, and clipped it to his collar. If these guys were armed and belligerent, the last thing I wanted was for Jay to go near them.

I took a step backward and was about to turn and retreat when his skinnier half stepped into full view. He grinned and raised his right hand in a gesture that didn't register at first. Then I realized he was pointing a finger gun at me. A thrill of electricity ran through me, but I resisted my inner chicken. What's the first thing to remember when faced with a dangerous animal?

Don't run!

TWENTY-EIGHT

I SQUARED MY SHOULDERS and walked to within speaking range of the two men. The skinny one's threatening gesture had confirmed my assessment of them as thugs, and a strange brew of fear and anger was whooshing through my veins. They might scare me, but I wouldn't let them scare me off.

"What are you doing?" It was a silly question, since Ray's truck door was open, and it was now obvious that they had jimmied the storage room door as well.

"Just out for a walk," said Skinny. He had eyes too pale to be called blue and a ragged scar from jaw-hinge to nose.

"In Ray Turnbull's truck?" *Shhh, Janet. Don't be foolhardy.* "This is private property," I said, surprised at how firm my voice sounded, "I've already called the police, so I think you'd better leave."

Skinny's buddy slammed the truck door and turned toward me, hands in his pockets. Jay stood up and stepped between me and the men, and I could almost feel his muscles tense through the air between us. The fat man glanced at my dog, then back at me. "You own this place?" I guess I expected him to have a Joe Viterelli sort of

104

voice, low and gruff, but he sounded more like Porky Pig. "Cuz if you don't, maybe *you* the one better leave."

"I have the owner's permission to be here." *Sort of. I would have if I had called him.* "And I'm sure you don't."

Fatman seemed to consider that, but Skinny let out a goofy laugh and turned deadly serious. "Maybe we should have a little chat, long as we're all here together." Before I could ask what on earth we would chat about, he continued. "Where's your friend, what's her name these days? Summer?"

Summer? Of course it made sense they knew her, or at least knew who she was, if they knew Evan and Ray, but what did he mean about her name? "I have no idea. I haven't seen her since Sunday."

"Know where we can find her?" It was the fat one, and I realized with a start that he had edged into a position slightly behind me, although well out of reach.

"As I said, no idea." I had just pulled my phone out and was trying to decide whether to call 9-1-1 or Hutchinson when it rang and I answered. "Ah, Detective Hutchinson. Good timing ... Remember those two men I mentioned?" The goons glanced at one another while I kept talking. "They're here at the crime scene ..." I turned my gaze past Skinny to the road. "Yes, I see you ... Good, you can talk to them when you get here."

Both men turned their heads toward the road. It was empty but for a black SUV approaching in the distance. Skinny tipped an imaginary hat at me before they climbed into their gray sedan and drove away, and I restarted my lungs and spoke into the phone again. "You still there?"

"What's going on? Are you okay?" It was Tom.

I filled him in.

"I think you should get out of there."

A giggling fit took me, but I managed to say, "I scared them away."

"You're sure they're gone?"

"I watched them drive away. I'm fine." Silence. "Really, everything's fine. Jay and I are going to walk around the property and then I'm outta here." I promised to call when I left.

I let Jay off his leash and started down the narrow grass-studded dirt lane that skirted the field. Jay trotted ahead but never got more than fifty or so feet away before he checked in with me. We had been walking for five minutes or so when he stopped short ten yards in front of me, head high, ears forward, body still. The cornrow stubble ran at a right angle to the lane and blocked my view of whatever had his attention. He glanced at me, then turned, crouching slightly, muscles tense. I scanned the field but saw nothing other than the broken gold of last year's crop. Then something moved. I caught bare glimpses as something black rose above the chopped-off stalks and disappeared. Again.

Bonnie.

TWENTY-NINE

JAY LEAPED OUT OF his crouch and raced into the field, and I started to run toward the spot where he had started. Then a scream, and an explosion of black against the pale blue sky. I stopped and swore. *Crows.* I walked on to where I could look down the row to where Jay was now sniffing something, his back end turned toward me. More dead things, I thought, stepping into the field. The ground was borderline muddy from the rain earlier, and globs of heavy clay glued themselves to my shoes. I stopped, debating whether to continue or retreat.

I called my dog, and he looked over his shoulder at me. "Come," I called. He looked at the thing on the ground, but turned and came running. "Good boy," I said, scratching his ear and squinting to make out what was so interesting to dogs and birds. My heart did a little flip when I saw that it, too, was black. I ignored the muck and walked on. Jay trotted ahead, again blocking my view. He stooped, turned toward me with something in his mouth, and trotted back. As he closed the distance, the object in his grasp became clear, and I whispered, "Thank God." Jay sat in front of me and dropped the dead crow at my feet. We left it there, and as we resumed our walk on the grass-strewn lane, I recalled reading that crows and other corvids mourn their dead. I felt a tinge of guilt for having crashed the funeral.

The rest of our reconnaissance was uneventful and unrewarding, and I felt sadness drop over me like wet wool. I stared at the ground as I trudged toward my van. *What else can go wrong?* I wondered. No sign of Bonnie. Her owner dead, apparently not by his own hand after all. And the joy of bringing a new puppy into our lives—*our* lives, I acknowledged—dampened by the city council's arbitrary pet limit. We now exceeded it, and Tom had two weeks to get out of his house. Under normal circumstances, we would just move forward and figure it out. But Councilman Martin's arrival next door made our situation anything but normal. One thing I knew for sure was that if the bill passed, Tom and I would rehome ourselves before we'd rehome any of our animals.

"Janet!"

The voice startled me out of my walking stupor. Giselle stood between my van and her own car watching Jay and her Maltese, Precious, say their doggy hellos.

"What are you doing here?"

"Same thing you are, I guess?" Giselle picked Precious up and I stroked the little guy's cheek. "I got out of class and thought we could take another look around for the dog. We walked around inside the building," she waved a hand toward the long pole building, "and the pens and arena." She heaved a long sigh. "I don't even know that dog, but I'd like to think someone would look for Spike if something happened to me."

I felt my forehead crinkle. "Who's Spike?" As far as I knew, Giselle had just one little dog, and he had just one horrifying name. Precious.

Giselle's carefully applied blusher deepened a shade and she giggled. "Oh, Homer says Precious is a ridiculous name for a dog, especially a boy." The little white dog in her arms let out a sharp *yip*, and I wouldn't be surprised if he agreed with Homer Hutchinson. "He's been calling him Spike, and, well ..."

"Spike's a fine name," I said, gripping Giselle's arm, "but tell me!"

A funny little smile took hold of Giselle's mouth, and when she looked into my eyes, bright lights were dancing in hers. "We had, umm, kind of a date?"

"Ha! That's great!" My sense of calendar time kicked in, and suddenly I was confused. "Wait. That was yesterday ..." *It was, wasn't it?* "I just gave Hutch your phone number ..."

"He called me yesterday and we, umm, met for dinner." She let out a long sigh and added, "He brought me flowers." Once she started talking, Giselle let the story rip, and by the time she finished, my cheeks hurt from grinning. "He didn't leave until almost midnight. And tonight ..."

A whoop that seemed to come out of my mouth cut her off. "Tonight? This is great, Giselle. I'm so happy for both of you." I'm not much of a matchmaker and I would never have thought to put the two of them together, but in retrospect, they were perfect for each other.

"Me too," Giselle said. We girl-chattered a bit more, and then she shifted to a less cheerful topic. "So I guess someone knocked that man ..."

"Ray."

"Yes, Ray. Someone hit him, you know, his head, with something and then hanged him, and apparently he had a record, a police record? And I guess he was a gambler so maybe that's why ..."

"Hutch told you all this?" That seemed odd to me. The investigation was very new, and in my not-as-limited-as-I-would-like experience, the police didn't share many details with civilians.

"Not exactly?" Giselle has obviously not completely conquered her habit of speaking in questions when nervous. "I heard him on the phone, I mean, he didn't really know I could hear because I came back from the bathroom and ... I heard a little?"

Jay was lying near the fence, and as I gazed at him, I thought about how he had always been happy to see Ray when we went to the Winslows' place. In fact, all the dogs liked the man, including his own, and I tend to trust canine and feline assessments. To Giselle, I simply said, "Ray wasn't the friendliest guy around, but I never picked up any, I don't know, 'bad guy' vibes. Are you sure Hutch was talking about Ray?"

"Pretty sure?" said Giselle. "I mean, who else could he have meant? He said, 'So it wasn't suicide,' and then he listened for a while, and then ... I don't remember exactly what he said, but something about getting a copy of the records from the Reno police and then he said, 'picked the wrong bookie,' and then he saw I was back and he cut off the call."

"What about the sheep?" But even as I asked, I knew it might make sense. Summer had quoted a price of four hundred dollars a head for Rambouillets. The twelve missing sheep could go for almost five grand. Not a great fortune, but for a man in debt it might be significant. Could Ray have stolen and sold the sheep after all?

The wind was beginning to blow the heat out of the remaining light, so I suggested we call it a night and get together in a few days for coffee. Just as we turned toward our cars, my phone rang. Giselle was looking over the top of her car at me, her head tilt a question mark.

Goldie's first words were unintelligible, and when I began to understand, my pulse jumped. "We're at the vet's office. Can you meet me here?"

"What's happened? Totem?"

"No! The missing dog, Bonnie! I found her!"

THIRTY

WHOEVER SYNCHRONIZED THE TRAFFIC signals on the main roads in Fort Wayne did a bang-up job, because I sailed from the Lahmeyer property to my vet's office on a sea of green lights and whipped into the parking lot twenty-two minutes after Goldie called. Peg, the office manager, had left for the day, and the new receptionist—Amanda according to her name tag—wouldn't tell me which exam room Goldie was in. I was about to start opening doors when Ravi, Dr. Joiner's veterinary technician, led a woman carrying an elderly terrier mix to the checkout desk. I told him why I was there.

"They must be with Dr. Douglas." He looked at the receptionist and asked, "Which room is the Sheltie in?"

Amanda hesitated, but finally gave up their location. As I opened the exam-room door I heard Ravi say, "Very good client and friend of the doctors." It was true. Paul Douglas had been my vet for years, and his wife and partner, Doctor Kerry Joiner, trained her Pomeranian at Dog Dayz with me and Tom and, well, most of my dog-crazy friends.

Goldie was alone in the exam room, twisting the end of a scarf and bouncing slightly on the wooden bench. Jay hopped right up beside her and looked into her eyes. Goldie worked her fingers into the thick silvery fur behind his ears and touched her forehead to his for a moment. When she turned her attention to me, Jay hopped onto the floor and lay down, panting, ears back and eyes half-closed.

"Oh, my, I'm glad to see you." She patted the bench and I sat beside her. "I'm kind of out of my depth here. I haven't had a dog since I was a kid."

"How is she?"

Goldie let out a long breath and patted her chest before she answered. The lap of her pants was smeared with muck and I picked a burr off the front of her sweater as she began to speak. "The poor little thing. She's just filthy but doesn't seem to be hurt, except her nose. It's bright pink. Sunburn, probably. That's what Dr. Douglas said. He's so kind. He took her in the back to … well, I'm not sure what."

Goldie's face was flushed so I asked if she wanted some water.

"No, I'm fine." She patted my leg. "Just, you know, excited and relieved and a bit surprised."

I was a bit surprised, too. There must have been thirty people looking for Bonnie off and on since Sunday. "So what happened? Where did you find her?"

"My garden club, of all things," she said. "Not *at* the meeting, but Marjorie Heffernan lives near where your roundup was. Is that right? Roundup?"

"Close enough. So then what?"

"I was driving home, had just passed that place with the big long red building. That's the place, right?" I wondered how Goldie knew that, but before I could ask she said, "They gave the address, well, the road at least, in the news about the man who died, and there was a photo of the building, and I recognized it from visiting Marjorie."

I nodded.

"I saw something on the berm up ahead, and I slowed down. First I thought it was a cat, but it was a bit too big, and then I saw her tail, and I knew."

"What time was that?" I couldn't believe that neither Giselle nor I had seen Bonnie.

"I don't know. A little more than an hour ago, I guess." Goldie glanced at her wrist, but it was bare. "Forgot my watch. But I came straight here." She lowered her voice and said, "I hope the little dear didn't see ... Well, you know, when her owner, Ray, yes? When the poor man—"

The door opened and Dr. Paul Douglas came in, a bedraggled black-and-white Sheltie in his arms. The tender area on top of her muzzle just behind the black of her nose almost glowed, it was so pink.

"Janet!"

"Hi Paul. How is she?"

I expected him to set the little dog on the exam table, but he held her snuggled into his chest. Bonnie seemed content there, but her eyes and ears were focused on Goldie, and Goldie was gazing back at her with a look not unlike the ones I'd seen on Giselle's and Hutchinson's faces. They're falling in love, I thought, smiling and a tad relieved. I wasn't sure I could afford to take in an orphan right then, with Councilman Martin on the neighborhood warpath.

Paul's voice drew me back to the room. "She's thin, probably hasn't eaten much for a couple of days. She has a microchip, but it's registered to Ray Turnbull, who I understand is deceased. There's no backup contact." He set her on the table and rested one hand on her shoulders. With the other he brushed the front of his lab coat and laughed. "As you can see, she's pretty dirty, and," he lifted her paw to show the tangled feathers, "she's packed with burrs." Goldie had moved to the exam table and leaned her face toward Bonnie, who gave her a series of quick kisses.

Paul said, "I cleaned a couple of minor cuts on her pads, so I'm sending antibiotics with her." He hesitated, looking at Goldie and then me. "That is, if one of you …"

Goldie waved him off. "Don't be ridiculous! Of course she's coming home with me."

THIRTY-ONE

WITH A LITTLE ENCOURAGEMENT from me, Goldie decided to have the clinic's groomer do the clean up since she had the tools and the know-how and could do the job light-years faster than I could. "Good thing it's your late night," I told Paul.

"We'd make it a late night for this one," he said, and disappeared with Bonnie.

Goldie refused to go home, so we decided to slip a few doors down to Dom's Deli for a cup of tea. It was on the edge of chilly outside, so I put Jay in my van with a chewy toy and off we went. When the fragrance of Dom's signature eggplant Parmesan hit me, I remembered I hadn't had dinner.

"I'm too excited to eat," said Goldie, "but you go ahead. I need to clean up a bit." She looked like Bonnie must have ridden on her lap all the way to the vet.

I found a booth and started making calls. Tom didn't answer, and I figured he must be outside with Drake and Winnie. I left a message and moved on to Hutchinson. When he said he knew about Bonnie, I blurted, "Oh, of course, Giselle called you." If a man's voice could blush, his would have when he said Goldie was the one who called him. I asked if there was any more news about the investigation, but he gave a completely irrelevant answer that told me he couldn't talk about it. I said I'd see him soon, hoping I'd be able to get more out of him then. If I couldn't, I knew Giselle would.

No one answered the Winslows' landline, and since Summer didn't like to give out her cell number, I left a message. I also called Marietta Santini, owner of Dog Dayz, and asked her to pass the word that Bonnie was safe and sound. Quite a few members had helped with the search and they'd want to know.

I was just finishing when Goldie sat down. Her clothes were still a mess, but her face and hands were clean and she had taken a semi-successful stab at tidying her hair. The food arrived and I dove in while Goldie sat and watched me with a beatific smile on her face. When I could do it without tomato teeth, I smiled back and said, "Well done, my friend."

"I believe I've received a gift."

"Are you thinking of keeping Bonnie? I mean permanently?"

"If she, I mean, did he, you know, Ray, did he have family, or someone who would, you know..."

"Someone who might want her? No idea."

"Well, if not, I'd like to keep her." Her eyes were wide and wet.

"From what I saw in the exam room, she'd like to keep you, too."

"Imagine what that little soul went through."

I *had* thought about that. A lot. I knew a little something about memories of violence. Bonnie would recover from her time on the loose, but if she had witnessed Ray's murder, who knew how long that vision would haunt her dreams. The man may have been surly to his fellow humans, but his dog clearly had loved him. So had my dog, for that matter. Goldie looked as close to tears as I felt, so I excused myself to get a to-go box and order some carryout lasagna for the next evening.

By the time I returned, Goldie was making a list. "I'll feed her some of Jay's food from that bag you gave me if that's okay until I can get to the store. Is that food okay for her? And she needs a bed, and a new collar and a leash and some toys although I guess Jay won't mind if she plays with the ones I keep for him .... " She caught me grinning at her and said, "What?"

"Jay will be happy to share his food and his toys, and I can loan you a leash. I probably even have a collar that will fit her to tide you over." The bell over the door tinkled and the tinted mirror tiles behind Goldie offered a distorted impression of two people sliding into a booth across the room. Closing time was ten minutes away, and Dom's wife was gathering the cheese and hot-pepper shakers from the tables, but I heard her welcome the latecomers.

I was about to tell Goldie that I'd check with Summer about any claims on Bonnie when her expression changed and she leaned into the table. She spoke, keeping her voice low and looking at something behind me. "Let's go. Something about those guys over there gives me the creeps."

Not much makes Goldie want to cut and run, so I had to fight the urge to turn around. Instead I told her to meet me outside. I went to the counter for my carryout order, figuring I would peek at the creepy guys on my way out. I was lifting the to-go box from the counter when a voice boomed next to my right ear. "Heard this is the best Italian in town. That right?"

It was the skinny goon, and he was well within my comfort zone. His pudgier buddy was jammed into a booth, nodding his head as he spoke into a cell phone. *Are they following me?*

"I, uh ... I don't know if it's the best, but it's good."

"Yeah? Whaddya recommend?"

I recommend you back off, bozo. "The eggplant is good." I side-stepped away from him.

"Hey, ya know, our conversation got cut off earlier." He made "conversation" sound sinister. He squinted at me, and when he spoke again, his voice was fringed with threat. "You get a lot of pictures at that dog thing?" He put all the emphasis on *pictures.*

At that, his buddy shifted his bulk and stared at me, the groan of the bench under him sounding like I felt. Skinny stepped in closer and I half expected him to poke me the way he had poked Evan on Sunday.

My brain jumped into gear, trying to remember if I had pointed my camera at him and his buddy. I didn't think so. In fact, I was pretty sure I hadn't had my camera with me when I saw them with Evan. I knew I hadn't downloaded any photos of them—I would have remembered—but I didn't see any reason to discuss my work with this guy. As I turned away, the fat man's Porky Pig voice followed me.

"Hey, where can we find your friend Summer? She ain't answerin' her phone."

Summer? They want Summer, not Evan? I stepped past Skinny and said, "I can't help you."

"Yeah, sure," came the cartoon voice. "Catch ya later."

I almost knocked Goldie over as I bolted out the door.

THIRTY-TWO

BY THE TIME I was halfway home, a vise had attached itself to the base of my skull and begun to squeeze. I hadn't had a migraine in months, but once you've had one, you don't ignore the prelude. I pulled into the first drug store I spotted and fished around in my tote bag for my meds. The bottle finally emerged from under the spare kennel lead I always carry "just in case," and I shook it hopefully. Not a single rattle from within. I looked at the glare of the store's name over the door and looked away as the light twisted the vice tighter around my temples. It was not the chain I use for prescriptions.

Despite the pain, I couldn't get my after-dinner encounter out of my head. What was up with that goon in Dom's Deli? *I'll catch you later?* Was that some kind of threat, or was I overreacting? Why were they looking for Summer? And why had the guy mentioned photographs? I was sure I hadn't had my camera when I saw him poking Evan in the chest. Had he and his pal been up to something when I *was* taking photos over the weekend? If so, I didn't remember seeing them, but maybe I had caught something by accident. Or maybe they just thought I had.

120

I leaned my throbbing skull against the headrest and debated whether to tough it out with an over-the-counter dose of something or drive to my regular drug store. On a normal evening, the drive would be no big deal, but all I wanted to do was escape the lights and traffic and banging in my head. Maybe I had something in my tote bag. To speed things up, I dumped the contents onto the passenger seat. My phone bounced once and played a tune, making me wonder whether the pain was making me hallucinate. It played again. The Beatles "From Me to You." Tom's ring.

"How's the dog?"

"She's fine, mostly. A few cuts, a sunburned nose," I said. "And she's filthy and full of burrs."

"That should take you a while."

"The clinic's groomer is doing the job. Goldie's waiting there. She won't go home without Bonnie." I closed my eyes and massaged the back of my neck with my free hand, then grabbed my billfold and got out of my van. "How are Drake and Winnie getting along?"

"Drake's not keen on having his head jumped on," Tom chuckled, "but he seems a little cheerier than he did in the car." He paused, then asked, "Something wrong?"

The last thing I wanted to do right then was tell Tom about the two goons, so I skipped our encounter at the deli and focused on the result. "Migraine coming on. I forgot to refill my prescription and I don't want to drive anywhere but home. Which I'm going to do as soon as I get a box of caffeine." I figured some stay-awake pills would do for now.

Tom offered to pick up my refill and come over to nurse me, but I said I'd be fine and see him the next day. It was all I could do to navigate the fluorescent nightmare of drugstore lighting, but I found the caffeine tabs and a bottle of iced coffee. When I got back to my van I washed down a double dose of pills and chugged the coffee. Twenty minutes later I pulled into my garage feeling a little less pain and a lot more buzz.

Jay hit the ground bouncing and spinning, and when I opened the service door into the house, he blasted into the kitchen and, crouched to brake, slid *bang!* into the cupboards. Pixel ran in from the other doorway and dropped a felt mouse on my foot. She rubbed her cheek against my jeans, then bounced across the vinyl and rubbed her cheek against Jay's muzzle. A long *mmrrrooowwwllll* sounded behind me, and I turned. Leo sat in the doorway, tail wrapped around his front feet, ears pulled partway back, eyes squinted.

"You're right, Leo *mio*. Too much racket."

In one liquid motion, he glided from floor to chair to table and held a paw toward me. I bent toward him for a nose bump and ran my hand over his head and down his silky back. It was a mistake. Leaning over revived the timpani in my head and made me a tad nauseated. I considered popping another caffeine tablet, but decided to give the two I had taken a little more time.

A light from the living room made me turn. Headlights. But I wasn't expecting anyone. I started toward the picture window, but caution caught up with me halfway across the room, and I turned down the hall and into my dark office. The curtains were open, and I had a clear view of the driveway, where a gray sedan sat idling.

THIRTY-THREE

SOMETHING MADE A LITTLE skipping motion in my chest, and I ran to the front door and checked the locks. I checked the kitchen door as well, and relaxed a tad when I saw Jay stretched out on the floor with Pixel straddling his head. If he saw no reason to worry, I probably shouldn't either.

I went back to my office and peered out again. The sedan was still there. I thought there were two people in the front seat, but I couldn't discern more than that with the headlights in my eyes. Mr. Hostetler's porch light was on across the street, and for a second I considered calling him, but I let that go in a hurry. He wouldn't be satisfied to keep an eye out and call for help if necessary, and at ninety-two, he didn't need to confront any thugs from Reno. *Should I call the police?*

I moved to my bedroom, phone in hand, to see whether the angle from there would soften the effect of the car's headlights. The curtains were open and I was afraid to attract attention to the room by closing them, so I crawled under the sill to the farthest corner and slowly peeked past the window frame. The glare wasn't as bad, but I still couldn't see inside the car. At least I hoped they were still in the car. *Find a weapon*, whispered my guardian troublemaker. *But what?* Jay would protect me, of course, but I needed to protect myself, too. And my dog. I crawled under the window again and went to the closet. I fished around in the dark and finally felt cool, hard wood in my hand. I could clobber at least one of them with my old softball bat.

When I peeked out the window again, the sedan's interior light was on, and a gray-haired couple appeared to be studying a map. As I watched, the dome light went out and the car backed away, crept past two more houses, and turned the corner. I leaned against the wall and slid to the floor and sat there laughing until I thought I might be sick.

You're overwrought.

I was also glad I hadn't embarrassed myself with a call to the police, but I still checked all the locks again. When everyone was fed and cuddled and calmed down, I grabbed an ice pack from the freezer, ran a hot bath fragrant with lavender bubbles, and sank in to warm my body and chill my head. As I lay there feeling the muscles in my neck loosen and the pain dribble from my head, I tried not to think, but questions and images filled it back up.

How could a dozen sheep just disappear? Especially with their owners—and their owners' dog—sleeping close by? The Winslows' camper trailer had been parked just past the end of the holding pen. As far as I knew, the sheep hadn't been delivered to any area slaughterhouses. The police had put out an alert, and I was sure Giselle would have told me if she'd heard anything like that. Could they have been stolen for their value as wool producers? At four hundred a head, the tiny flock could go for nearly five thousand dollars. If Ray really did have a gambling problem, as Giselle had surmised from overhearing Hutchinson on the phone, he could also have had a debt problem. Did he steal the sheep to pay a gambling debt? Possible, I supposed.

And what about the Winslows' money problems? The argument I had overheard suggested they could use five grand, but they could have just sold the sheep. What would they gain by staging a theft, especially away from their own farm? Insurance money? Could the sheep be insured for more than their value on the open market? That might be something to check out, if I were playing amateur detective, which I reminded myself I was not.

Besides, I had enough on my plate. If the pet-limit bill passed and Tom couldn't move in with me, we would have to figure out an alternative lickety-split. Plus my mother's wedding was less than two weeks off. I smiled at the memory of dress shopping with Goldie, and was grateful once again that I hadn't been the one to take Mom shopping for *her* dress. My brother's partner, Norm, had far more fashion sense and patience than I had, and he had virtually taken over as wedding planner and bridal consultant.

The white noise of the exhaust fan quieted the drumming in my head, and I realized that most of the pain was gone. Happy that I'd stopped the migraine before it took over, I drew in some deep, slow, lavender-heavy breaths and tried to decide whether to add some hot water to the tub, or get out. A lovely, deep muzziness enveloped me. *Hot chocolate.* I pictured myself snuggled on the couch with a cup of hot chocolate, a fleece blankie, a good book, and my animals. I was still relaxed, in the thinking-about-it phase, when something *wham wham whammed* against the wall behind my head.

THIRTY-FOUR

I BOLTED STRAIGHT UP in the tub, sending the ice pack flying toward the mirror over the sink and a bubbly lavender tidal wave onto the rug and my bath towel. I had checked all the locks, so how ... I remembered the jimmied doorknob on the storage room and looked around for a weapon. Why hadn't I brought the softball bat in with me? I carefully stepped out of the tub and opened the cupboard under the sink.

Scrubbing powder wouldn't be much good as a weapon unless I could throw it into an assailant's eyes. *Oh, sure,* said Janet Devil, *ditch the aerosols. They're dangerous.* I grabbed an old toilet brush from the back of the cupboard, but the plastic wand had no heft and was loose. *Aha!* I wrapped my trembling fingers around a spray bottle of Goldie's homemade glass cleaner. It might be nontoxic, but a blast of detergent and vinegar in the eyes should slow ...

My brain kicked in about then. The hammering against the wall was accompanied by snuffling, and as I reached for a dry towel, two white paws appeared under the door. The banging stopped and a pair of black paws pushed in beside the white ones. I wanted to be angry, but what kind of person doesn't smile at the love letter of dog feet under the bathroom door? Besides, I was a tad embarrassed for myself.

"Janet, are you okay?"

At the sound of Tom's voice I shoved the bottle back under the sink and wrapped the towel around myself. "Yes, although that Labrador tail scared the bejeepers out of me." I dried myself and dropped the towel onto the puddle my first towel hadn't sopped up. "What are you doing here?" I asked as I pulled my jammies on and ran a brush through my hair.

"We're here to help," Tom said. "I'm a doctor, you know."

I opened the door and walked into Tom's open arms. "You're not that kind of doctor, Doctor."

"Sure I am. I know all kinds of herbal concoctions." It was true. Tom's anthropological specialty is ethnobotany, and he has studied traditional uses of plants for purposes of all sorts. "How's your head?"

"Better. Between the caffeine, the ice pack, and the hot bath, I think I'm fine, although I may not sleep the rest of the week." I disengaged and bent to snugglekiss the two dogs who were sniffing my legs. "Where's Winnie?"

"I put her in the x-pen in the living room so the cats can check her out without getting trounced."

As if to confirm his story, a series of sharp yips erupted from down the hall. Drake and Jay trotted off in that direction, and we followed. When we got to the living room, Winnie was bowing at Pixel, who was arched into an "h" with her tail as the upright and skitterjumping back and forth in front of the imprisoned puppy. Leo was lying on the couch, a *whose brilliant idea was this* look on his face.

"Things seem to be under control in here," I said. "I was thinking of hot chocolate."

Tom put his arm over my shoulder and steered us toward the kitchen. "Sounds good."

"More to the point," I said, "now that you're here, I was thinking of that Mayan hot chocolate you do so well."

Twenty minutes later we had settled onto the couch with spicy hot chocolate and a lot to talk about. We started with Bonnie's condition and Goldie's elation. I considered not worrying Tom with the story of my encounter at Dom's Deli, but I was itching to double check my images from the weekend to see whether I had in fact photographed Skinny and Porky without realizing it. "Remember those two thugs I saw talking to Evan?" I asked as I retrieved my laptop and booted it up.

"We don't know they're thugs."

"Yes, we do," I said, and by the time I had described my interactions with them, Tom was sure they were hit men from Jersey. *Or Nevada.*

"Wait a minute!" I looked at Tom as I waited for the machine to wake up. "What if they really are connected?"

"Connected?"

"To gambling or organized crime or something. Ray was from Nevada. And Summer is from somewhere out west."

"But you saw them talking to Evan, and that was after Ray…"

Tom didn't finish the thought, and we sat in silence as I opened my photo file from Saturday and scrolled through the images, focusing on backgrounds and peripheries. Tom scooched in close and draped his arm over my shoulder, and I leaned into his warmth. The photos flew by. Most of the early ones were just dogs and sheep with no people at all. There were several dozen shots of Bonnie and Ray organizing the sheep early Saturday morning when the world still seemed normal.

"I'll have to print some of these for Goldie," I said. "I'm sure she'd love to have some photos of Bonnie working."

"What if someone, you know, Ray's family, wants her?"

I handed Tom the computer and extricated myself from the depths of the couch, wincing at the aches beginning to settle into my sheep-bruised flesh. "May as well find out right now."

"Right now" meant as soon as I rounded up my phone, which took a few minutes of searching my tote bag, camera case, and pockets. Jay and Drake did their best to help me, but after I tripped over them three or four times, I sent them to lie down in the living room. As they toddled away and I started re-searching my jeans pockets, I heard "From Me to You" playing somewhere in the vicinity of my feet. I lifted the bed skirt, and picked up my phone.

"Thank you," I said.

Tom chuckled. "You're welcome. Hurry back."

When I rejoined him in the living room, I felt as if a great load had been lifted. "I talked to Evan. He says Ray had no family, and no one has any claim on Bonnie."

As I took the laptop back, Tom covered my hand with his own and directed my attention to the x-pen. It had gotten so quiet, I'd forgotten we had two babies in the house. But there they were. Winnie was pressed up against the wires of the pen, and Pixel was snugged up to the outside, one paw pushed through the wires and tucked under the puppy's chin.

"Where's my camera when I need it?"

THIRTY-FIVE

WE JUST SAT FOR a few minutes, holding hands and watching the sleeping babies. Then I went back to the photos. The only people in any of the herding photos were the judge, the dogs' owners, and Ray. The scene shifted to the disc area, and although the focus of most photos was on the leaping, running dogs, there were more people on the fringes. It was, after all, set up as a spectator event. I found a terrific shot of Edith Ann, the little black-and-tan dog whose owner had helped me look for Jay, catching a disc mid-air, and made a note to send Kathy a copy. "Some of these are keepers," I said, "but no shady characters that I can see."

"You want to call it a night and do the rest tomorrow?" asked Tom.

"I won't be able to sleep if I don't get through them. Wait! What day is tomorrow?"

"Wednesday. All day."

"I have a herding lesson in the morning," I said. "Maybe I'll learn something then."

Winnie woke up and whined, so Tom left me to finish with the photos while he took her and the big dogs out. The images in front of me had shifted to the parade of herding breeds, and there were some good ones. I knew most of the dogs and people, since they were nearly all local and many of them trained at Dog Dayz.

I knew I had nearly reached the end because I hadn't taken many photos after the parade. There were some random shots of the crowd and the vendor booths, and an occasional human-interest shot. My eyes were beginning to itch and my brain was fogging up when headlights panned the wall across from me, as Goldie's lights did when she pulled into her driveway at night. I wanted to run over to see Bonnie after her makeover, and to tell Goldie that, according to Evan at least, no one else was asking for the little dog. Tom brought the dogs in and set Winnie back in the pen with a giant teddy bear, while I rushed through the last two dozen images.

And I almost missed it.

In fact, I did miss it, but my subconscious didn't, and I scrolled back, leaning into the screen at first, then zooming in on the image. It was meant to be a shot of the Indiana Collie Club's information booth, and if I used it, I would crop out the part I now found most interesting.

Tom slid in beside me. "Goldie's home."

"We'll go see her in a minute. But look at this first."

A man with a dark blonde ponytail was turned forty-five degrees away from me. Evan. I couldn't see his left hand, but his right was held palm out toward the heavier of the thugs. The skinny guy stood beside his buddy, head thrust forward and mouth open as if he were talking.

"That doesn't look very friendly," said Tom. "Are those the guys you mentioned?" I nodded, pointing at another figure turned away from the men, but looking back toward them. Her long copper hair was bright as ever, but even at that distance, Summer's expression was dark. I always take several shots of a scene, so I clicked through to the next image, and the one after that. By the third one, Summer still appeared to be looking at the men while moving away from them, away from her husband. In the final shot, her torso was angled forward and her elbows were bent. She was running away.

THIRTY-SIX

THE WINSLOWS' FARM WAS bucolic in the morning light, and more perfect spring weather would be hard to find. Wooly clouds scattered themselves across a robin's-egg sky like a reflection of the sheep grazing here and there in the rolling meadow behind the house, barn, and yarn shop. It wasn't until I had parked in the shade of an ancient beech between the shop and the barn that a few oddities struck me.

First was the size of the flock in the pasture. A week earlier, it would have seemed normal, because Summer typically kept about fifty sheep. A quarter of the flock had disappeared the previous Saturday, and yet at a glance there seemed to be as many animals as ever. Could they have replaced the stolen sheep in four days? I had the impression they didn't have that kind of cash lying around, and the insurance claim—if there was one—couldn't have been settled yet.

As I tried to wrap my mind around the number of sheep in evidence, I spotted Luciano, the Winslows' Maremma, lying toward the center of the scattered woollies. Summer usually locked the big dog up before her herding students arrived because he got to be quite the handful, even for her, when other dogs appeared on the property.

Had she forgotten I was coming? It was certainly possible, given the stress of the past few days.

I opened the windows, the side doors, and the back hatch to keep the van cool for Jay, and left him in his crate while I walked across the yard to Summer's wool shop. A rustic painted sign hung above the door—Hole in the Wall Yarn Shop. The door was unlocked and the lights were on, but there was no one there. Thinking she must have stepped out for a moment, I walked around the shop and looked at the merchandise. There seemed to be thousands of skeins of gorgeous yarn in bright colors, heathers, darks, blends. There was sheep's wool, alpaca, and blends of all sorts. I can't knit two rows with the same number of stitches, but I enjoyed imagining the possibilities embodied in that wall of fibers.

The center of the shop was taken up by a double-sided display rack. The side facing the wall of yarn held three rows of craft and pattern books. Here were instructions for sweaters and shawls and comforters, caps and mittens, wall hangings and scarves. At one end of the display there were even a few patterns for needlepoint projects, and I wondered whether my mother would enjoy working on one. Then again, I wouldn't dare choose for her. Besides, she was busy these days with the therapy garden at Shadetree Retirement, and with Tony Marconi, her bridegroom-to-be.

I heard barking, but by the time I stepped out the door the only sound was a mixed chorus of chickadees, cardinals, and crows. The sheep were calm, and Luciano was still in place. I pulled my phone out to check the time and found that we should be starting my lesson in seven minutes. I walked around the shop, thinking Summer might be in the little dye garden she kept at the back, but there was no one there. Her truck was in its usual place, though, and Evan's rusty old Toyota pickup was parked in front of the house. Even if Summer had forgotten my lesson, she must be around. I shaded my eyes with my hand and squinted at the sheep-dotted slope to see if I had missed her up there, knowing even as I did that Luciano would be on his feet if anyone were out there with his beloved sheep.

The house. They must be in the house, I thought, already walking that way. In fact, since the shop was unlocked, it seemed likely that Summer had run "home" for something. The house was oriented with the front door facing away from the barn and shop, and a herringbone brick walk through paired borders of different kinds of lavender led around the privacy fence that enclosed the back and sides of the house. The plants were just greening, but I had seen this walkway in August when the beds were rivers of white and violet and the air was heavy with fragrance and a-dance with bees. I stopped and drew a deep breath, and smiled at the promise carried in the faint lavender scent.

The curtains were drawn over the front windows, which seemed odd and gave my stomach a tiny squeeze. I glanced back at my van, wondering if I should go back and lock Jay's crate, but that seemed a little silly. No one coming to the yarn shop would bother my dog, and besides, I'd only be a minute.

I stepped onto the long wooden porch. One end was framed and screened, and Rosie, the old ewe who slept there and had occasional house privileges, was watching me. She lay on a braided rug and had a flower-print bandana around her neck. "Hi, Rosie," I said. "Your people around?" I flinched at the loud squeak of a loose board and a louder flurry of barking from inside the house. Nell. Summer must be inside, then, because Nell was always at her side. I knocked on the door and waited. Nothing. Even the barking had stopped, as if someone had hushed the dog. I knocked again, a bit harder, and called, "Summer? Evan? It's Janet MacPhail."

Evan's voice came from behind the doorframe. "Janet?"

"Yes." When the door didn't open, I said, "I have a herding lesson scheduled. Maybe Summer forgot?"

Another couple of seconds went by before I heard a deadbolt pop and the door opened a few inches. Evan peered past me, then opened the door a bit wider. "Come in," he said, and when I did, he looked out again, then slammed the door and locked the deadbolt. As I bent to greet Nell, the corner of my eye caught something that made me turn my head. A shotgun leaned into the corner behind the door.

"Is something wrong?" I asked. *Of course something's wrong,* whispered my scoldy voice.

Evan turned wide, red-rimmed eyes my way. "Wrong?"

"You seem a little jumpy, and you have a shotgun by your front door."

His eyes flicked toward the gun and back to me, and he said, "Oh, yeah. Coyotes. We've had coyotes around."

That was certainly possible. In fact, that was a big reason Luciano was out there guarding the sheep. Still, as I registered again the closed curtains and Evan's attention to locking the door, I knew there was more to his jumpiness than coyotes on the prowl.

"Where's Summer?"

"Summer." He murmured the name so softly I could barely hear him.

Yes, Summer. Your wife. I half turned back toward the door and said, "If something came up, that's fine. I'll just reschedule my lesson."

Evan just stared at me, and I got the same creepy sensation I'd had with the skinny goon at Dom's Deli, dialed up a few degrees. My salivary glands seemed to have stopped working and my voice came out a bit squeakier than I would have liked. "That's what I'll do. I'll call her." *Right after I run to my van and peel out in a storm of flying gravel.*

I turned and pulled the doorknob, then remembered the dead-bolt. Blood was thundering in my ears, each beat coming a little faster, but not so loud that I couldn't hear Evan breathing close behind me. I grabbed the deadbolt with my other hand and tried to turn the two bits of metal in unison. The knob turned easily and I felt the door move toward me a fraction of an inch, but the cold metal in my other hand held fast. I hit it with my palm and tried again, panic rising like acid in my chest.

The deadbolt wouldn't turn.

THIRTY-SEVEN

THE METAL HANDLE OF the deadbolt wouldn't budge. As I spun around to face Evan, my right hand slipped into my pocket in search of keys to use as a weapon and my left arm rose to block whatever might be coming. But Evan wasn't looking at me, and as his hand moved past my ear he said, "That damn thing. I thought I had fixed it."

I sidestepped and nearly tripped over Nell, who jumped out of my way and wagged her tail at me. I looked at Evan's hand. His thin fingers gripped the deadbolt handle and turned it, and he said, "You have to sort of pull and twist to make it work." He turned toward me, and the muscles of his face shifted as if he'd been shocked. "Janet?"

My voice wouldn't work.

"What's wrong?" A series of emotions danced across his face and his eyes softened. "Oh, jeez. You're frightened." His hands gripped the back of his head and seemed to pull it toward his chest. "I'm sorry. I didn't mean to scare you. I … It's been …" He let his hands drop and stood straight, looking into my eyes. "I'm sorry."

As I watched a muscle in his cheek twitch, I could barely resist the urge to grab his shoulders and shake him. The need to run had been replaced by a need to know what was going on. "Is Summer available? I saw her truck—"

"No."

I waited, and finally he spoke again.

"I mean, she's not here. She's, uh … she's out." *Out? As in "not home," or as in "out cold"?* Evan signaled me to follow him to the kitchen. I hesitated to go deeper into the house, but Nell seemed relaxed, and her master's demeanor was more defeated than threatening, so I followed along.

The kitchen walls were a dingy pink-yellow putty color that probably needed painting a decade earlier. A single chipped mug sat next to a tipsy pile of catalogs, mail, and miscellany on a wooden table that might have been called shabby chic in another setting. In the gloom of the curtained kitchen it was just shabby. The soles of my shoes made soft sucking noises with every step.

"Would you like some coffee?"

"Sure." I didn't really want coffee, but my curiosity meter had hit tilt. *Don't get involved,* a little voice screeched at me, but the other one, the *oh, what can it hurt?* one, was louder.

Evan refilled his mug and poured one for me, moving as though he had sandbags strapped to his limbs. Neither of us spoke. He set the mugs on the beat-up table, gestured to a chair, sat down across from me, and leaned his crossed forearms on the table. It rocked in response, and I lifted my mug before the contents could add to the pattern of stains on the tabletop. Evan didn't seem to notice.

"Do you think Summer will be back soon?" What I really wanted to ask was where in the world she had gone on a Wednesday morning without either of their trucks. Nell laid her head on my knee and gazed up at me as is to say, "I've been wondering that too." Evan didn't answer, so I went on. "I mean, it's fine if something came up."

"If I'd known you had a lesson scheduled, I would have called you," Evan said. "I, uh … I don't know where she is."

"No problem. I'll just call later to reschedule."

Evan stared at me for a moment before he said, "No, I mean I really don't know where she is. I haven't seen her since Monday morning."

Something tingled in my chest. "Monday?"

He nodded.

"Have you called the police?"

He shook his head and pulled an envelope from under a catalog and laid it in front of me. "I ripped it, you know, opened it, thought, well … I lost the other part, but you can still get the gist of it." I recognized Summer's neat round letters and began to read.

> did some things back in Reno, bad things, me and Ray. They found us, those
> uys. I'm sorry they hassled you Ev. Don't worry, I'll be fine. ~~I'm going~~ I can
> art over. Sell the sheep if you want - Al Russell's number is in my phone. He'll
> d sell the shop inventory too. Don't try to find me. Be safe. Forgive me. S.
> <u>n't call the police.</u>

I read it twice. When I looked at Evan, his expression was blank. I picked the envelope up and looked inside, but it was empty. "What's she mean? Was there something in here?"

Evan shook his head, but he didn't meet my eyes. My first thought had been that she left him some money, but that made no sense. I had always gotten the impression that they got by with not much to spare. If there had been a letter inside, she wouldn't have written the note on the outside. Then an image of Ray's body hanging in the storage room intruded, and a cold shriek filled my head. I remembered the look of terror on Summer's face when she saw the two thugs on Sunday, and couldn't help thinking that their appearance and Summer's disappearance were not coincidental. Had they done something to her? Had she done something to herself?

"So she knew Ray before, back in Reno?"

"Seems so."

Another thought intruded. What if she hadn't been afraid of the two men? What if she thought the thugs had told her husband something that made her afraid of *him*? Something about her and Ray. My self-defense instinct reawakened and my thigh muscles tensed. *The husband is always the first suspect when a wife dies or disappears. Leave.*

But Evan stopped me.

THIRTY-EIGHT

I was about to excuse myself when Evan spoke, and his voice was so placid, I didn't move. "I went to pick up printer cartridges on Monday, and when I got home ..." He tilted his head back and seemed to collect himself. "I figured she was in the shop. Around one I made lunch and called her cell, but it was here, on the table."

"She left her phone?"

He sniffed hard and nodded.

Her phone. Her truck. Her dog. Who leaves home without at least one of those?

"So I went to get her. She forgets to eat sometimes when she's busy."

I should be so lucky. "And she wasn't there?"

"I checked the barn, and then the pastures. She was nowhere." He touched the envelope with his finger. "This was in the bedroom. I didn't find it until later." He sniffed. "She's just gone."

Silence held us still for a moment. When I finally broke the spell, Evan flinched as if I had snuck up on him.

"Evan, I saw you with those two men on Sunday." When he didn't answer, I pressed on. "I saw the guy poke you in the chest."

"Just guys I know."

"Look, if you can't tell me, maybe you need to tell someone else. Maybe you need to talk to the police."

He shook his head but said nothing.

I set my mug to the side and leaned toward him. "I saw Summer's reaction to those guys." I was stretching the truth a bit, considering I hadn't noticed Summer watching them until I saw my photos, but the revised version was close enough.

"Summer wasn't there," Evan said, staring at me.

"No, but she was watching. And then she ran away."

Evan frowned. "I don't know why she'd do that."

Yes, he does. "Are you sure?"

"Yeah. I …" He seemed to drift away.

I thought of my little encounter with the men at Dom's Deli and was suddenly angry. "Evan, who are those guys? I need to know, because the skinny one sort of threatened me—"

"What do you mean?" Evan came back to life. "Threatened you how? Why?"

When I retold the story for the second time, it didn't sound quite as scary and I ended by saying, "I guess it wasn't really a threat, but it felt, I don't know, strange." *Scary.*

Evan stared at me for a long moment before he said, "That does sound like a threat. Do you really have photos of them talking to me?"

"Yes." I told him about the photos of his encounter with the men, and of Summer watching and, apparently, running away from them.

"That can't be right," Evan said, peering out the window and then grabbing the coffee pot to refill our mugs. "She doesn't know them."

"Maybe she was looking at something else," I said, knowing I was right about her reaction to the men. "Evan, you still haven't told me who they are."

He dropped into his chair with a thud, sighed, cleared his throat, and spoke. "A while back I got into a little trouble. Gambling. Money." Something like a laugh punctuated the last word, and he went on. "Isn't that rich? I never gambled at all when I lived in Nevada."

"Wait. You were in Nevada?" Maybe the conversation Giselle overheard wasn't about Ray. What was it she heard Hutchinson say? "He picked the wrong bookie," if I remembered correctly. We had assumed they were talking about Ray. Had they meant Evan?

Evan's brow crinkled. "Yeah, for a while. I went to Reno with my brand-new computer science degree to find work, but without a master's, I ended up waiting tables in a casino restaurant."

"But you didn't gamble? So where—"

"A client in Cleveland ..." He slumped into the back of his chair and sighed long and hard. "I was there setting up a system and one night ... I was drinking and trying to be one of the guys, throwing money around at a bar. I ended up at a back-room poker game with some guys who were, well, let's just say they weren't computer geeks. Jack Daniels did my thinking for me, and before I knew it I was in deep."

"How deep?"

"Forty-six grand and change."

"Whoa! And you borrowed money from the wrong people?"

He shook his head. "I signed a note for this place."

"The farm?"

"And those two guys are here to collect?"

Evan let out something between a snort and a groan, but didn't say anything. I was about to ask how he could sign over the farm without Summer's agreement, both legally and morally, but Evan looked like he might burst into tears. I decided to change directions.

"Did you know Ray in Nevada?"

Evan shook his head. "No. He answered Summer's ad for a part-time stock man. Just a coincidence that he's from Nevada."

Sure it was. "Small world." I turned my mug in circles while I thought, and then said, "Isn't Summer also from somewhere out west?"

He nodded. "North of Reno, near Winnemucca. Her family raised sheep."

"Did you get married in Reno?"

"No, we ... I got sick of waiting tables and decided to leave." His forefinger started tapping the side of his cup and he pursed his lips before speaking again. "We're not actually married. We're planning to ... well, we were planning to get married eventually."

And unless you added her to the title, that's how you signed the farm away all by yourself. "Then Summer's name isn't Winslow?"

"No. She just thought it would be easier to call herself that."

That seemed very odd to me, unless Summer was hiding from someone.

"What is her last name?"

"Smith."

Really? "Did you really meet in Reno?"

For the first time since I'd arrived, he smiled. "Yeah. Talk about a whirlwind. I was actually waiting for the bus to Salt Lake City and she sat down beside me at a diner, you know, at the counter. She had all that wavy red hair and those green eyes and ..." His cheeks reddened and he cleared his throat. "It wasn't just, you know, physical. I mean, she was—is—gorgeous, but that wasn't it. We started talking and hit it off, and when I told her I was leaving town, she said she'd go with me."

"How romantic." *How completely crazy!* I got that Evan was ready to move on for a better job, but what about Summer? Now I was sure she had been running from something, or someone.

"Yeah. I thought she was kidding, but an hour later we had cashed in my bus ticket and were roaring east on U.S. 50 in her truck." The muscles in his face softened, and he went on. "They call it the loneliest road in America, but it sure didn't feel that way."

"I imagine not," I said, thinking about the first flush of love. I knew I was lucky to still feel that with Tom after a year together. As I considered the pain Evan must be feeling, I knew it was time to take our conversation down another road, so I said, "And then you came to Indiana?"

"We spent a week camping in Great Basin National Park, and by the end of that, we were in love. I could hardly believe how lucky I was to have a woman like Summer fall for me."

I could hardly believe it either. In fact, I was pretty sure Summer had seen him coming and had taken full advantage. He was her ticket out of whatever she had fallen into in Reno.

Evan continued the story. "We spent another month taking odd jobs across Utah and Colorado, and then came here." He looked around the kitchen. "My aunt needed help after her husband died. This was her place, and when she passed away a year later, she left us the farm, an ancient mule, and a dozen barn cats." He let out a long sigh. "It was a no-brainer. I love this place. When I was a kid, we'd come to visit for a few days at a time. Me and my brothers. My aunt had no kids and she liked having us around."

"Sounds like fun."

"We had a ball." Evan chuckled. "And my mom got some rest. Raising five boys couldn't have been a picnic."

We sat quietly for a few moments, and then I remembered the Purdue diploma that hung in Summer's office. "When did Summer go to Purdue?"

"Oh, that." A puff of air escaped between Evan's lips. "That was Summer's idea. She thought having a degree would make her more credible, but ... "

I waited, but Evan's story had stalled. I said, "She never went to Purdue?"

"She went for a weekend seminar on managing sheep. She got a certificate, and she used that ... " He faded away again.

"She faked a diploma."

Evan nodded. "She learned about sheep and weaving and all that other stuff as a kid, but she felt, I don't know, embarrassed about not having a college degree. Or high school." He finally looked directly at me, the light in his eyes throwing out a challenge. "She's smart. Really smart. And she reads a lot."

"You don't have to convince me," I said, and it was true. I had never thought of Summer as uneducated or uninformed.

"The sheep and wool and all that were her thing, and she's been making money the past couple of years. I get enough freelance gigs with software companies to keep things running. We're doing okay." He laid his head on his arms and mumbled what sounded like, "At least we were."

THIRTY-NINE

EVAN AND I SEEMED to have exhausted conversational topics and ourselves, so I told him I needed to get going. I was surprised when he offered to walk me out, but he seemed to have shed his earlier terror, at least for the moment. "Summer has a dog here for training. His owner's picking him up this weekend, but I need to take him out for a run."

Evan stopped by the front door and picked up the shotgun. He started to reach for the doorknob, but stopped and thrust the gun toward me. "Could you hold this? I need to change shoes."

Without thinking, I wrapped my fingers around the gun's barrels. Surprised by its weight, I took the stock in my other hand and ran my gaze along the length of the weapon. A long ragged scratch marred the otherwise sleek finish of the wooden stock. "You're taking this with you?"

He laughed. "No, the coyotes don't come around until dusk." He took the gun from me and set it out of sight in the living room. "I just don't think that's the best place for it."

We said our goodbyes in the yard between the house and the barn, and I went to my van. Jay shook his travel crate with his wiggling, but I signaled him to lie down and said, "Sorry, Bubby, no sheepies today. We'll go for a walk on the way home." He grinned back at me, ready as always to accept whatever I suggested.

Movement near the barn caught my eye as I fastened my seatbelt. Luciano was trotting down the hill toward Evan, who held a stainless steel dog bowl. The two of them disappeared into the barn, and I assumed Evan was locking the big dog up to avoid any problems when he let the client dog out. I started the van, and as I reached for the shift, a big charcoal-gray dog bounded into view, leaping and spinning and bouncing. A Bouvier des Flandres, a big one and obviously young. Evan followed.

I was about to drive away when the Bouvier ran toward Evan, who swung his arm up and forward as if to direct the big galoot toward a gate at the end of the path they were on. The gate opened into an empty pasture, and I assumed Evan meant to use it to exercise the dog without disturbing the sheep in the other field. The purposefulness with which the dog trotted toward the gate held my attention. I waited and watched. The Bouvier stood on his hind legs and reached for the gate latch. It took him a couple of tries, but he finally did it.

He opened the gate.

Evan had pulled a clump of hairs from the gate latch on Saturday morning. They were dark, and six or so inches long. About right for a Bouvier's beard. In the distance, Evan caught up with the dog, pulled the gate shut behind them, and disappeared over a small rise in the field. I sat for a moment, then shifted into gear and turned toward home.

Had someone sent a dog to open the gate and fetch the sheep from the pen? Could that be why the security cameras hadn't caught anyone around the pens during the night the sheep went missing? They were undoubtedly set to human height to avoid accidental triggering by wild animals. Had Summer trained that Bouvier to do that neat little trick? It made sense that Summer would prefer to use a dog she didn't own if she had larceny on her mind. It wasn't as if he'd tattle on her. But I hadn't seen a Bouvier around the event grounds, and a dog that size would be hard to miss. And why steal her own sheep? And if Summer was the rustler, then Evan had to be in on it. He would have known she was gone from their camper.

Then another question popped into my head. Did we know for sure that both Summer and Evan had spent Friday night in their camper? What if one of them had gone home? Someone had to care for the animals on the farm. I hadn't given it any thought before, but as I drove away with the Bouvier's gate-opening trick fresh in my mind, I started to wonder.

And what about Ray? How was he involved? I had the impression that Ray had stayed on the event grounds, although I wasn't sure why I thought that. Maybe because I had arrived early and he and Bonnie were already moving the remaining sheep. If the Bouvier had been on the farm for more than a few days, Ray must have known the dog. Maybe he was the one who trained him to open the gate and round up the sheep. But again, why? And if the dog did take the sheep from the pen, what did he do with them?

I thought back to the huge paw prints Tom and I had found, and considered the size of the Bouvier. I had a hunch his feet would fit into those marks. Could someone have parked a stock truck somewhere on the property and used the dog to commit the crime? I remembered an old movie, *The Doberman Gang,* about a crook who trained Doberman Pinschers to rob banks. But that was Hollywood, and this was Indiana, and real, live sheep with no retakes. Still, I'd seen the dog open the gate with my own eyes, and a good sheepdog—Nell or Bonnie, for instance—could have moved the flock to a waiting truck. The more I tried to untangle the possibilities, the woollier my thoughts became.

FORTY

I HAD MEANT TO stop for a walk with Jay on my way back, but I'd flown right into town and found myself driving south on North Anthony. If I kept going another five or so miles, I would end up at Shadetree Retirement Home. Why not? Jay was clean, so we could pop in for a visit and see how the bride was doing. And we could still get a walk in on the St. Mary's Rivergreenway if we didn't stay too long with Mom.

Jay was thrilled to get out of his crate, and we took a little relief walk among the maples and oaks along the side of the building. When he was finished, I clipped Jay's therapy dog ID tag to his collar and in we went. Jade Templeton's office door was closed and the lobby was empty but for a quartet of rummy players at a table near the gas fireplace. I looked into the solarium, Mom's favorite hangout, but she wasn't there. My next stop was the reading room, a bright space with several comfy chairs and a long library-style table with desk lamps and a computer at one end. Harlan Overmeier, a bespectacled gentleman of indeterminate old age, hunched toward the screen. He wore earphones and worked a humongous game gadget with his right hand, apparently controlling the spaceship that careened around the screen.

Mom sat at a table near the windows, holding hands with Tony Marconi, her soon-to-be husband. Bill and his partner, Norm, were there as well. Bill is my brother by birth, Norm my brother by natural selection. I'm ever thankful that they have one of the most loving and stable relationships I know of, because if they ever broke up, I'd be hard pressed to choose between them. In the moment before anyone noticed me and Jay, Norm and my mom were smiling and chattering like kids with a new toy, Tony was finger-punching his e-tablet with his free hand, and brother Bill was leaning back in his chair and scowling. Norm and Mom were no doubt thinking of ways to spend Bill's money.

Jay pulled me forward until he could lay his chin on Mom's lap, raising a squeal from his favorite old lady. "Jay!" She didn't bother with me until she'd finished smooching my dog. Tony saw me and began creaking to his feet, but I signaled him to stay sitting. Bill said hi, and Norm jumped up and hugged me silly.

"We're just finalizing plans," said Norm. "Can you help me decorate the Solarium Friday a week? I've ordered garlands, simple but beautiful. Jade offered to have her guys set up the seating, and …" He rattled on and I smiled to see everyone so happy. Everyone but Bill.

Conversation and laughter intermingled for another half hour, and even brother Bill lightened up and joined in. The best thing was that Mom was fully present, and I credited Tony with at least some of her cognitive improvement. Even if it lasted only a few months, it was good to have her mostly back.

Our noses eventually told us that lunchtime was almost upon us, and Bill, Norm, and I said our goodbyes and walked toward the lobby together. "I need to make a short stop," I said when we reached the entrance to a small alcove off the hallway. "I'll talk to you later, and Norm, I'd love to help decorate."

When Jay and I emerged from the restroom and started to cross the main lobby, I heard the receptionist say, "Here's a brochure with quite a bit of information. We can arrange a tour of the facilities if you like, too, and you're welcome to talk to some of the residents to see how they like ..." I glanced at the information counter and felt a shiver race up my spine. A heavy man in an ill-fitting gray suit had his back to me, but I knew the set of his shoulders. It was the fat thug. *What the ...?*

I backtracked out of the lobby, my heart thumping as if I'd just run a 5K. "Come on," I told Jay, "we'll go out the side door." I had put Jay in his crate and was about to climb into the driver's seat when a voice said, "Heard this is the best nursing home in town. That right?"

I whirled and found myself face to face with Skinny.

FORTY-ONE

THE SKINNY GOON HAD a smirk on his face and was standing too close for comfort but just beyond slapping distance. Fury rose like hot foam in my throat and smothered the fear I had felt a few minutes earlier.

"Are you following me?" Of course they were following me. How else could they show up at Dom's Deli and my mother's nursing home? "And who the hell are you?" I kept my hand in my pocket and worked my keys between my fingers to make a weapon of them.

He pulled something out of his pocket and began to finger it. "Janet, is it?" He gave me a look that might have been playful in a cat-playing-with-mouse sort of way. I looked more closely at the thing in his hand. It was a business card. *My* business card. He must have picked it up at the information booth at the Dogs of Spring event. "How about you turn over that roll of film. The one you took with us on it."

What century are you living in? "I don't use film, and why in the world would I take pictures of you? I don't even know you."

"If you don't use film, I guess you'll have to let us buy your camera from you. How much?" He pulled a roll of bills from his pocket, slipped the rubber band off, and began peeling fifties away. "Two hundred?"

If I hadn't been caught somewhere between roaring mad and scared spitless, I would have doubled up laughing. I had more money tied up in cameras and lenses than I had in my van. "Two hundred wouldn't even cover my camera case. Anyway, it's not for sale and I didn't take any pictures of you. Now unless you'd like to talk to the police, leave me—"

"Everything okay here?" I heard the voice before I saw the car pull up behind my van. Bill stepped out and stood with his feet slightly apart and shoulders squared. He kept his eyes on the other man, and when he spoke again, his voice was clear and low. "Janet, I'll just follow you home instead of coming over later. Ready?"

"Yep." I got into my van, buckled up, and started the engine before I looked out again. The goon was walking away, and Bill was still there, watching him go. The gray sedan pulled up beside the guy and he got in, and Bill stepped to my window.

"What was that?"

"Long story, and I only know part of it, but thanks." I've never really thought of Brother Bill as an action hero, but he'd come through this time.

"You know that guy?"

"No, but I've seen him before." I hesitated, but finally told him about my encounter with the two men at Dom's Deli, and about seeing them with Evan and Ray.

"The dead guy?" Bill's voice was no longer clear and low. It was more of a masculine screech. "You saw that guy threatening the dead guy?"

I shrugged, but didn't feel as calm as I was trying to look. Skinny had my business card. My address wasn't on it, but my email and phone number were, and I knew that it just isn't that hard to find out where people live if you have some basic information.

"I don't think you should go straight home. Come to our house, or go see Tom."

Good idea. "Don't be silly. I'll be fine."

Bill scowled at me.

"Really, I will. Besides, he thinks you're following me home." I tried to smile at him, but my mouth was too dry to work properly. "Anyway, I need to drop Jay off and get my gear. I have a portrait shoot this afternoon." *And I want to back up those photos I accidentally took of the two thugs.* In fact, I wondered whether I should email them to Hutchinson, and I knew I should tell him those guys were definitely stalking me.

"Call your policeman friend and tell him those guys are stalking you," said Bill.

Does everyone read my mind? "I will."

"Please."

He waited while I called Hutch. The detective answered, and he asked me to send the images as soon as I got home. "I have a friend in Washoe County sheriff's department. He lives in Reno. I'll see if he can find out anything about the guys." Hutch said he would reach out to the Cleveland police, too, and have a patrol car cruise by my house at intervals. He reminded me to lock my doors and be careful.

No kidding.

When I finished, Bill said, "I *am* going to follow you home." He must have thought he was expressing too much affection, because he added, "Mom would kill me if anything happened to you before her wedding."

FORTY-TWO

BILL FOLLOWED ME HOME and I made him lunch. That may not sound like much, but it was the first time my brother and I had spent an hour and half alone together since grade school. I made grilled Swiss and tomato sandwiches and, after I scraped the charred edges off, they were pretty good. By the time Bill left and I got my camera and other gear ready to go, I had shoved recent events to the back of my mind and was feeling pretty mellow.

And then Hutchinson called.

"I thought you were sending me pictures of those guys?"

I forgot. "I will when I get home. I'm on my way to a photo shoot, but it shouldn't take long."

My session was with three physicians new to a practice about ten minutes from home. When we made the appointment, I had told the office manager that I was on a tight schedule and that in addition to my regular fee, I charge extra per quarter hour I'm kept waiting. It was my little revenge for all the hours I've wasted waiting for doctors of various kinds. They were ready when I arrived and I was home ninety minutes later.

I let Jay out and turned on the computer, but had to take time out for some cat cuddling. Pixel squirmed and wiggled when I picked her up, clearly more in the mood for some catnip-mouse hockey on the bare floors. Leo, though, hopped onto my lap and stretched his torso against mine, tucking his paws against my collarbone and purring his satisfaction. "Leo *mio*, I've neglected you." He opened his mouth but no sound came out. "We'll get the agility equipment out one of these days and have some fun." Leo and I had entered our first feline agility competition five months earlier, and he was a game little competitor.

Pixel apparently tired of the little felt mouse, and when she started grabbing Leo's tail, cuddle time was over. He jumped off my lap and chased the little pest into the living room. I let Jay in, grabbed a diet root beer, and opened my photo file from the weekend. I had copied the images with the two tough guys into a separate folder, so I checked them and then sent the whole folder to Hutchinson. An "ok, got them" email came right back.

For an hour or so I was able to focus on work, organizing several sets of proofs to send off to potential buyers, including a magazine editor and an author looking for book illustrations. When I got to the herding photos, though, everything came rushing back—the missing sheep, the runaway sheep owner, the hanged sheep handler. Not to mention the increasingly menacing pair of goons.

"Come on, Jay," I said, getting up and shaking off the black mood that was trying to ruin the afternoon. "Let's go see how Bonnie's settling in."

My phone rang just as I was snapping Jay's leash onto his collar. Giselle. I wasn't sure I wanted to hear about dead guys or anything else connected to the weekend right then, so I let it go to voice mail. I'd see her in a few hours, anyway. It was obedience training night at Dog Dayz, and we were among the never-miss die-hards.

Bonnie met us with a rousing Sheltie rendition of "there's some-one at the door!" but she turned it off as soon as Goldie appeared and let us in.

"Wow!" I said. "She looks great."

"Doesn't she?" Goldie beamed at the little dog, whose coat was fluffed and shiny as anthracite, the white trim gleaming. Bonnie pranced around, wagging her tail and spinning a "let's play" invita-tion to Jay.

I followed Goldie and the dogs into the kitchen. "I can't even tell where she trimmed out the tangles and burrs."

"I know," said Goldie, setting a plate of cookies on the table. "These have no flour and no sugar other than the fruit."

Who can resist that? "Just one. I have to fit into that dress in nine days."

"Have they learned any more about ..." Goldie paused and glanced at Bonnie, and whispered, "Ray's death?"

My phone rang before I could respond. Giselle again. "This might be important. She—Giselle—just called a few minutes ago. I should—"

"Answer it," said Goldie, getting up to make some tea from her own herb garden.

"I wanted to warn you before tonight!" It was Giselle, and her voice was pitched high and fast. "Before training, I mean."

Her words conjured the menacing faces of the two thugs, whose names I realized I still didn't know. Were they planning to attack me that night? *And how would Giselle know that?* "Warn me about what?"

"I got an email from my friend in Muncie. Some animal rights nuts showed up at their training club last night and let a couple of dogs out of their crates, and it happened in Indy and Lafayette, too, last week."

"Did they find the dogs?"

"At Muncie, yes. There were two of them—people, I mean. One opened the crates and the other held the door open and they tried to let them out the door but," she paused, and for a second I wondered whether she had hyperventilated, but then she went on. "One dog was Judy Clifton's Golden Brill, you know him, and he ran to the ring where Judy was training her Lab."

"Good boy."

"Yeah, And the other was a Jack Russell, and I guess he started barking at the woman who opened his crate and raised a real ruckus, and then I guess they, you know, the intruders, ran for it, because you *know* how mad everyone was."

A wave of nausea passed through me as I remembered how I had felt on Saturday when I thought the demonstrators had let Jay loose.

A humorless laugh came through the phone, and Giselle said, "Good thing the dogs weren't hurt or we might have had another murder on our hands."

FORTY-THREE

THE DOG DAYZ PARKING lot was jam-packed with dogmobiles when I got there Wednesday evening, so I parked on the grass across the driveway. I had put Jay on his leash and let him out and was gathering my gear when I heard my name pronounced with a soft, breathy J.

"*Hola*, Señorita Janet." It was Jorge Gomez, the groundskeeper. A half-grown tortoiseshell kitten was cradled in his arms and staring down at Jay, who was craning his neck for a sniff.

"*Hola*, Jorge. *¿Como esta?*" I stroked the kitten's black-and-gold cheek. "And how is Linda this evening?" Jorge had cared for *la linda* and her mother, dubbed *Acoiris* by Jorge but translated to Rainbow by the rest of us. When the kitten was weaned, Jorge had taken her mama to be spayed, and now Linda's belly was sparsely covered as the fur grew back from her own surgery.

Jorge rubbed his cheek against the top of the kitten's head. "Leenda is naughty kitten. She leave *raton* on desk in office and make Mees Marietta scream." Marietta Santini was the woman I'd have voted least likely to scream about a dead mouse. Jorge grinned at me. "I geev Leenda little beet sardine with dinner."

"I think you're the naughty one, Jorge." I left him giggling and headed for the door.

The basic obedience class was just wrapping up, and Marietta Santini, owner of the facility, had her "Alpha Bitch" hat on—we all chipped in and got it for her the previous Christmas as a joke, but she loved it and wore it whenever she taught a class. It was the final class of the eight-week session, so Marietta was handing out certificates of completion and encouraging everyone to continue training their dogs for life, even if they didn't come back for more classes.

I was surprised to spot a familiar face among the single row of spectators arrayed alongside the ring. Goldie waved and scurried over to see me. At least that's what I told myself, since Jay was first to get her attention. When she'd finished smooching my dog, she stood up and grinned at me. "This is all so exciting, and so much fun! I've just signed Bonnie up for the next session, although she already knows what she's doing, but I don't, so ..." She braked for breath, rubbing her hands together and bouncing almost imperceptibly.

"You'll love it," I said, "and you couldn't have a better dog to learn with."

"Is it okay for me to stay and watch you masters of the art for a while?"

"Absolutely, although I wouldn't call myself a master. But there are some great trainers here," I gestured toward the far end of the training room, "including that man down there."

Tom stood ninety or so feet down the building from us, surrounded by our fellow dog nuts and a few of their four-legged friends.

"What's going ... Oh!" She pulled me toward the group. "Did he bring the puppy?"

As we got closer, Giselle circled the crowd and pulled me aside. "Janet, what's going on with Summer?"

Who knows? Then again, a lot could have happened in an afternoon. Maybe Summer had surfaced and Giselle knew something I didn't. I wasn't sure how much I should say and bought a little time by petting the little white dog snuggled in Giselle's arms. "How you doing, Precious?"

"Spike. He's officially Spike now. Janet! What about Summer?"

"What do you mean?"

"I've been trying to reach her all day." Giselle pulled me toward the wall farthest from the ring and lowered her voice. "I found a little notebook that I think must be hers. Actually, Spike found it when we were looking for the dog. I just glanced at it, looking for the owner's name. It has a lot of notes about sheep, you know, individual sheep? And some notes about money. I didn't really read it, you know, just glanced enough to figure out whose it is. I think it must be Summer's. I've been trying to call, but no one answers at her house or her shop."

At that moment a big man came through the front door and headed toward us. Hutch. Giselle smiled and turned as Hutchinson wrapped an arm around her shoulders and pecked her cheek. Spike pushed himself up and licked Hutchinson's chin.

"Could you give me and Janet a few minutes?" His voice was tender, but when Hutchinson turned to me he was all business. "We need to talk."

My throat tightened a notch, and Jay must have sensed a change because he pressed himself into my leg as if to say, "It's okay, I'm right here."

When Giselle had returned to the puppy klatch, Hutchinson spoke again. "Good news, sort of. We couldn't ID the heavy guy in the photos, but my connection in Reno recognized the other one."

So Skinny is from Reno? Like Ray? My wheels started to turn as I pondered how two—no, three, with Summer—Nevada transplants wound up in northeast Indiana.

Hutch continued. "Name's Mick Fallon. He's not local to Reno, but he got into a little trouble out there a couple of years back. Roughed up a woman who pulled a con on his boss, a thug from Cleveland named Barry Cucinelli. She managed to get away, and security grabbed Fallon when he chased her through a casino full of people."

"Knowing he has a history roughing up women, or anyone else, doesn't make me very happy."

"No, but you'll love this." His mouth twisted into a half smile. "She nailed him. Pulled off her stiletto and walloped him right in the face."

"I figured the scar was from a knife fight." A smile grabbed my mouth. "That's even better."

Hutchinson chuckled. "He probably doesn't do much bragging about how he got it." Then he turned serious. "Anyway, the guy works for some hood in Cleveland. His buddy probably does too. I've reached out to the Cleveland police, so we should have an ID on him soon."

Tom was watching us, Winnie cradled in his arms, her mouth agape in a huge yawn. I smiled at him, thanked Hutch for the information, and started to move toward Tom.

"Janet, the photos helped a lot," said Hutchinson, placing a hand on my arm. "And that's what those guys were worried about."

He didn't have to tell me to be careful, but he did.

FORTY-FOUR

Dog training is a bit like meditation with movement, noise, and fur. It's all about the moment. Becoming one with the dog. Calming what the Buddhists call our monkey mind, the one that flings one thought willy-nilly on top of another. At least that's how training feels when I focus, which wasn't easy after my chat with Hutchinson. Once Marietta started calling commands in the practice ring, though—forward! slow! about turn!—my monkey mind settled down and my dog-handler brain kicked in. Jay was attentive as usual, and feeling him prancing beside me pushed scar-faced thugs and dead bodies out of my consciousness.

Our training community is fairly stable, so when a new dog-and-handler team shows up for anything other than basic obedience classes, they stand out, especially when the dog is as gorgeous as the one I spotted in the ring. Her person was warming her up with a series of tricks—sits, downs, spins, paw waves—and the grin on the dog's face showed how she enjoyed the game. *Maybe those nuts who think owning and training animals is abusive should see some of this.* As I watched, I realized that I'd seen this pair before. It was the cute black tri-color Aussie I'd seen at the herding event wearing sunglasses and a pink floppy hat with her name embroidered across the front. Lilly, if I remembered correctly.

Lilly's owner spotted Jay and smiled, then shifted her attention to my end of the leash and walked toward us. Her reaction was not unusual. Dog people are a bit tribal, and people with the same and similar breeds tend to pack together. Conversations often begin with reference to the dogs, as this one did.

"Nice Aussie," she said.

"Ditto!" We introduced ourselves and our dogs, who were busy wiggling and sniffing as well as they could through the accordion fence that edged the ring. Lilly and her owner, Jean, were in Fort Wayne for a four-month work assignment. I added Jean's phone number to my contact list and we promised to get the dogs together soon for some Aussie fun.

Aside from an occasional loudly voiced opinion from a couple of canines and a few squeals from human members getting their first glimpses of Winnie, it was a quiet session. No "loose dog" alerts, no knocked-over ring barriers. There wasn't even much gossip, which surprised me in light of Ray's death. Granted, most Dog Dayz members were not involved in herding and hadn't known Ray or the Winslows, but a death at any sort of canine event was news.

It wasn't until we were lining the dogs up along one side of the ring for the stay exercise that I realized I had forgotten to tell Hutchinson what I had seen at the Winslows' farm. In my own defense, my chat with Evan seemed days rather than hours earlier. I considered skipping the stay practice, but Tom moved Drake into the line next to me and Jay, winked, and said, "This sit taken, ma'am?"

On Marietta's drill-sergeant bark we told our dogs to sit and stay and walked the forty feet to the other side of the ring. Members of the group ranged from novices fresh from basic obedience to dogs with advanced titles and handlers with many years of experience. As a result, some people stayed in the ring to supervise their novice dogs, and six of us left the ring to hide behind a barrier set up for that purpose. At least we said we were hiding, but since the dogs watched us with the focus they'd give frolicking squirrels, we all knew it was a shared fiction.

"Winnie is quite the hit," I said, picking a clump of black hairs off Tom's sweatshirt." "Where is she?"

"In her crate. She's worn out."

"She's very quiet for a puppy in a strange place," I said.

"For now," Tom said. "Don't jinx it!"

We whispered with the rest of the out-of-site dog owners and, after a long three minutes, returned to the ring on Marietta's command. Five of the dogs were right where we left them. The sixth, Sandy Braun's Wire Fox Terrier, Diva, had chosen to confirm her breed's reputation for being fun-loving free thinkers. She was in the middle of the ring, on her back.

"Don't laugh at her," Sandy said in a stage whisper. "It just encourages the little devil." But Sandy was smiling when she went to get her dog.

As soon as we had finished the down-stays, I found Hutch. He was sitting outside the ring with Spike, formerly Precious, on his lap.

"I see you have a new buddy."

He grinned. "He's a cool little dog."

"What does Amy think of him?" Amy was the calico litter sister to my Pixel and Goldie's Totem. Hutch had fallen head over paws for her when the kittens were about five minutes old.

"They get along great." He looked at me with wide eyes. "I'm amazed. I always thought, you know, dogs and cats—" Jay poked

Hutchinson's arm with his nose, and Hutch looked at him and said, "You're right, Jay. The joke's on me."

"So, Hutch," I said, watching Giselle approach from the back of the building. "If you have a minute, I forgot to tell you something."

He gave me an uh-oh look but held his tongue. Giselle took her dog, and Hutch and I found a relatively private place to talk. I told him first about the number of sheep in the Winslows' pasture. "I've never counted them, you know, but I have a sense of how big the flock was. It looks like it always looked. I mean, not like a quarter of the sheep are missing but—"

"Jeez, I know nothing about sheep. How would we even tell one from another? I mean, they all look alike."

I stifled a laugh. "They don't, actually, but more importantly, they all have ear tags that identify them. So I guess that could be checked."

"I'll get somebody to look into it." He started to turn away.

"Wait! There's more." I told him about watching the Bouvier open the pasture gate.

"But it's not their dog?"

I shook my head. "Evan said Summer had it there for training."

"Okay, I'll get up there first thing in the morning and talk to her. If she's the one training the dog—"

"That's the thing, Hutch. She's not there."

"What do you mean?"

"Evan hasn't seen her since Monday. At least, that's what he said this morning. But her truck and her cell phone are there, and her dog." Now I had his attention. "And then there's the notebook . . ." I knew as soon as it was out of my mouth that Giselle hadn't told him about finding Summer's notebook. She probably didn't think it was important. *Well done*, whispered my inner nag. *You've set up their first lovers' spat.*

168

FORTY-FIVE

WINNIE HAD HER SECOND wind by the time we arrived home, so in the interest of getting some sleep when the time came, we all went outside for a game of tennis ball. I had installed lights halfway down the backyard after a break-in the summer before, so visibility was no problem.

Despite her size, Winnie was game. Tom or I would throw the ball, the three dogs would chase it, and the boys would stand aside and let the puppy win almost every time. When she tried to engage one of us in a game of keep-away, we ignored her, and she was quickly learning that if she wanted the game to go on, she had to deliver the ball to one of our hands. By the fifth race down the yard and back, her battery seemed to be running down a bit, so we put the ball away and just enjoyed the brisk spring air and starlight.

We were ready to go in when Goldie's back door opened. Bonnie woofed once when she saw us, glanced back, and when she saw that her new mistress was right behind her, trotted to the fence to greet our gang.

"I'm so excited!" said Goldie. "Bonnie and I start class next week. Janet, do you have any good books I can read about basic training?"

I promised to get her set up with reading material and videos, and added, "Bonnie's used to having a job, you know, and unless you plan to put a few sheep in your garden, you might want to try agility after you get the basics down."

We chatted a few minutes more, but when Winnie lay down and curled up to sleep, we said goodnight to Goldie and Bonnie, took the dogs in, and settled in to watch a movie. The first few minutes were chaotic as Pixel reached from my lap to bop Winnie on the nose, and Winnie tried to squirm free of Tom to respond with a wrestling match. Drake didn't want any part of that nonsense, but Jay hopped onto the couch beside me and started to lick Pixel. By the time the previews had finished, Pixel had slid from my lap and curled up between Jay's lovely white paws, Winnie was snuggled against Tom's chest, Leo was purring behind my head on the back of the couch, and Drake was sprawled across the big round dog bed.

I tried to lose myself in the movie, but it was no use. My mind wandered first to Ray and then to Summer. Summer, who had created a fiction about herself in Indiana. She and Evan weren't married, and Winslow wasn't her name at all, and her diploma from Purdue was a forgery. What had she been running from in Reno, and what else had she made up? More to the point, why? And why had she been frightened by the two goons from Cleveland? They were there to collect from Evan, not Summer. Or were they?

"What's the matter?" Tom's voice broke into my reverie.

"Nothing. Why?"

"You've been fidgeting since the movie started." He picked up the remote control and hit pause. "So what's up?"

I gave him the abbreviated version, and when I finished, he said, "Okay, let me put Winnie to bed and we'll do a little research." He turned the television off.

"You'll help?"

He gave me a one-armed hug in reply, then carried Winnie to her pen. She barely opened her eyes when he laid her up against her giant teddy bear. I got up as carefully as I could, leaving Jay and Pixel where they were. I set my laptop up on the kitchen table and Tom sat next to me. Drake traipsed in and thunked down on the floor beside him.

We started with Summer Winslow, and several references came up to her yarn shop and herding lessons. I had never seen her website before, and it was lovely, illustrated with lots of great photos, including a few that I had taken of her herding students and their dogs. When we had clicked through all the internal links, Tom pointed out that there were no photos of Summer herself.

I returned to her "About Me" page. "Her bio begins with her studying at Purdue, which she didn't." And Tom was right. There was no photo of her.

We tried again, this time looking for Summer Smith and adding and subtracting search terms as we went—Nevada, weaving, wool, sheep, Reno. Nothing came up. Then we tried "Summer" with the other terms in various combinations. That brought up the kinds of page links I could get lost in—Basque shepherds and cowboys of Nevada, sheep farms and weaving workshops, herding and guardian dogs. But nothing about the woman we knew as Summer Winslow.

We were scrolling through a list of links to weaving workshops much like the ones Summer offered at the farm when Tom stopped me. "Wait! Go back a page." I did, and he pointed at a listing for Summertime Woolens in Winnemucca, Nevada. "Didn't you say Summer was from Winnemucca?"

The link led to a bare-bones site. The home page showed a store-front with a dark-haired woman standing in front with a basket of colorful yarns in her hands and a Border Collie at her feet. I clicked the About Us link and found two more photos. In one, the same woman sat at a loom. The second picture showed a flock of sheep in the distance, and the back of a little girl with her hand on a different dog, this one a blue merle Aussie. The girl had her back to the camera, and the only clue that she was female was the pink boots she wore. I leaned into the screen for a glimpse of the girl's hair. Her straw hat hid it, but something in her build and stance, even though she appeared to be about ten, was familiar.

Tom and I looked at each other, and we both said, "That's her."

FORTY-SIX

WINNIE GOT US UP before dawn on Thursday morning. Normally I'd have burrowed under a pillow and let Tom deal with his baby, but I'd already been awake for what seemed like hours. I'd been thinking about the web photo I was sure showed Summer, or whatever her name was, as a little girl, and about Ray Turnbull. What were the odds that two people from Nevada, both of them involved with sheep and herding dogs, would end up in this little corner of northern Indiana? Even more incredible, if they had both been working with livestock and competing with sheepdogs in the sparsely populated land north of Reno, how could they not have known each other?

I pulled on some sweats and started down the hall to the kitchen. As I passed the room I'd been clearing out for Tom's new office, something moved on top of a stack of boxes under the window. Pixel's tail. It was twitching as if possessed, but the rest of the kitten crouched perfectly still as she watched the activity in the backyard.

"Good morning, Ms. Pixel." I picked her up and she butted my chin with her forehead and let me hold her for two seconds. Then she tried to turn back to the window, protesting with long, squeaky meows. "You're right, the dogs are more interesting than I am this morning," I said, setting her back on her perch.

In the kitchen I set four eggs on the counter, told Mr. Coffee to get busy, and opened my laptop. But before I could type "Ray Turnbull" into the search engine, Leo hopped onto the table and sprawled across my keyboard. We bumped noses and I stroked his soft marmalade fur. "Leo *mio*," I murmured. He squinted at me and purred. I know there are people who find such animal behaviors annoying, but I'm thankful that my furry friends think enough of me to ask for attention. Cats and dogs are here such a short time, and that time passes so quickly, that I find it hard to begrudge them a few minutes of petting or play. They seem to feel better for it, and I know I do.

The back door opened and the three dogs exploded into the kitchen, little Winnie in the lead. Jay and Drake stuck with Tom, knowing he'd be dishing up breakfast. Winnie didn't know the morning routine, and when she saw me and Leo she tried to change direction. Still at full speed, her feet scrabbled one way while her plump little body slid the other, and she came to rest up against my foot. Half a beat later she had her wet paws on my knees and her wet mouth on Leo's leg. Leo pulled his ears halfway back and opened his mouth, but Winnie missed the warning. At eight weeks, she barely spoke Dog, let alone Cat. She poked her nose at Leo, yipped, and grabbed his leg again. Leo arched back from her, flattened his ears, hissed, and socked her in the snoot. Winnie froze for a second, then seemed to decide it was a game. She came back for more, grabbing Leo's tail. He leaped from my lap and I tried to grab the bouncing puppy, but she was too quick for me. She made another grab and Leo whirled on her, all patience gone. Winnie bowed at him, tail spinning, and pounced. He hissed and spat and whacked her little black nose. *Yip yow!* Winnie rolled over backward, recovered, and sat looking at Leo but not moving.

"When the cat says no, little girl, dogs should listen," Tom said. Jay and Drake sniffed Winnie, apparently decided she was fine, and went back to staring at chef Tom.

I looked at the puppy's nose. Something was sticking up from the top of the moist black tip. "Did he scratch her there?"

Tom laid a hand over Winnie's shoulder and neck and pinched something from the top of her nose with the other. He put it in the palm of his hand, looked at it, and held it for me to see. "A bit of his claw sheath." He turned back to where Winnie had been, but her round little fanny was racing down the hall in search of more fun with Mr. Cat.

I went back to my laptop while Tom retrieved the puppy. He set up a baby gate to keep her in the kitchen, dished up the three doggy breakfasts, and put a leash on Winnie to keep her out of the big boys' bowls.

"Need any help?"

Tom handed me Jay and Drake's bowls and grinned at me. "I think she's going to be a two-handed project for a while."

Drake and Jay both had drool-globs dangling from their lips by the time I set the bowls down, but they waited for my "free" command before they inhaled their grub. Winnie took a little longer, particular the "sit and wait" phase of breakfast service, which was new and frustrating for a hungry puppy. But Tom is nothing if not patient, and when she managed to sit for five full seconds, he let her eat. I went back to my computer while he handed out carrots for their post-breakfast treat.

My first search was simply Ray Turnbull's name. Aside from recent news of our Ray's death, I found links to a curler and broadcaster from Manitoba and a plumber from Florida, but no stockmen from Nevada or anywhere else. That didn't mean much, though, since Ray didn't strike me as a guy who would have a website or spend much time on social media. Next I typed in Turnbull + sheep and found someone, but he had a different first name and he lived in England. I found some Turnbulls in the Reno area, but no Rays.

Tom took the dogs out again and I started to shut down my computer, but decided to take one last run at finding Ray. If Summer was hiding behind a pseudonym, maybe Ray was, too. I leaned back and closed my eyes. My mind was still flailing around for a starting point when Tom brought the dogs back in. Winnie took a couple of laps around the kitchen, but her morning romp and full belly had taken the edge off her energy, and she soon flopped down between Jay and Drake, rolled onto her side, and heaved a big sigh.

"Looking for more on Summer?"

"Ray. But no luck so far, at least not under Ray Turnbull."

Tom poured our coffee and said, "Okay, ten-minute limit, but let's take one more stab at it." He grinned at me. "I'm not sure we should be playing detective, but it is kind of fun puzzling out the details."

We brainstormed search terms and watched the results for anything remotely promising. *Raymond Turnbull* found nothing new. *Ray + Nevada + sheep* was equally disappointing.

"Try just 'Ray Turner,'" said Tom. "I read somewhere that people often choose new names similar to their old ones."

"That seems pretty obvious," I said, but I tried it. Nothing. Ditto *Ray Turn + Nevada.*

The ten minutes and our coffee were nearly used up when I had another idea. "You know, I always thought 'Turnbull' was the perfect name for a guy who handles livestock. I mean, lately he's been working with sheep, but what if he used to work with cattle and just made up the name?"

Tom finished his coffee and set the mug on the table. "I bet there are a lot of cowboys named Ray, if that's even his name."

"Maybe something else?" I type *Ray + Nevada + bull* and found a man who braided bull ropes. "What the heck is a bull rope?" We both leaned in to read and learned that a bull rider grips a braided bull rope for the eight-second attempted ride in a rodeo. I typed again—*Ray + Nevada + bull rider.* That brought up several names, but none fit our guy.

"Rats," I said, fingers poised for another search string, if I could think of one.

"Time's up and I'm starving." Tom stood up and kissed the top of my head. "I need more than two eggs and a piece of toast. Let's go to the diner."

He didn't have to ask twice.

FORTY-SEVEN

WE HAD SUCH AN early start that it wasn't yet eight when Tom dropped me at home and took off with Drake and Winnie to pack more books. I resisted the urge to do more Googling and focused for a couple of hours on tasks that would pay the bills. As I hit publish on the last set of proofs and they posted to my website, I looked around to see where all the very quiet creatures were. Leo and Jay didn't worry me, but a silent Pixel could mean trouble. But there she was, curled into a sleeping gray ball inside the bigger curve of Leo's body. They were on a chair in a shaft of sunlight, and their fur shone like pewter and gold. I carefully lifted my camera and took several shots. The soft clicks of the shutter release woke Jay. He stood, stretched, yawned, and laid his head on my thigh.

"You're right, Bubby. Time for some fun." He cocked his head. "Maybe Goldie and Bonnie would like to go with us. What do you think?" Goldie was game, and twenty minutes later we parked at the River Road Trailhead for the Rivergreenway, unloaded the dogs, and headed east along the chocolaty Maumee River.

"She's such a good girl," said Goldie, "I don't know that she even needs that obedience class."

"She probably doesn't, but it will be good for you, and help you build a stronger relationship."

"Oh, I'm going!" Goldie's laugh blended with the birdsong rising from the beeches and sycamores and oaks along the riverbank. "I'm really excited about it. And I know Bonnie will get me through." At the sound of her name, Bonnie turned toward Goldie and wagged her bushy tail, then rejoined Jay. The two of them trotted at the ends of their six-foot leashes, but they didn't pull. "I have very few regrets, but I'm beginning to regret all the years I've lived without a pet."

"Maybe the time just wasn't right," I said, although other than college I couldn't imagine a time in my own life when an animal didn't fit in. "And you have a pair of lovelies now."

We walked in silence for a while, the kind of silence that, between simpaticos, feels like communication. The air had that early spring mix of fresh leaves and new grasses and cool mud. We turned around at the one-mile marker and were just in sight of the parking lot when a little white dog trotted into view followed by a woman in leggings and a tunic. Her face was obscured behind big sunglasses, and she was too far away to see clearly at any rate. The dog stopped short and barked at us. "Quiet!" I knew the voice, and waved.

"Giselle! You cut your hair!" When I had first gotten to know Giselle, she'd been very overweight, unhappy, and not very nice to be around. She had tried to hide behind baggy dark clothing, lanky hair, and garish makeup. I still had trouble reconciling that woman with the stylish person in front of us now.

"Do you like it?" She pulled her sunglasses off and smiled when we both said we loved it. "I just had it done this morning. I went for a trim, and saw a picture on the wall of the salon, and, well, ta-da!"

Maybe you should try something like that. It was my pesky inner nag. Every so often she reminded me that I didn't have to go four months between trims and wrestle with my curly mess for three of those months.

Conversation quickly shifted to the murder investigation and missing persons and sheep, and I knew when Giselle narrowed her eyes at me that she was going to suggest something crazy.

"Janet, maybe we could find an excuse to go look around the Winslows' place."

"Oh, no, I don't think that's a good—"

Goldie piped up. "You know, I've been thinking about taking up knitting again." I stared at her. "What? I used to knit … When I was a little girl … A little."

"I knit!" Giselle said. "Let's go to the yarn shop and see what's going on!"

"The last time we did something like this—"

"It was great fun and we solved the case," said Goldie.

"We got in trouble, and no, we didn't!" Then again, I thought, we did learn things that helped move the investigation along. "I'll drive."

An hour later, we pulled into the parking area in front of the Hole in the Wall Yarn Shop. Jay and Bonnie were in the big crates in the back of my van, and Spike was snuggled up on a fleece pad in his tiny carrier on the backseat. It was fifty degrees outside and breezy, so we cracked all the windows for the dogs and locked the van.

No one seemed to be about the place, but Evan's beat-up old Toyota truck was parked where it had been the last time I was there, although now it faced out, as if set for a quick getaway. A flock of starlings flushed from a trumpet vine that festooned the woven wire fence between the two pastures. Like the last time I was there, the hillside was dotted with sheep, but the sky this time was dappled with pewter and lit by a cold sun.

Goldie stood facing the pasture directly behind the shop and barn, the one with the sheep. "How lovely!"

Giselle and I flanked her and I scanned the flock scattered across the green. I didn't see Luciano.

"Maybe we should check in the shop?" Giselle said, turning toward the building. Goldie and I followed a few paces behind but stopped when Giselle said, "They're closed." She pointed at the sign in the window, then crossed the porch, made blinders of her hands, and pressed them against the glass to peer in. "I can't see much. The lights are off. Oh!" She knocked on the door. "I thought I saw someone." We waited. She knocked again, and finally said, "Weird. It must have been a shadow. It looks like a great place. Darn it."

Goldie snorted. "We didn't actually come to shop."

"I know, but still . . ." Giselle turned toward us and shrugged. "Should we look around?"

Adventure Janet shouted *Yeah! Let's look around!* while Sensible Shoes Janet wrung her hands and said *Oh dear oh dear, I don't think we should.* The decision was out of my hands, though, as Goldie and Giselle were already crossing the yard toward the pasture gate.

Goldie gripped the gate latch and said, "Maybe they're out there. Let's—"

"Stop!" I ran toward her and covered her hand with my own. "Luciano might be out there."

"Who?" Goldie asked.

"Sounds like a Mafia hit man!" Giselle elbowed Goldie and they started to laugh.

"You won't think it's funny if he catches you in his pasture." I studied the animals on the hillside again and saw no dogs, but I wasn't about to go into the pasture until I knew for sure where Luciano was. "Let's check the house and the barn before we go traipsing up the hill."

The house wasn't buttoned down as tight as it had been the last time I was at the farm. The curtains were open, and a pot of Johnny jump-ups sat on a blue ladder-back chair by the front door. I didn't recall seeing them the day before, but couldn't be sure. No one answered when I knocked, and as we turned to backtrack, my gaze swept the area. At first nothing seemed out of place, but when the sun peeped out from the cloud cover it caught on something near the porch.

"What's that?" asked Goldie, peering over my shoulder as I picked the object out of the grass.

I looked at Goldie and said, "Shotgun shell."

FORTY-EIGHT

"A SHOTGUN SHELL?" GOLDIE and Giselle asked at the same time.

"Evan said they've been having trouble with coyotes," I said, but knew that shooting right outside the front door seemed odd. The predators would be after the sheep, especially the lambs, and would have no reason to hang around the house. *Canine predators, at least.* I thought of the thugs from Cleveland and my fight-or-flight response kicked in. One little voice screamed "Get out of there! You're all in danger!" while the other insisted on looking for Evan and his dogs. I stared at the empty shell for another few seconds and set it back where I found it.

"Let's check the barn," I said, and we hurried back around the house and across the yard.

The sliding door at the end of the building was half open and we stepped onto a dirt floor strewn with bits of hay. It was too dim inside to see well, but the musty warmth of hay mingled with animal scents filled my nose and warmed my soul. A dove cooed somewhere in the rafters, and something moved in a stall ahead and to my right.

"There must be a light switch around here," said Goldie from somewhere behind me.

A few seconds later a pair of dusty bare bulbs came on above us and I walked farther into the barn. Luciano's stall was at the far end. I was about ten feet from it and convinced he wasn't there when a barrage of *basso profondo* barking knocked me back a step. Something heavy whammed into the wooden barrier between us and Luciano's big head appeared behind the chain link that formed the upper part of the stall. He kept barking, and I didn't want to imagine what he was threatening to do to me.

"No problem, big guy," I said. I backed away slowly until the barking slowed to sporadic, then turned and walked back to Goldie and Giselle. "That answers that question," I said. "Let's go."

"If anyone's around, they must know we're here after that ruckus," said Goldie. "Not very friendly, is he?"

Giselle said, "He's just doing his job. He's guarding his sheep and his farm." She glanced back and added, "But I see why you wanted to be sure of his whereabouts."

Maybe it was the shot of adrenaline Luciano gave me, but I started to laugh. "Whereabouts? Have you been hanging out with a cop or something?"

We had stepped out of the barn by then and I could see that Giselle's cheeks had gone bright pink. Goldie saw it, too, and something seemed to click. She said, "Oh my gosh! You're Hutch's new lady love! He told me he was seeing someone, but he never mentioned your name." She elbowed Giselle. "Quite a gentleman. Doesn't kiss and tell." Goldie studied the other woman's face as we walked and added, "You know, he's really quite smitten with you." Then, as if to take the pressure off Giselle, Goldie pointed toward the far pasture. "Someone's up there."

At first, I saw nothing. Then movement. Something dark, and hard to make out against the silver-green backdrop of Russian olive along the far fence line. "Maybe it's Evan. Let's go."

We reached the gate I had seen the Bouvier open the previous day. It stood open again. There were no sheep in that pasture, though, so it didn't seem unreasonable to leave the gate unlatched, and I didn't think much about it as we trudged up the slope toward whoever was up there. The grass was still sopping from the night's dew, and the clay soil beneath was muddy and slick. We had fought our way almost to the top of the hill when a big charcoal-gray dog appeared from the other side. The Bouvier. And close on his heels was Nell, the Winslows' English Shepherd.

"Oh my," said Goldie, a thread of fear in her voice.

"Just stand still," I said. "I think they'll be okay." I pitched my voice higher and said, "Nell. Come, girl. Nell, come." She did, tail wagging a happy hello. Her big buddy followed her lead, but he seemed to misjudge his braking distance and sideswiped me. "Whoa!" My feet slid backward along the slick grass. I flung my arms out and tried to stay upright, but my toes hit a grassless patch of clay and accelerated faster than the rest of me. My knees hit first, still sliding, although a bit more slowly. I caught the balance of the fall on my hands and collapsed against the wet grass and muck.

"Careful!" said Goldie.

Good idea. I laid my forehead against the ground for a few seconds, gathered myself, and pushed onto my hands and feet. A huge shaggy head knocked into my own, the black nose leather-cool against my cheek. "You big galoot." I pressed a hand against the dog's back for support and got to my feet. The Bouvier leaned his thigh into mine and peeked up at me from under his bangs as if to say he was sorry.

Giselle and Goldie started to laugh. I tried to give them a dirty look, but when I replayed the sight of that big goofy dog slipping down the hill toward me, I laughed as well. I smeared the mud from my palms onto my jeans, patted the dog's neck, and said, "Who's out here with you guys, eh?"

Giselle handed me a crumpled but clean tissue and said, "You might want to wipe your forehead." She cooed to the big dog and reached for the tags dangling from his collar. "What's your name, fella? Ah, Hugo. Good name."

Nell had begun running a few yards ahead, turning back to us, running ahead again. "Come on. She wants us to follow."

"Oh, man, I hope Timmy hasn't fallen in the well again," said Goldie. We all laughed, but I secretly hoped it wasn't something worse.

The downward slope flattened into a small pasture backed by an old-growth stand of hardwoods. Even from a distance I could see that a patch of ground near the corner of the fence had been disturbed, and the closer we got, the colder the air seemed around me.

"What is that?" Giselle whispered.

"Odd place to put in a garden," said Goldie.

We stopped. Nell sat down and whined at one end of the rectangle of brown earth so at odds with the spring grass around it. We were silent for a moment, and then I found my voice.

"It's a grave."

FORTY-NINE

WE WAITED FORTY-FIVE MINUTES on the porch of the yarn shop. Giselle had put Hugo in the empty kennel in the barn for safety but Nell, I knew, was used to having the run of the place. I opened my van doors and she hopped onto the backseat to meet Spike through his carrier door, and then climbed over the crates in back to say hello to Jay and Bonnie. Judging by their waving tails, Nell and Bonnie were delighted to see each other, and as I looked on a tickle of panic started just north of my stomach. *What about Nell?* The rest of the thought was slippery, but felt a lot like another dog soon to be in need of a home.

Deputy Johnson, the same sheriff's deputy who had been sent to investigate the missing sheep over the weekend, was the first to arrive. He stepped out of the car and approached us as another vehicle pulled in behind him and I heard Giselle murmur "uh-oh" behind me. It was Hutchinson.

"You go explain yourself," I said, retreating to the barn to make myself scarce until she was finished.

By the time I got back, Giselle and Goldie were closing the van doors and Hutch was taking to the deputy. He nodded at me and said, "We need one of you to show us what you found." All three of us stepped forward, Goldie in the lead and Giselle somewhere behind me. Hutchinson glanced at the deputy before he spoke again. "Just one, ladies. And no dogs."

"We and the dogs have already been back there," said Goldie, suddenly in Question Authority mode. "I don't see why—"

"Goldie, please," said Hutchinson, holding his palms out in a calming gesture.

Giselle rushed by me. As she passed Goldie, she leaned toward the older woman and I heard her half-whisper, "Stop it. It's Homer." She walked past the two men and, without breaking stride, said, "I'll show you."

Goldie's next two steps were twice as fast, and warning bells went off in my skull. I hurried forward and caught her elbow. "Goldie! What's the matter with you?"

She glanced at me, took another three steps, and then slowed, stopped, and turned toward me. "Hell if I know." She closed her eyes and gave her head a little shake, then stared at me. "Must be the uniforms."

"What are you talking about?"

"I don't like being told what to do by men in uniforms."

I let out a long breath. "Okay, I get that, but we need them. Besides, it's Hutchinson."

"Right." She shrugged and turned back toward the van.

We were sitting on the shop's porch step with Nell between us when Goldie nudged me and gestured down the driveway. A big man in muddy work boots and bib overalls over a long-sleeved shirt was trudging our way. His pant legs sagged at the pockets, which I assumed served as portable toolboxes. Nell trotted out to greet him and he chucked her chin and said something I couldn't make out. When he reached conversation distance he touched the brim of his green-and-yellow John Deere cap and said, "Ladies." He pulled a bandana from his pocket and wiped his red nose. "What's happening here? I seen the police cars." He looked around, then back at us. "Where's Evan or Summer?"

"We, uh, found something out back and called … Have you seen Evan this morning? Or Summer?" I didn't want to explain about the grave, if that was in fact what we'd found.

He shook his head. "Not in a couple of days." He pulled the cap off and wiped his forehead with his shirt sleeve before fitting the cap back over buzz-cut gray hair. He studied my face for a moment and then said, "I live right there," he pointed across the road and down a farm. "If, well, I'm there if anything needs seein' to, you know, the animals."

"Thank you," I said, and told him my name.

"Wayne. Wayne Meyers." He turned watery eyes toward the back pasture, and said, "If you wouldn't mind, I'd like to know if anything's …" He couldn't seem to find a way to end the sentence.

"I think it might be a while," I said, and left it at that.

He turned to walk away, Nell on his heels. Wayne stopped and gestured toward us and said, "You stay here, Nell." The dog hesitated, then rejoined us on the porch. Wayne looked at us and said, "She was born in my kitchen and likes to visit from time to time."

We watched him go, and Goldie said, "That's a relief. I was worried about who would take care of the animals if, well, you know …"

Silence hung over us like a low, dark cloud for another quarter hour until, finally, we heard voices. At the same instant, I spotted a truck topping the small rise in the road and heading our way, a cloud of smoke spilling out behind like a blue tail. Evan's truck. Deputy Johnson and his crew crossed the yard and climbed into their vehicles.

Giselle stopped and leaned against the gatepost, pulled off a shoe, and shook it, but Hutchinson kept walking. He reached Goldie and me just as the truck turned in and bumped up the driveway. It passed the shop, and as the rear window came into view, so did a long-barreled gun stretched across a gun rack at the back of the cab. I assumed it was the shotgun I had seen earlier in the house, but wondered if Evan had it for self-defense.

"Is that the guy? The owner?" Hutchinson's tone was as calm as I was jumpy.

"That's him. But what did you f—"

"I'll be back." He strode toward the car from which Deputy Johnson was re-emerging and watched Evan pull in. The truck's usual spot was blocked, so Evan pulled onto the grass and jumped from the cab and said, "What's going on?"

I started to walk toward Evan and Hutch, but thought better of it and redirected myself toward Giselle. She was bent over, tying her shoe.

"Did he tell you?" Her voice was pitched higher than normal and seemed to need more air behind it.

"No! Tell us! Is it a body?"

She stood up and looked at me.

"Yes, it's …"

Oh God! Summer? I was suddenly so dizzy I almost missed her next words.

"… a sheep."

"A sheep?" Goldie and I asked in unison.

"She must have been special," said Giselle. "She was wrapped in a blanket, and there were roses scattered over her. She had a bandana around her neck."

"Aww, Rosie," I said, feeling a pang of loss for a friend I'd barely known.

"Who?"

"They had an old ewe named Rosie," I said. "She was a pet, slept on their screened porch. I just saw her yesterday." *Was that only yesterday?* So much had happened, it seemed like weeks since I had been here talking to Evan. Rosie, I remembered, had been lying on the porch with a flower-print bandana around her neck, a nice pile of hay nearby.

Hutchinson started back toward us. One of the uniformed officers stayed with Evan while another looked through the open window of Evan's truck.

"You can go now." Hutch looked at Giselle. "I'll be a while. I need to talk to Mr. Winslow."

"About a dead sheep?" Goldie asked.

"About where his wife might be," Hutch said, and then, "as if it's any of your businesses." Giselle smiled, but seemed to think better of policing his grammar at the moment.

We rode in the silence of our own thoughts until we got home, unloaded the dogs, and went our separate ways.

FIFTY

I took Jay out for a tennis-ball game. We'd been in the backyard for about five minutes when Jay ran to the fence and stood up against it. He barked once, a greeting, and our jolly new neighbor, Phil Martin, yelled, "Shut up!"

"Jay, come," I said, forcing my voice to be calm as I walked toward the fence. My dog met me, fell into heel position, and sat at my side when I stopped. "Hello."

"I hate barking dogs," said Martin, forgoing all semblance of neighborliness.

"I wouldn't call him a 'barking dog,'" I said. "He was just saying hello." As if someone had planned the timing, the Washingtons' spaniels, Flo, Mary, and Ross, exploded out their back door and ran in full cry to the fence on the other side of Phil Martin's yard. "Now *those* are barking dogs" I said, and laughed. "But they're never out for long, and I think if they get to know you, they'll settle down."

A cross between a harumph and an obscenity came out of Martin's mouth before he turned his back and started to walk away. Maybe it was the stress of the morning, of wondering whether another person I knew had died a violent death, of learning that a sweet and gentle animal was gone and that her absence left a hole in someone's heart. Maybe it was just the belligerent rudeness of the man. Whatever it was, it set me off.

"You know, Mr. Martin, we're going to be neighbors for the foreseeable future." He stopped, but kept his back to me. "I've been nothing but friendly to you, and my animals are healthy and well-trained, and they are definitely not a neighborhood nuisance." He turned slowly, and I waited until we made eye contact. "So whatever it is you sat on, I suggest you have it removed."

I waited for him to respond, and when he didn't, I said, "Have a lovely afternoon," and walked to my back door with Jay at my side. I stopped at the kitchen table and ripped up a couple of pieces of junk mail, muttering a few choice comments about Councilman Phil Martin. From there I went straight to the couch and stretched out. Jay hopped onto the other end, wrapped a paw over my calf, and laid his chin next to it.

I closed my eyes and tried again to sort through the tangled threads of information I'd taken in over the past few days. What little I had known about Summer and Evan seemed to be all wrong, an elaborate fiction they had spun for local consumption. The more I thought about it, the more I realized that the bulk of the falsehoods were Summer's creations—the forged Purdue diploma, her nonexistent marriage, her adopted name—but Evan had gone along with them. Ray was even more of an enigma, but since I hadn't known him other than to say hello and pet his dog, the mystery of his past didn't feel like such a betrayal.

Something landed on my belly. "Leo *mio*," I said, stroking Leo's soft tawniness as he settled his torso against mine. A second presence hopped onto the arm of the couch next to my shoulder and purred into my ear. "Miss Pixel." She maneuvered herself between

Leo and the back of the couch, quiet for once. I closed my eyes again, calmed by the touch of animals I loved.

But my mind kept working, and the more I thought about it, the more I was sure that Evan didn't know the whole story, either. In fact, I was pretty sure he'd been played. But why? If Summer wanted to leave Reno, why not just leave? Why hook up with a stranger in a diner? And what about Ray? Evan had said it was a coincidence that Ray and Summer were both from Nevada, but that just didn't ring true. Besides, Nevada wasn't the only thing they had in common. They both knew sheep, and herding dogs. Weirder yet, neither one seemed to have any traceable history.

The phone rang in the kitchen. Only a handful of people ever use that number anymore—my mom, my brother, Giselle, Goldie, and an occasional telemarketer. I pulled my cell phone from my pocket and found it was dead. I'd forgotten to charge it. I slid Pixel between me and the back of the couch, extricated my legs from under Jay, swung myself into a sitting position, set Leo onto the couch beside Jay, and got up. Giselle had hung up by the time I reached the kitchen. I called her back.

"Oh, Janet, I just called you."

"I know. I was trapped under a pile of animals."

"I found something." She sounded a bit breathless. "About Ray. At least I think it's him." Giselle didn't want to tell me the rest on the phone and asked if she could come over on her way to class.

"I'll do you one better," I said. "I need dog food, so why don't we meet at the Firefly?" It was one of my favorite coffeehouses, and was close to the university and my dog-food source. We agreed to meet in an hour, which gave me just enough time to change out of my Hugo-besmeared duds and drop seventy-four bucks on the kind people at Blackford's Farm and Garden for a forty-pound bag of grain-free premium dog food. I had to rearrange a few things, including a new

194

planter and two medium bags of potting soil that had been waiting for a couple of days, before the bag would fit behind my dog crates.

Somewhere I had read that switching a ring from the customary hand to the other can be a useful reminder, an updated version of tying a string around a finger, so as I walked into Firefly, I switch my silver-and-turquoise band from right to left to remind me to get the dog food, planter, and dirt out of the van when I got home. I settled in at a quiet table toward the back of the café. I had just turned my laptop on when a loud male voice from behind me exploded over the usual coffeehouse background murmur. It was followed by another, and the echo around it said the second guy was on speaker phone. I tried to ignore the conversation, but after about three minutes I knew it was impossible. A quick look around the room showed other people scowling and shooting eye-darts at the guy with the phone.

"Excuse me." I had stood and turned toward the guy. He wore a wrinkled blue suit and his maroon tie had a dark stain four inches beneath the knot.

The guy said, "Hang on a sec," and frowned at me.

I smiled and said, "That's really distracting. Would you mind turning the speaker off and lowering your voice a little?"

"Look, lady, I'm making a multi-million-dollar deal here, so get a grip."

A young woman at another table looked at me wide-eyed, and I decided it was time to set an example for the next generation. Besides, to quote Woodrow Call in Larry McMurtry's *Lonesome Dove*, "I can't abide rude behavior in a man." I stepped up as close as possible to where the guy's phone lay on the table, leaned toward it, and said, "Sir, does whoever is on the other end of that call know that you're broadcasting it in a crowded coffeehouse?"

The guy grabbed the phone and covered the microphone. "Look, lady, just stick it."

And that was the funniest thing I'd heard in quite a while. I laughed. I looked around, still laughing, and said, "Folks, does this guy's conversation bother you?" Several affirmatives, many nods. "Me too. So I asked him to please turn it down and he told me to stick it." I looked back at the guy, whose face had gone fire-engine red. Around me I heard, "Take it outside, guy," and "Freakin' annoying," and a few things more forceful than "stick it."

The guy grabbed his stuff and passed Giselle in the doorway as she came through. She stopped and placed an order, and ten seconds later she sat down. She was practically vibrating.

"You sure you need coffee?"

"I ordered tea. Herbal." She plunked her purse onto a third chair. It tipped and emptied half its contents, and I marveled at how organized everything still was. If that had been my bag, coins and pens and a ratty tennis ball would have been scattered among miscellaneous bits of paper, my unsnapped billfold, and desiccated-liver dog treats. Giselle's stuff was all neatly arranged in see-through zippered bags and they dropped more or less together next to the chair's leg. She put them back in the purse, zipped it shut, and said, "Man, I'm so disorganized these days."

"Please, Giselle. You'll give us organizationally challenged a bad name." I turned my laptop so she would have a better view just as the barista called our names. By the time I sat back down, Giselle had re-entered the search terms that pulled up the information she wanted to share—Ray + Reno + sheep + police. "There," she said, pointing at the third entry, a link to a social media post that began "Have you seen this couple?" Giselle clicked the link and we landed on the original post.

Have you seen this couple around Reno? Theyre con artists. I need 2 find them SOON & get my money back. IM me if you have info.

A grainy picture of a man and a woman appeared above the post. The resolution was so low that it was impossible to make out details, but the man looked vaguely like Ray Turnbull. The woman wore a scarf and sunglasses, and had the collar of her coat pulled up past her jaw line. A band of dark hair peeked out between her forehead and scarf.

"Can you fix that picture somehow?" Giselle asked.

"I doubt it. It was probably taken with a cell phone on low res." Giselle's sigh echoed my own disappointment. "What about the comments? Anything interesting there?"

"Maybe." She scrolled past the first few comments and pointed to one. "He mentions their names."

Who knows theyre real names. He went by Ramon Torres. Claimed to have a ranch near Ely. Complete BULL! He said her name was Bella Verano.

Giselle tapped a nail against the screen. "Ramon Torres. Ray Turnbull. *Torres* means 'towers' in Spanish, but it *sounds* like *toro*. Bull. And Ramon is Raymond."

A little tingle started in my brain.

"And *bella verano* is 'beautiful summer,' assuming the guy misspelled *bella*."

These two had to be the people we knew as Ray Turnbull and Summer Winslow. "I think you found them," I said, touching Giselle's arm. "We—you—need to tell Hutchinson. If he goes back to the police in Reno with these names, who knows?"

"Right!" Giselle was bouncing in her chair and her face was flushed.

Finding the clue *was* exciting, but if Ray and Summer were running con games together in Reno and came here separately on the run, something had obviously gone wrong. And now Ray was dead, and Summer was missing, either running again, or ... The pieces of the puzzle were swirling around my brain like leaves in an April wind, but one thing seemed clear. They had conned the wrong person.

FIFTY-ONE

Tom called as I was waiting for a carry-out coffee and sandwich for Joe, a homeless man who hung around the area. I had noticed him when I parked my van. Tom offered to bring supper. "Something light," he said. "I hate to run on a full stomach." I didn't tell him I'd completely forgotten about agility practice. Lapses like that scared the bejeepers out of me, and made me wonder if I had inherited by mother's problems. I'd been going to agility classes and practice on Thursday evenings for almost two years. I shook it off and decided I wasn't demented quite yet. My sense of time was simply bent. The past five days felt like months, and my day-sense was distorted.

"See you tonight?" I asked Giselle as she started her car.

"Yes, I get out of class at five, so I'll have just enough time to run home, change clothes, and grab Pre…, er, Spike." She glanced at her watch. "Eeek! If I don't leave now I'll have to speed, and I don't want any trouble with the police." She winked at me and started to back out of her space, but stopped and said, "Janet, could you call Homer and tell him about what we found? I won't have time to call before class." *And you don't want to tell him you've been snooping around.*

Joe was sitting on a boulder concrete retaining wall next to the parking lot, and I waved and walked over and said hello. "Say, I bought this to take home for supper, but my friend just said he's cooking. These sandwiches aren't very good reheated. Would you like it?" He smiled and took the sack and coffee from me.

When I parked in my driveway, something moved in my office window and Leo's lovely face peered out at me. I had planned to call Hutchinson and then slump on the couch and ponder the many mysteries of Summer Winslow and Ray Turnbull, but Leo gave me a better idea.

The call to Hutch took about ten minutes, and by the end of the conversation I wasn't sure whether he was glad to have the lead on Ray and Summer, or miffed that I was corrupting his girlfriend by encouraging her to, as he put it, "poke your nose in police business." Apparently we hadn't ditched all the baggage of our early relationship.

When that was finished, I went outside and set up some agility equipment. Three jumps, a tunnel, four weave poles, and the obstacle I've come to call the "dog-and-catwalk" since I started doing feline agility. To be accurate, Leo and I have competed in exactly one trial, but the little guy loves training with me and has no problem with the canine course.

Within minutes, we had an audience. Goldie was cheering us on from her yard, while Phil Martin glared at us from his. This time, he wasn't alone. A woman who looked to be in her mid-twenties and borderline anorexic stood beside him, and judging by the matching frowns on their faces, I guessed she was his daughter. I waved at them but kept going with my cat. He soared over two jumps, raced through the tunnel, ran up one end and across the dog walk and trotted down the other slope. He hopped onto the pause table, where he sat and waited. I wanted to pick him up and smooch him, but restrained myself. I counted down ten seconds, then off we went again. He carefully wove himself through the poles and flew over the final jump. I said, "Good boy!" and opened my arms, and he leaped into them and bumped my chin with his head.

Goldie was clapping and cheering, and I grinned at her. I turned to see what the reaction was in the Martin yard and found both watchers still frowning. I walked to the fence, smiled, and said, "Lovely afternoon, isn't it?"

"It was." The woman with Councilman Martin was a little older than I had thought at first, maybe early thirties, and she looked familiar. I have an eye for faces since I photograph so many of them. I'd seen this one before. "It's shameful to force an animal to perform just to feed your ego." She tilted her head toward the man beside her. "See, Daddy. You need to pass a law."

I had it. She had been with the protesters at the Dogs of Spring event over the weekend. I met her scowl and held it until she shifted her target from me to Leo. Phil Martin wouldn't meet my eyes. In fact, he was looking at the ground and his face had reddened.

"You want to make it illegal for people to play with their pets?"

"You're forcing that creature to perform for your pleasure."

I couldn't help myself. I laughed, even knowing that people with such extreme views can be terrifying. "Lady, first of all, this 'creature' is a cat, and his name is Leo. Second, is your head too far ..." I started to make an anatomical reference, but forced myself to change direction. "... into extremist propaganda to miss how much fun he was having out there?"

Something nudged me gently from the right and I realized Goldie had joined me. "Hello, Chelsea," she said.

"You know each other?"

"Chelsea is in my yoga group." Apparently Goldie made the same assumption I had, because she said, "I didn't realize that you and the Councilman were related."

Chelsea hooked her arm through Martin's and her voice changed to little-girl vamp. "We're friends."

But you called him "Daddy." Demon Janet jabbed me and whispered, "Oh, too weird."

"Ah," said Goldie. "You should know that Janet is devoted to her animal companions. As am I." There was a challenge in the last three words, and Chelsea took a half step back.

"Speaking of animals," I said, turning to Goldie. "Jay needs a nail trim before class." I turned back to the couple across the fence. "You should pop into Dog Dayz training facility sometime and watch the human-animal bond in action. You might learn something."

Goldie followed me into my kitchen. "I guess we know why he moved out of the mansion on Old Mill."

"And where the pet limit bill came from."

"'Oh, Daddy, make this law for me,'" I said, imitating Chelsea as well as I could. We were still wiping the laugh-tears away when Tom arrived with the pizza.

FIFTY-TWO

"THIS IS A LIGHT bite to eat?" I asked, lifting a piece of pizza onto my plate.

"Depends how much you eat," Tom said. He punctuated by stuffing half a slice into his mouth, rolling his eyes, and moaning.

Goldie had declined our invitation to join us, so Tom and I had a few minutes alone. Goldie and I had already told Tom about my encounter with Councilman Martin and his friend Chelsea, so I moved on to Giselle's discoveries and conviction that the people in the article were in fact Summer Winslow and Ray Turnbull. "If they really were—or are—con artists, I wonder if they staged the theft of the sheep to defraud the insurance company."

"But it seems like Evan was the one most in need of money," Tom said. "He's the one in debt to the loan shark, right?"

"Maybe they were all in it together." I thought about that for a moment and backtracked. "No, I don't think so. The arguments I overheard didn't sound very cooperative. And unless Evan is a better actor than I think he is, he doesn't know that Summer and Ray knew each other in Nevada."

We had to get moving to make the seven o'clock practice session, so we tabled our speculation for later. Tom ran home for Drake and Winnie, but it was more or less on the way to Dog Dayz. I changed into my running shoes, put Jay's leash on him, and started for the door, but backtracked to the dryer for his crate pad, which I had washed. He sniffed it and I thought I detected a little *ewww* nose wrinkle. I imagined him thinking the dryer sheets made it smell funny, and just when he'd gotten his own scent plus a bit of grass and mud nicely worked into the fabric.

I opened the side door of the van and told Jay to sit and stay while I leaned in to squish the crate pad into place. Whoever designated these pads to "fit" crates must never have tried to install one. It was at least half an inch too long and too wide, and I had to crawl halfway into the crate to flatten the thing to the floor. As I backed out, a reflection in the rearview mirror caught my eye, but disappeared even as I looked. When I had both feet on the ground, I told Jay to hop in. I had just started around the front of the van when I sensed movement again on the street. I turned my head and my breath caught.

A gray sedan was creeping past my house, the passenger side to me. I couldn't see the occupants through the tinted windows, but the Cleveland thugs had been driving a gray sedan. Was this the car? I can tell a Shih Tzu from a Lhasa Apso and a Birman from a Ragdoll, but one gray sedan looks like another as far as I'm concerned, and I'd been wrong before. Still, seeing the car sent a chill through my bones. I jumped in behind the wheel and grabbed my tote bag from the floor, thinking I'd call Hutchinson. I rummaged for my phone and listened to the blood pounding in my ears. The gray car was visible in my rearview mirror and seemed to be barely moving now.

For an instant I thought I might open the garage door and pull in, but that wouldn't work. The garage was half-filled with boxes Tom had moved from his place. I could still run in, but no way would I leave Jay unprotected in the van.

The only sounds I could hear were Jay's soft panting and the pounding of my heart. I don't think I was even breathing. I turned in my seat to watch the sedan and felt a lump between my thigh and the seatbelt. My phone. I squirmed around and reached into my pocket, still watching the creeping car, and froze as the passenger-side window opened a couple of inches. Every gangster movie I'd ever seen came rushing back. Would they shove a shotgun or an Uzi through that window?

I didn't have time to call Hutchinson. I pressed 9-1-1, held my breath.

FIFTY-THREE

Two things happened simultaneously. A voice asked through my phone, "What is your emergency," and the gray sedan made an excruciatingly slow right turn into Goldie's driveway. *They're lining up for a clear shot!* screeched my inner fraidy cat. "Hello? What is your emergency?"

I almost had my tongue moving when the front doors of the sedan opened and two women got out. The one nearest me, the passenger, wore emerald green slacks and a marigold sweatshirt. She opened the back door and pulled out a huge flower-print tote bag, walked around the front of the car, and, with her friend, disappeared in the direction of Goldie's front door.

"Is anyone there? I'm dispatching police—"

"No! Sorry! I'm sorry, I dialed by accident. Very sorry."

"Police are on their way, ma'am. I can't cancel until they confirm that there is no emergency."

I disconnected the call, gripped the wheel, and leaned my forehead against my hands. Jay sat up and turned around in his crate, and I looked back at him. "I'm losing it, Bubby." He cocked his head and closed his mouth, catching his upper lip on a canine tooth. The combined effect looked as silly as I felt when the police cruiser pulled up four minutes later. "Accidental speed dial," I said, and the officer assured me it happened all the time.

When I arrived at Dog Dayz, Jorge was walking across the parking area, a pooper scooper in his hand and two calico cats on his heels. He waved and signaled me to park on the short gravel driveway that snugged up to a sliding door in the side of the building. I rolled my window down and he said, "You park here, Mees Janet. Best spot."

"Are you sure, Jorge? Marietta parks there."

"No, ees good. Her truck ees in shop."

Tom was already there, taking advantage of the few minutes before the seven o'clock sessions began to let Winnie see the agility tunnel, which was collapsed to about six feet. Sylvia Eckhorn was holding the squirming puppy at one end of the tunnel and Tom crouched at the other end, calling "Winnie! Winnie!" Winnie let out a sharp *yip!* Sylvia let go, and Winnie shot through the tunnel into Tom's arms. He scooped her up, and she licked his face and squirmed to be put down again.

"I think she wants another turn," I said from the sidelines.

Tom turned the puppy so she faced the tunnel again, and this time Sylvia called her. She raced back through, ears flapping like Dumbo's, and Sylvia caught her and gave her a treat.

"One more," said Tom. When he caught her that time, he gave her three little treats and a full-body rub-and-scratch, snapped her leash to her collar, and stood up. "That's it, little girl."

Sylvia stepped over the ring barrier and gave me a hug, then scratched Jay behind the ear. "I hear you had quite the weekend and more," she said.

"Where did you … Giselle?"

She nodded. "I met that guy, what was his name? Ray? Met him once at the hospital." Sylvia was an emergency room nurse, and had been an angel when my mother needed care a year earlier. "Came in for stitches. Said he walked into a rake in the barn, but it looked like someone hit him …" She stopped, and grabbed my arm. "Wow, look at my big mouth. Don't repeat any of that, Janet. I could lose my job."

"I'm sorry, did you say something?" I removed Jay's collar and slipped a kennel lead over his head. I always run him "naked" in agility, meaning without a collar, and the slip-lead works as a leash outside the ring.

"Say, Sylvia," I said, remembering something. "Your husband is in insurance, isn't he?" It was embarrassing, but I never could remember the man's name. I was sure it started with "J." John? Jason? Jim?

"Ron?" *Right, Ron.* "He works for his dad's agency. Eckhorn Home, Farm, and Business. Why? Are you shopping?"

"No, nothing like that. I'm just curious about the missing sheep."

"They were stolen, right?"

"They were *reported* stolen," I said, picking my words. "But what if …" I couldn't find my way to the end of that thought, at least not out loud.

Sylvia got it. "You think the owners might have staged a theft to collect insurance?"

I nodded. "They're worth about four hundred a head, so the missing flock could go for almost five grand."

"Wow. I had no idea lamb was so pricey."

I thought of sweet Rosie and cringed. "No, not for meat. For their wool."

"Ah."

"But I don't know whether a flock could, or would, be insured."

207

"I can ask," Sylvia said. "I do know that animals in other kinds of performance events can be insured. I think it's pricey, but if they knew they were going to be 'stolen,' it might be worth it."

"Don't spread that theory around, okay?"

"I'm sorry, did you say something?" She winked at me and promised to ask her husband and get back to me.

Agility practice went great. Fewer people were there than usual, and we each got three practice runs. On his first two, Jay was fast, accurate, and responsive to my signals, and I was reasonably coordinated other than one stumble over my own feet. Tom and Drake had two and a half good runs, and then Drake hit the bar on a jump and came down limping, so they quit. Tom brought Drake to where I was watching. He sat on the floor and ran his strong fingers up and down the dog's leg, feeling for heat or tenderness, massaging as he went. When he let Drake up, the limp was gone.

"I'm going to do the contacts, and then quit," he said. When his turn came, he dropped all the jump bars to the ground, and ran the course contacts—obstacles the dog walks on or through. Drake seemed fine. When they finished, Tom took Drake out to relieve himself and put him in his van. Jay and I went into the ring for our third and final run. I set Jay up at the start line and turned to walk toward the first obstacle when I saw the front door open and my heart jumped into my mouth. This time I wasn't imagining things. It was the two thugs from Cleveland. *Are they stalking me?* The fat one just stared at me. The skinny one—Mick Fallon, if I remembered correctly—gave me a mock salute.

"Janet, do you plan to run?" It was Marietta.

"No, I don't," I said, gathering the leash in my hand and walking out of the ring with my dog. No one but Jay heard my next words. "I can't say they don't scare me, but I don't plan to run."

FIFTY-FOUR

WHEN MARIETTA ASKED IF I was planning to run, she meant the agility practice. I had planned to do it once more, but the appearance of the goons in their rumpled suits changed my plans. When they walked into Dog Dayz, fear was my first response. Fury was next. Fury born of fear is a powerful emotion, and I knew even as I stomped toward them that reasonable caution was being smothered by my urge to shove the guys back out the door and out of my life.

"Are you stalking me?" I stood about six feet in front of them, staring first at one, then the other, my heart thumping. Several men were sitting in chairs nearby, spouses of Dog Dayz members, and they turned their heads our way. Jay placed himself between me and the goons, and a quick glance showed me his hackles were up, giving him a lion-mane look.

"We got a puppy," said Fallon, a slap-me smirk on his thin lips. "We wanna see about training it." He looked at Jay. "Nice dog you got there. Looks real healthy." He turned colorless eyes back to me. "Hope you keep him that way."

I can't say Jay understood the words, but he took some meaning from the man's tone and his muzzle wrinkled into a lupine snarl. I laid a hand on his neck and he stopped the threat but stayed alert.

The men both smiled at the canine warning as if to show their bravado, but they edged back a few inches. "Say, your friend Summer here?" It was the fat one. "Know where we can find her? Got something for her."

His buddy, Fallon, looked into my eyes and lowered his voice. His next words were just for me. "We want those pictures you took, too. We want to know you'll keep them private. Sort of a health issue, know what I mean?"

A cold tickle started down my spine. I thought maybe I wanted to run after all, but Tom's voice close on my right held me in place.

"What's going on here?"

Two of the men who had been watching their wives and dogs in the practice ring stood and turned toward the strangers, and another shifted in his seat to face them. Fallon raised his palms and let out a whiny laugh. "Nothin', man. Just talkin' here."

"I don't know where Summer is, and I was photographing dogs." I glared at them. "I'm not remotely interested in taking your picture, so leave me alone."

A fifth man stepped up on my left. Hutchinson. He stared at the two goons for a moment, then showed them his badge and said, "Mr. Fallon, is there a problem here?" Fallon's face reddened, making the scar through his cheek more obvious. His buddy shot him a sidelong glance. They were surprised that Hutch knew Fallon's name. Hutchinson stepped toward the door, forcing Fallon to move out of his way. "Gentlemen, let's have a word outside."

"We just came to see the dogs, officer, but we don't want no trouble." It was the heavy one.

Hutchinson opened the door and said again that he'd like a word with the pair outside. Fallon looked back at me and said, "See ya 'round."

I sat down and pretended to tie my shoe to camouflage the transformation of my knees to jelly. Jay shoved his head against mine, and I wrapped an arm around him and buried my face in his fur for a moment. The men I didn't know were talking, but I couldn't make sense of their words. Tom sat down beside me and I felt his hand on my back.

I looked at him and said, "How dare they?" I kept the rest of my thoughts to myself, but they were spinning like the vanes of a pinwheel. How did they know where to find me, if it was me they were looking for? A shudder rolled through my body. If they knew about Dog Dayz, they knew where I lived. My paranoia wasn't entirely unfounded.

Tom glanced out the front window, then looked into my eyes. "Hopefully Hutchinson will discourage them."

We gathered our belongings and got up. I thanked the other men for their show of support, and turned toward the back of the building and the parking lot.

"I'll walk you out and we'll caravan home, okay?"

"I'm not scared."

"I know."

"Okay."

"Wait here while I put Winnie in the car. I'll be back for her crate and then we'll go."

Hutchinson came back in and said, "We had a little talk, and I'm checking for outstanding warrants."

"So you got Fallon's friend's name?" I thought it might be time to stop thinking of him as a cartoon character. He wasn't that funny.

"Zola. Albert Zola. I don't think you'll have any more trouble from them. But call me if you need to. Any time."

Tom insisted we take a roundabout route home in case the guys tried to follow us. He led, I followed, singing along as Bruce Springsteen belted out "Dancing in the Dark." It was better than thinking. Tom signaled us into a Kroger parking lot about a half mile from my house and we pulled up window to window.

"Seems like a butter pecan sort of night."

"Cookies and cream."

Ten minutes later we pulled into my driveway and I raised the garage door. The porch light illuminated something stuck to my front door, but first things first. I took Jay and Drake into the house while Tom put Winnie on her leash, picked up his grocery bag, and walked around to the backyard for a pit stop. I let the boys out, then went to the living room. I looked out the window but nothing seemed to be moving other than the "Welcome" flag waving from Mr. Hostetler's front porch across the street. I scanned the street again for strange gray cars as I stepped out to grab the envelope that was taped to the door. My name was scribbled in the center, and the Fort Wayne Police Department's address was printed in the upper left corner.

I tossed it on the kitchen table. I figured it must be from Hutch, although why or when he had left me a note I couldn't imagine. He hadn't mentioned it at Dog Dayz. Before I opened it, I wanted to change into sweatpants and put moisturizer on my face. I felt dehydrated. The bathroom door didn't latch properly and the dogs burst in and jostled me into the sink, making me squeeze a quarter cup of moisturizer into my hand. I rubbed it into my arms and said, "Okay, you guys! Let's go!"

The boys ran back toward the kitchen, but Winnie was busy pulling the end of the toilet paper through the bathroom. I scooped her up before she got out the door, took the paper from her, and made sure the door latched behind us. I pressed my face into Winnie's warm blonde neck wrinkles and said, "You're a little devil, you know it?" She wriggled and licked me in agreement.

"What's that?" asked Tom, pointing the ice cream scoop at the envelope.

"Must be from Hutchinson," I said. I set Winnie down, put the baby gate up to keep her in the kitchen, and tore the envelope open. "What the..." I read it twice before I shoved it at Tom.

It was a citation for allowing my dogs to run loose. According to the paper, the author of the citation had seen my dogs "at large" in the neighborhood at seven forty-two that evening, and "efforts to capture them were unsuccessful." I was being fined seven hundred fifty dollars. That was two-fifty "per dog." It was signed by an Officer Dave Jeffers.

"This won't be hard to dispute," said Tom.

"Oh, I'll dispute it all right." I took the paper from him and stuck it to the fridge with a magnet. I picked up the envelope and, after I ripped it to bits and threw it away, I said, "I need an extra scoop of that ice cream."

FIFTY-FIVE

FRIDAY MORNING DAWNED GRAY, cold, and wet. Tom was up early to take Winnie out, but I burrowed under the covers and declined to get up. Wet weather means wet dogs, so Jay, Drake, and Winnie were confined to the kitchen, and even the cats left me alone for another ninety minutes of welcome sleep.

Then my phone rang. By the time I found it in my jeans pocket in the hamper, the message indicator was flashing. I listened to my brother-in-law's voice. "Janet, it's Norm. Sorry to wake you. I wanted to catch you before you take off on safari." It was Norm's term for my photo shoots, whether non-human animals were involved or not. "There's a bit of a situation with the cake, so call me this morning if you can. Love you!"

What kind of situation could there be with a wedding cake? I staggered to the kitchen in search of coffee and found Tom reading the morning paper with three dogs and two cats watching him. Dawn's gloom had given way to a dappled sky and promising sunshine, although the trees seemed to shiver in the wind. Jay, Drake, and Winnie made it all but impossible to step over the baby gate, and once I did, I had to go into "ignore the puppy" mode until she stopped trying to climb my leg. When she finally had all four paws on the ground, I gave her a good shoulder-to-butt scratch. I kissed Tom, then the doggy boys, and wrapped up the morning greetings with kitty nose bumps. Finally I poured my coffee and sat down. The first hot mouthful hit my stomach and I felt alive again.

"What's on your agenda this morning?"

"Cake, apparently."

Tom raised an eyebrow at me. "You're baking a cake?"

"Heavens no." I hit Norm's number on my phone and spoke as I waited. "Norm called. He says there's a 'situation' with the wedding cake."

Norm explained that he had taken Mom with him to look at cake designs and she had ended up insulting the baker. "I'm going to talk to a new cake lady at ten-thirty and wondered if you'd like to go with me."

"Is Mom going to be there?"

"Not this time."

I agreed to meet him there, and went to my desk to write down the address. The bakery was only a couple of blocks from the police station, so I planned to have a word with Officer Dave Jeffers or his supervisor first about the sham citation he'd left me the night before.

"Breakfast?" asked Tom.

I remembered the state of my larder the previous morning and said, "I haven't been shopping yet."

"Not to worry," said Tom, pulling a dozen eggs, butter, milk, and raisin bread from the fridge. "Raisin bread French toast, coming right up. How many slices do you want?"

Why don't you give up and marry the man? asked my conventionally practical voice of reason. *Why buy the cook when you can have the French toast for free?* my fiercely independent voice countered.

Fiercely scared, you mean. In reality, I was still caught somewhere in the middle, and having Tom move in with me seemed a big enough step for the moment. Maybe too big. As angry as I was about the arbitrary pet limit bill, a tiny bit of me saw it as a way out of the commitment I'd made. Not that I didn't want a committed relationship with Tom. I just wanted it without giving up my independence.

"A raisin for your thoughts," said Tom, popping a raisin between my lips.

I looked around the kitchen. "How come it's so quiet in here all of a sudden?"

Tom chuckled and turned to the stove. "Winnie wore her little self out. She's asleep in her pen and the boys are out on the patio catching some rays. Last time I saw the cats, they were sacked out on the couch…" He set a plate of French toast in front of me and sat down. "See. The beginning of domestic bliss."

An hour later I walked up to the desk sergeant at the police department and asked to talk to Officer Jeffers. The Sergeant asked my business, and I gave him an abbreviated version, ending with, "Officer Jeffers has made a mistake."

He turned to his keyboard, mumbling "That's what they all say" as he typed. I bit my tongue.

"Jeffers wasn't on duty last night," the sergeant said.

"Well, he signed this and left it on my door at seven forty-two last evening." I handed the citation across the desk.

The sergeant picked up his phone, punched in three numbers, and said, "Jeffers there?" Pause. "Can you come out here and speak to a lady about a citation?" He hung up and said, "He'll be right out."

Jeffers was not "right out." Maybe he hoped I'd go away, but I was still there when he showed up twenty minutes later. He looked about fourteen, and I wondered briefly if he was some sort of police scout, but he had the spit-polished shoes and a badge that looked legit. "What can I do for you, ma'am?"

"Did you leave this on my door last night?" I held the citation toward him.

He glanced at it but didn't touch it, and said, "Yes, ma'am."

"Then we have a problem. A couple of problems, actually."

Jeffers crossed his arms over his chest. "How so?"

"Well, first of all, I have one dog, not three." No need to complicate the matter by mentioning my frequent visitors. "And he wasn't running loose, not last night or any other time. Who told you he was?"

Officer Jeffers shifted his weight and there was the beginning of a catch in his voice when he answered. "I saw them, three dogs. They were running around."

"Yeah? What did they look like?"

He uncrossed his arms and shifted again. "Well, one was gray, one was ...," he hesitated, as if trying to remember. "Right, and one was black, and one was, I don't know, sort of hard to describe. It was getting dark."

The colors were close enough, but someone had obviously fed Jeffers the information. *Councilman Phil Martin.*

"Who told you to write this? Because it's crap."

"Ma'am, it's illegal to let your dogs run loose ..."

"Janet? What's going on?" The voice came from my left, and the next thing I knew, Hutchinson was beside me. I handed him the citation and he read it.

"You write this?" His tone was not friendly.

"Yes, sir. The dogs were—"

"No, they weren't. They were at a dog training class. I know that because I know Ms. MacPhail and her dog, and I know her friend Tom's dogs, and I saw them at the dog-training facility right at the time you say you saw them. So, Officer Jeffers, is it? We have a big problem here."

Jeffers squared shoulders seemed to deflate. "Sir, I …" He didn't finish.

Hutchinson asked to keep the citation and told Jeffers to meet him at his desk in ten minutes. Then he turned to me. "You have a minute?" Jeffers was still there, fidgeting. Without looking at him Hutch said, "Ten minutes, Jeffers," and then guided me to a bench along the wall. "You have a neighbor out to get you?"

"Councilman Phil Martin moved in next door."

Hutch's eyes widened slightly, and a funny little smile took over his lips. In addition to pushing the pet limits, Martin had been backing a bill to reduce overtime pay and benefits for the police. I didn't ask, but I had a feeling Hutchinson planned to hand this over to someone who could use it against the councilman, who must have strong-armed Jeffers into pinching me.

"I'll take care of it," he said. "And I have some other information you'll find interesting."

FIFTY-SIX

"I can't tell you much," said Hutchinson, signaling me to sit on a wooden bench along the wall of the police foyer, "but I can tell you that Ray Turnbull, formerly known as Rex Turnell, among other things, and his wife are wanted for a string of cons involving tourists in Nevada and Idaho."

"His wife?" It had never occurred to me that Ray was married. "What was her name?"

"Like him, she had a bunch of aliases. Hang on." Hutchinson searched for something on his phone. "Okay, my contact in Reno sent me a list of known aliases, but her real name was Udane Zabala." He pronounced the first name ooh-dane, and I couldn't imagine how to spell it.

"What kind of name is that?"

"I wondered that, too," said Hutchinson. "The guy said it's Basque. Lots of Basques in Nevada."

Of course, I thought, remembering some of what I'd read about the history of Jay's ancestors. Australian Shepherds are descended in large part from sheep-herding dogs brought into the western states by Basque shepherds who arrived by way of Australia with Merino sheep and their "little blue Australian sheepdogs." How ironic.

Hutchinson's voice brought me back to the moment. "Ray or Rex, whatever, got into some trouble when he was younger, and was arrested about fifteen years ago for stealing some horses, but the charges were dropped." He flicked his thumb against the screen. "Then he apparently hooked up with Udane and they were arrested for larceny and insurance fraud, but the case was also dismissed on some sort of technicality."

The missing sheep, I thought. "What kind of insurance fraud?"

"They filed a claim for a Rolex and a man's diamond ring they claimed were stolen." He chuckled. "I don't have all the details. Apparently the stuff was stolen, but not from them."

"You mean they stole the watch and ring, insured them, and filed a claim?"

"Something like that," said Hutchinson, putting his phone in his pocket. "But the owner changed his story, said they weren't actually stolen from him as he originally claimed. That he gave them to the Turnell's as payment for 'consulting.' The detective I spoke to figured they had something on the guy, maybe had set him up with, you know, compromising photos or video or something."

"But if Ray stole the Winslows' sheep …" I couldn't finish the sentence because I couldn't finish the thought. I shifted focus. "Wait. What happened to his wife?"

"She disappeared. They both fell off the Reno radar about four years ago."

I recalled that Summer's fake diploma was dated four years earlier, so the timeline fit.

I felt Hutchinson watching me. "What are you thinking?"

"Did they have photos? You know, of Rex or Ray and his wife?"

He pulled out his phone and opened the email attachment. I was afraid to look, but I did. A woman looked back at me. She had pale skin and very long, dark, curly hair. Her cheekbones were sharp above shadowed hollows, and I guessed she weighed at least thirty pounds less than the Summer I knew, but it was either Summer Winslow or her twin sister. I was sure of it, no matter what name she went by.

"Hutch, how do you spell 'Oooh …' What was that name?"

He spelled "Udane" for me and I scribbled it on an old dog-show premium list in my bag.

My head was spinning when I left the police station and walked down Main toward Darling Confections to meet Norm. No wonder Summer hadn't married Evan. She was already married. Even so, it was a strange set up, and I had to wonder whether Ray's arrival in Indiana had been a surprise or whether she had known he was coming. Either way, it seemed that Evan was the ultimate mark in their con to get away from someone they had wronged in Reno. Unless he knew more than he was saying.

I turned my phone off to prevent interruptions and walked into the bakery. The scent of the place enfolded me, and I closed my eyes and inhaled the swirl of fragrances that filled the small space. Yeast and cinnamon, vanilla and lemon, cloves and almond, and burnt sugar. Aroma therapy at its yummiest.

"Don't swoon," said Norm. I opened my eyes and saw him step out from behind a humongous wedding cake.

"Is that real?" The multiple tiers of the cake, each festooned with icing swags and doodads, reached from the top of the table it stood on to maybe six inches short of the ceiling.

"If it is," Norm said, tapping his finger against the nearest layer, "it's past its use-by date." He stepped forward and kissed my cheek.

"Thanks for coming. I didn't want to do this all alone, and Mom did enough damage the last time."

A woman bustled through the swinging doors behind the counter and smiled at me. "Good morning! Is this your sister, Norm?"

"Sister-in-law." Norm draped an arm across my shoulders and hugged me to him. "I'll take her as my sister, though. Janet MacPhail, meet Doreen Darling, the cake lady."

Doreen would have been chic if not for what looked like powdered sugar on her nose and chin and pink icing on her apron. She escorted us to a pair of pink metal chairs with ruffled pink cushions and pulled out a notebook with a fancy cake on the front. "Why don't you look through these and see if anything catches your fancy while I finish boxing up an order?" She pointed to the fancy coffee machine and told us to help ourselves.

Norm knew exactly what he, and presumably my mother, wanted, and I just nodded my head, tasted a few samples, and nodded some more. By the time we left, I was on a serious sugar-and-caffeine high. I hugged Norm and told him I owed him big for taking care of all the wedding details that made me hyperventilate.

My head spun all the way home with a collage of icing flowers, stolen sheep, marzipan fruits, threatening goons, and a thousand questions that could be summed up in just two—who knew what? and who did what? I wanted to get to my computer and look for a few things, including the meaning of Summer's real name. Somehow that seemed important. I also realized I hadn't asked Hutchinson whether anyone had checked the ear tags on the sheep now grazing in the Winslows' pasture to see if they were the animals Summer had reported stolen.

Hutch answered on the first ring and said he did plan to send someone to check the tags. "It's not high on the priority list, so it may be a day or two." He paused. "And Janet, don't get any ideas."

"I won't."

"And don't take Giselle with you."

"She does as she likes, Hutch." If he knew anything about Giselle, he should know that by now. "Get used to it."

I stopped at the grocery store for a salad and soup from their lunch bar. I was hungry, and needed some real food to counter Doreen Darling's sugar and caffeine. I pulled into my driveway and reached for the garage door opener without paying much attention. There was a pop and whir followed by a heavy thud, but the garage in front of me remained closed. *Oh, crap.* I'd opened the back hatch. I closed the hatch and opened the garage, slung my tote bag over my shoulder and my camera bag over my neck, and picked up the salad box and the soup. That thud I had heard must have been the dog food in the back. I glanced at my ring. Switching it to my other hand had not worked well as a reminder. I decided I'd come back for the dog food when my hands weren't full.

FIFTY-SEVEN

WORK CALLED TO ME, and for the rest of the afternoon I did my best to focus on the business end of photography instead of murder and mayhem. Leo and Pixel were curled up together in a shallow box next to my big monitor and the sound of their purring was like a mental massage. Still, my mind insisted on wandering, and try as I might, I couldn't keep the image of Ray's body out of my head. It came to me at unexpected moments and left me slightly nauseated each time. When I realized I couldn't push it completely away, I left my desk and lay down on the couch for, as my mother would say, a think. Jay was curled up at one end and his belly made a great foot warmer. I tucked one cushion under my head, hugged the one with the Aussie face embroidered on it, and returned to the scene of the crime.

I had been watching the sheep as they ate, and was startled by the clank of Evan's bucket hitting the concrete apron outside the door. When I turned around, Evan was bent forward and moving away from the door. He'd been sick in the grass, as I recalled, after finding Ray's body. If he was acting, the man had talent. Still, I could have overlooked something in the rush and horror of the situation, or he could have been responding to feelings of guilt rather than shock.

Jay lifted his head and cocked an ear toward the back of the house. It had been three-fifteen when I left my computer and I hadn't been on the couch more than fifteen or twenty minutes. It wouldn't be Tom. He had a meeting until four and then had to go home to pick up the Labbies and a few more boxes, so I didn't expect him until a bit after five. A burst of panic shot me off the couch and into the kitchen. *Did I lock the back door?* On normal days, I didn't lock it when I was home during the day, but ever since I'd met the boys from Cleveland, I had tried to remember to keep the house locked whether I was home or not.

The door was locked, and Jay was no longer interested in whatever had caught his attention. He was slurping water as if he hadn't had a drink in days, his tags clanking against the water bowl. I patted his shoulders on my way to the fridge and said, "Pace yourself there, Bubby." I stared into the refrigerator for a moment, looking for something to drink. I'd had the last diet root beer the day before. "Great, Janet," I said, taking stock. "Three beers and two hard ciders. And a partridge in a pear tree." Jay sat and watched me. "I don't even have any milk. Can you believe it?" Judging by the look on his face, I'd say the answer was no.

As I was putting my shoes back on for a run to the store, I wondered whether Tom had anything planned for dinner. For about five seconds, I considered cooking something, but by the time I tied the second shoelace, I had come to my senses. I grabbed my tote bag, checked that all the doors were locked, and went out through the garage. A sharp wind had risen since morning, and the sidewalks were empty of dog-walkers and joggers.

As I backed up, something bumped under the back right tire and I heard scraping and grinding. *What the…?* I hit the brake and the back of the van slid an inch or two to the right. I stared at my ring, there on the wrong hand as a reminder. *Now you tell me.* The scraping and grinding was the sound of a seventy-four-dollar bag of premium dog food being pulverized into my driveway. *Cha-ching!*

I pulled forward to the sounds of more scraping and grinding and a *thup-thup-thup* from under the van. Several raindrops tapped the windshield for emphasis. I yanked the gear shift into what I thought was park, jumped out, and scurried around to the passenger side. Kibble and raindrops were strewn like coins a third of the way down the driveway. I'd been trying to clean up my vocabulary, but it seemed like the perfect time to use a few of those words, and I did. I'd gotten several out of my mouth when I noticed that the bag seemed to be moving up the driveway's slope, toward the tire. At first, the image made no sense.

And then it did. My van was rolling backward. The tire bumpity-bumped again, tearing more paper and pulverizing more food. I hustled around the front of the van, raced beside it for a few steps, got past the open door, and jumped in. I hit the brake and jerked to a stop in the middle of the street. Something in my peripheral vision caught my attention and I turned just as a horn blared. A little red sports car waited for me to finish whatever I was doing. I mouthed "sorry" at the driver and turned to the gear shift indicator. The needle rested on N. I'd put it in neutral rather than park. *Way to go, Janet.*

The sound from under the van as I pulled forward was like a giant playing card in a bicycle's spokes. In the spirit of closing the barn door after the horses had left, I put the van in park, turned off the engine, and removed the key before I got out to reconnoiter. What was left of the bag was caught under the bumper and a river of dog food ran down the driveway into the middle of the street. The red sports car ground about twenty bucks worth into the pavement before wheeling up Phil Martin's driveway and into his garage. The rain was serious now, and little rivulets were running down the driveway, rolling bits of kibble like edible river stones.

I got back into the van and tried to give the door a good therapeutic slam. Instead, it went *thuk!* and bounced away from the latch. I yanked the seatbelt out of the door and added more dog food to my list of errands.

FIFTY-EIGHT

THE NEXT TWO DAYS were quiet, with rain showers scattered among periods of bright sun. It was also a rare weekend with no photo gigs or dog shows, no disasters, not even a phone call. Tom and I stopped to visit my mom for a few minutes on Saturday, and when Tom showed her a photo of Winnie, she insisted he bring her in. We left the boys in the van to keep the excitement factor to a minimum, and Winnie was exactly the sort of hit you'd expect of a roly-poly puppy. Then we took all five of us for a walk on the Foster Park portion of the Rivergreenway, where Winnie was transfixed by the site of a Great Blue Heron on the far side of the St. Mary's River.

Goldie and Bonnie popped in later with two kinds of fresh-baked cookies—raspberry yogurt and lemon-lime-oregano—and a separate plate of homemade carrot-ginger dog biscuits. Saturday night we cozied up in front of a movie with the three dogs and two cats, and I went to bed wondering why I had any doubts about Tom moving in.

"This could work," I told him as we drifted toward sleep in the wee hours. Of course, as soon as I said it, Demon Janet whispered, "But but but…" Worse yet, Phil Martin's wacko girlfriend popped into my head, dressed as the Wicked Witch of the West and whining, "I'll get you, my pretty, and your little dog, too!"

We stuffed ourselves with Sunday brunch at Spyro's Pancake House on West Jefferson and didn't eat again until late evening, when Tom brought out the box with Goldie's cookies. A slow afternoon of packing and pitching more of Tom's belongings punctuated by periodic puppy-training sessions oozed into another dog walk, a raucous game of backgammon, and an early lights out. I barely considered murder and mayhem all weekend.

Monday morning I unplugged my phone's charger and the screen lit up with messages. *At seven in the morning?* But when I looked at the time stamps, I found that the calls had come in over the weekend—three from Giselle, three more from Bill and Norm's landline, one from Hutchinson, and one I didn't recognize. "Stupid phone," I said, and then thought to check the settings. The master volume was turned off. I'd forgotten to reset it after I left the bakery. *Stupid Janet.* It was too early to start calling people, so I drank my coffee, kissed Tom goodbye in his driveway, and followed his van until he turned off toward the university.

Bill and Norm were early risers, so I called their number first. Norm answered, and said he was just tidying up wedding plans. He went through a list of To Dos that included a few for me. "And seriously, Janet, get your hair cut before Saturday." He recommended someone named Chas in place of my usual cut-rate place, and I promised to take the plunge. "I'll be able to tell the difference, you know." *Busted.*

Next on the call-back list was Hutch, but I had to leave a message. Then I called Giselle. "I have nothing new for you," she said in a voice that suggested she was pouting. "I think Homer is on to me. He's being careful not to talk about the investigation in front of me."

"That makes sense," I said. "I mean, it is police business."

"Right, but he talks about his other cases in front of me. Whenever he gets a call about Mr. Turnbull's murder or the sheep, though, he shuts himself in a closed room."

I could picture Giselle with a glass pressed against a door to listen in. "He just doesn't want you getting hurt or, probably, passing things on to me."

"So stupid," she said. "That could have been a real grave, I mean, you know, for a person."

I told her to call me if she accidentally overheard anything interesting.

Hutchinson didn't call back until almost noon. Jay and I were taking advantage of the crisp, bright spring day for a run through Franke Park. The wind was from the direction of the zoo, and Jay's nose worked overtime sorting out the scents he must have been getting. We slowed to a walk when my phone rang in my pocket. Hutch wasn't one for small talk.

"Good call on the ear tags. The sheep on the farm are the same sheep they reported missing."

"How could they think they wouldn't get caught?"

"Why are you breathing so hard?"

"Running."

"I don't know. Hiding them in plain sight, I guess."

"Still no sign of Summer?"

"Not that I've heard." Hutchinson told someone he'd be right there before continuing with me. "Anyway, my guy at the farm said the neighbor saw the cars and walked over. Says he's been helping since Summer's been away. Seems to think she's visiting family. He also told my investigator that the husband, Evan, doesn't know much about handling the sheep. That right?"

How would I know? I thought about what I did know, and answered carefully. "When I went for lessons, I only ever saw Evan in passing. Summer's the one who knows sheep and sheepdogs." I sat down on a bench and signaled Jay to lie down. "Ray was there sometimes, doing odd jobs or shearing the sheep or whatever."

"So Summer and Ray were the ones who managed the sheep." It was more statement than question.

"Evan is comfortable with the animals, and I think he probably helped with some of the work. You know, feeding and mucking and stuff." I thought again about the photo I had taken of Evan with the newborn lamb, and of him and Rosie, the old ewe who had lived on their front porch until she was buried in a bed of rose petals. "I think he's a nice guy who got in too deep."

"You mean the gambling?"

I said yes, but I thought that might be the least of his problems. Summer and Ray had played him, and he still seemed to be clueless about their relationship, their history, their motives. Thinking about that spun me off in other directions. What did I not know about Tom that might hurt me as Chet, my ex, had? What had I not told Tom about myself that might cause a problem between us a week, a month, a decade in the future? How much do we really know about anyone else, even people we've known all our lives?

"You still there?"

"Sorry, yes," I said. "Just thinking. What did Evan have to say about the tags, the sheep?"

"Nothing yet. According to the neighbor, Evan went out of town to visit his sister for a couple of days. Needed to get away."

That made me squeeze my eyes shut to find a memory. It came slowly. Evan and I had been sitting in their kitchen. In the midst of bewilderment and loss, Evan had brought up happy memories. Visits to the farm, his aunt's farm. Five brothers.

"Hutch," I said, "I don't think Evan has a sister."

FIFTY-NINE

APRIL IS NOTHING IF not muddy in northern Indiana, and the weekend's rain had sloshed puddles and muck across portions of the paths through Franke Park, but our run cleared my mind, at least for a couple of hours. Jay and I were a mess when we got home, so I stripped off my muddy shoes and pants in the garage, put Jay in a down-stay, and grabbed some ratty old capris and a headband from my bedroom. I reached for the garage doorknob, dog shampoo in hand, but snatched my hand back, detoured to the fridge, and returned to the garage. Jay was exactly where I'd left him, so I tore the slice of cheese into three bits and gave them to him one by one before I told him he was free.

"Not completely free, Bubby," I said. He eyed the bottle in my hand and hung his head. In a cheery voice I confirmed that yes, he was going to have a bath. I kept up the happy chatter, opening the overhead door and explaining again that I'd had the adaptor hooked up to the wash tub in the garage so I could use the garden hose for warm-water doggy baths on the driveway. The voice didn't fool him. I tried again as I worked shampoo down his legs, asking why a dog who happily ran through mud puddles and swam like a retriever was horrified by a simple bath. He just hung his head lower.

I set my grooming table up just inside the garage, hoping some of the fur would land outside, raw material for bird-nest linings. A little red sports car crept past the end of the driveway while Jay was being blown dry. It looked vaguely familiar, but I wasn't sure why. I didn't pay much attention at first—people are always slowing down for a look when they see a dog being groomed—but the car stopped and the driver's window rolled down, so I looked more closely. It was Councilman Martin's arm candy. "Hello," I called, waving the dryer nozzle at her. I would have added her name, but I couldn't think of it. *Chastity? Charity?* She scowled at me and gave her golden locks a theatrical shake, as if bathing and drying a dog were the height of animal abuse. *Chelsea.* That was it. She hit the gas, screeched into Martin's driveway, slammed her door, and flounced up the front sidewalk and out of sight. Half an hour later Jay was a clean, fluffy, blow-dried stunner, and I was a wet, frizzy mess with Aussie fur stuck to my skin and clothes.

"I'd better get a move on, Bubby," I said as I wound the cord around the dryer handle and stashed it under my workbench. "Winnie and Bonnie start school tonight, and we need to cheer them on." Jay bounced up and down in front of me in agreement and followed me to the bathroom, as if to make sure I subjected myself to the horrors of a bath, too.

Jay was loaded into his crate and I was about to get behind the wheel when I heard a voice bark, "Just a minute there!" It didn't come from my side of the van, so I stepped toward the front of the vehicle to see over the hood. Phil Martin was stomping across his lawn toward me. He was all puffed up like a rooster, no doubt for the benefit of Chelsea, who stood in front of his house with her arms crossed.

"I'm on my way out."

"It's illegal to run a business in this neighborhood, you know." Martin squinted at me, and when I didn't respond he added, "It's a zoning violation." His Daffy Duck voice was beginning to wear on me, and there was something else. I'd heard that voice somewhere, and not on TV or radio. But where?

My mind was reaching for a response, but I couldn't imagine how running a photography business out of my home could be a violation. All my sales were done online or by mail, and I went to my clients for their photo sessions. Before I could ask what the heck he was talking about, he told me.

"Pet grooming businesses must be regulated and meet certain, uh, standards." He slowed down at the end of that just enough to tell me he was winging it. He didn't know what special regulations applied to professional groomers.

I considered setting him straight right away, but I couldn't help myself. I smiled and used my best flipping-him-off voice. "I don't think a little shampoo down the sewer will be a problem, especially considering all the petroleum and lawn-care products that wash into it."

"Argue all you like. It's not going to work." *It's not going to work.* That's what the man I had accidently called from Summer's phone had said, and I was almost certain it was the same voice. But why would Summer Winslow have Councilman Phil Martin on speed dial?

I stared at him for a moment, and suddenly a few more pieces fell into place. Martin was in insurance. Had Summer been in cahoots with Martin on an insurance scam? I let it go for the moment and said, "You're right. Because I don't have a grooming business. I'm a photographer." I nodded toward Chelsea. "Your girl there has misled you."

He sputtered and said, "She saw you, with a table and dryer and a strange dog…"

"Like the cop who saw my dog running loose the other night when my dog and I weren't home?" We stared at one another. I finally said, "By the way, my dog isn't strange, he was wet. And I'm late." I got in the van and left the councilman red-faced in my driveway. For my part, I wasn't sure whether the whole incident was hilarious or infuriating, and settled on half-and-half until I realized what it meant for Tom and me. If Martin and his girlfriend were already harassing me, they were bound to escalate when Tom moved in with two more dogs, especially if the new pet limit passed. Who knew? Maybe they'd even hire a couple of enforcers, like the goons from Cleveland.

SIXTY

THE NEW CLASSES WERE assembled in their respective rings by the time I had parked and taken Jay for the obligatory pre-training walk. Goldie waved as we passed the beginner ring. Goldie was sitting cross-legged on the floor with Bonnie sprawled across her thighs as if they'd been doing that for years. I hoped that Ray, wherever he was, knew his dog was safe and loved. I also hoped I'll be that limber at Goldie's age. *Who are you kidding?* It was that annoying little nag in my head. *You wish you were that limber now.*

The puppies were in the next ring. Tom was on his knees, giving Winnie eensie bits of chicken as rewards for keeping her focus on him. He also had the attention of the bouncing baby Boxer on one side, and the spinning and bowing Poodle-mix puppy on the other.

The third ring was open for individual training, so I stashed my equipment bag on a chair and buckled my treat pouch around my waist. Jean, whom I'd met at the Dogs of Spring event, was in the center of the ring talking to Giselle, and Jean's lovely Aussie, Lilly, was leading Spike in circles around the two women, his leash gripped firmly in her mouth. "That's cute," I said.

"I don't know where she learned that," said Jean, "but she loves to lead other dogs around by their leashes. And people, if you let her!"

As I began warming Jay up with some heeling, Giselle said she needed to talk to me before I left, and I nodded but didn't break training. Jay and I would be trying for our first utility-level obedience leg in less than a month, and I had been slacking off with everything else going on. We had a great session, though, and practiced several open and utility exercises—the drop on recall, the scent articles, a few directed retrieves.

The last exercise I wanted to work on was Jay's favorite—the retrieve over the high jump. On my command, Jay went over the jump and grabbed the dumbbell. As he flew back toward me over the jump, a familiar puppy voice spoke up from the next ring. Jay sat in front of me as expected, but as soon as I took the dumbbell from him he cranked his neck toward the source of the racket. Winnie was bouncing and squealing and twirling on her leash and pulling toward Jay, who was clearly having a lot more fun than she was. Tom smiled at me, shrugged, and made a trilling sound that finally got her attention. As soon as she looked at him he clicked his clicker and popped a bit of chicken into her mouth.

Jay and I had been at it just over twenty minutes, but I decided that was plenty since he had made no major mistakes. Always better to quit on a high note if possible. Great advice, and not just for dog training. Giselle was waiting, so I stashed my paraphernalia, gave Jay an extra couple of treats and a kiss, and sat down to listen.

Giselle's face was flushed and her eyes were wide. She checked that no one was within eavesdropping distance and leaned toward me, her voice barely audible. "We were having breakfast at Cindy's Diner downtown and Homer got a call."

I waited.

"I didn't really pay attention, but then he mentioned Blackford's Farm and Garden. I buy my dog food there."

"So do I." She just nodded at me, wide-eyed, so I asked, "Were they robbed?"

"No." Giselle clamped her fingers around my wrist. "They found a body out back, behind the dumpster."

My first thoughts were of Ralph Blackford, the owner, and Ed and Phyllis, the long-time clerks who always rang up my dog food and garden supplies. Then I thought of Joe, a homeless man who hung out in that part of town. "Did he say who it was?"

Giselle shook her head and tightened her grip on my wrist. "Homer said there was no ID on the body, and..." She swallowed and pressed her eyes closed, then looked into my eyes. "He was shot in the face." I was just absorbing that information when Giselle shuddered and added, "With a shotgun."

SIXTY-ONE

By the time we got back to my house, my nerves had landed me somewhere between nauseated and ravenous for carbs. Tom was right behind me and Goldie's car was already in her driveway. When I stepped out of my van she waved from her front porch.

"Come on over for dessert when you get everybody settled in!" I knew she wanted to talk about her first-ever dog-training class, and although I didn't really feel like socializing, how could I say no?

Tom took the dogs straight out back, mostly for Winnie's benefit, and we rendezvoused in the kitchen. I was sitting at the table, my face buried in Leo's soft neck, when man and dogs came in. Winnie leaped against my knees, poked Leo with her nose, and rolled back into a sloppy sit. The cat ignored her, and she shifted her four-second attention span to Pixel. They wrestled at my feet while I told Tom about the body found behind Blackford's Farm and Garden.

"I'm afraid it's Joe."

"Who's Joe?"

"The homeless man who lives in the area."

Tom nodded. "You know his name."

"Yes." I didn't bother to add that I often bought him some food when I saw him.

We sat with our individual thoughts for a few minutes before Tom said, "Goldie's waiting," and we found our way from my kitchen to hers. The contrast was startling. Mine smelled of old coffee and the lingering scent of canned vegetable soup. Goldie's was rich with a complex swirl of yeast and cloves and something like licorice that wrapped around me like a cashmere shawl. Bonnie pitty-patted back and forth between me and Tom, her lush tail waving. Totem, Pixel's litter brother, watched from atop a stack of cookbooks on an antique sideboard.

"How about a glass of wine to toast my return to school?" Goldie held a bottle of Infamous Goose Sauvignon Blanc and had I not been bound by social convention, I might have grabbed it for a quick chug. Instead, I said I'd love some. We toasted Bonnie and friendship and new ventures, and for a minute and a half, I felt better. I guess it didn't show, because Goldie said, "What are you so glum about?"

"No, nothing," I said. "Just tired." I muscled my mouth into what I hoped was a smile and she let it go, but with a look that told me she knew me better. The intermingled fragrances that filled me up when we arrived turned to ecstatic flavors when Goldie set her fennel and clove sweet rolls in front of us. By the time we left an hour later, the carbs and alcohol had done their work and I was out almost before I rolled into bed.

It was a good thing I got a decent sleep, because I needed my strength on Tuesday. We were just having a second cup of coffee when my cell phone rang and I saw Hutchinson's number on the screen. "Hutch? At eight in the morning?" I asked, looking at Tom before I answered.

"Janet, you're going to get a call from a detective named Tim Wainwright." He was talking fast.

"I am?"

"He's going to ask you to go to the station for a talk. They—"

"About what?" I set my coffee down as the cup and a half in my stomach began to churn.

Hutchinson's voice was softer when he spoke again. "There was a murder last night."

My inner smarty pants wanted to blurt *just one?*, but another part of my brain urged caution, even with Hutch. "The one at Blackford's?"

"You know the place?"

Tom was watching me, a crease forming between his eyes.

"Yes. I've shopped there for years. Hutch, who—"

"You didn't get this from me, but don't go in alone." He paused, came back. "Hang on." A few seconds passed, and he was back. "Your brother's a lawyer, right?"

The coffee in my stomach was now splashing its way up my esophagus. "My brother-in-law."

"Take him with you."

Something cold gripped the back of my neck. "Hutch, who was killed?"

I heard a male voice in the background and Hutchinson told me to hang on again. I turned to Tom, "The police want to talk to me."

"Why?"

I shrugged as a carousel of possible victims cycled through my mind—Summer, Evan, Joe the homeless man, Councilman Phil Martin. My spinning thoughts were cut short by Hutchinson's voice. "I gotta go. I won't be there when they talk to you, but I'll be around if I can."

"Wait! Hutch, who was it? Who was killed? And why talk to me?"

"It's Mick Fallon. They have witnesses to your altercation with him the other night. Hell, Janet, even I saw it."

"But—"

"I gotta go."

He was no sooner off the line than my other phone rang. It was Detective Tim Wainwright, and he asked me to come to the station at my earliest convenience. I wanted to say I couldn't think of a convenient time, early or late, but that didn't seem like a good plan, so I said I would try to be there around ten. Then I called Norm.

"I'm not a criminal attorney, Janet."

"Well, that's okay, because I'm not a criminal." I tried to laugh, but it came out more like a gargle.

Norm sighed. "I'll meet you in front of the police station at ten."

Tom had classes all morning, but he told me about a dozen times to call him as soon as I was finished and he'd call me back. I promised. He took Drake and Winnie home and I stood in front of my open closet for what seemed like an hour pondering the right clothes to wear to a police interrogation. My innards felt like they were set on spin as I cycled through fear, anger, and apprehension about what was coming. I also felt a touch of relief that Mick Fallon wouldn't be threatening me anymore, and guilt for feeling relieved at the death of another human being, no matter how odious.

Detective Wainwright was younger than I expected, and friendlier. He had red hair and freckles and reminded me vaguely of Alfred E. Newman, the guy on the cover of *Mad* magazine. The conversation was relaxed at the start—did I know Fallon, when did I last see him, had we had any difficulties? I had to remind myself several times to follow Norm's advice—"Just answer the questions they ask. Don't offer anything extra." He was right, of course, and telling them that Fallon had threatened me more than the one time they knew about would not help my cause.

I thought we had covered everything when Wainwright said, "I'll be right back. I want to show you something." When he came back, he laid a shotgun on the table in front of me. A ragged scratch ran half the length of the stock. "Look familiar, Ms. MacPhail?"

A little shot of adrenaline sparkled along my nerves. "It's a shotgun."

"Have you seen it before?"

My face went cold and I felt Wainwright assessing my reaction. "It looks like one that belongs to Evan Winslow. If so, then yes, I've seen it at their farm. Why do you have it?"

"That's the thing, Ms. MacPhail. We found it in a dumpster behind the Firefly Café, just down the street from where we found Mr. Fallon's body." He pinned me to my chair with a cold eye. "You know the place." Wainwright now made me think more of Chucky from the horror films than of Alfred E. Newman, and the axe he wielded was what he asked next. "Ms. MacPhail, why are your fingerprints on this weapon?"

SIXTY-TWO

MY FINGERPRINTS WERE ON the shotgun—the murder weapon. I had a perfectly good explanation to offer Detective Wainwright, if I could get my mouth to operate. Trust me, I don't lose my ability to speak very often, but at that moment, with the detective staring at me and the gun on the table between us, I was dumbfounded.

"Hang on a minute," said Norm. "Why do you have Ms. MacPhail's fingerprints?"

Wainwright gave Norm a dismissive look, but he answered the question. "They're on file from a case last year." He crossed his arms over his chest and stared at me.

"They fingerprinted a lot of us," I said, ignoring Wainwright and speaking to Norm. "For elimination purposes."

Norm had already jumped to his next question. "Detective Wainwright, what time was Mr. Fallon killed?"

Wainwright hesitated, but finally answered. "Between six-thirty and seven-thirty."

Norm seemed surprised. "That's pretty precise."

"Yeah, well, the manager at Blackford's said he helped load some feed into a customer's truck at six-thirty. Had to walk back and forth past the dumpster, and Fallon wasn't there." By "manager," I was sure he meant Ralph Blackford, the owner. "When he went out there an hour later to toss some trash, there the guy was. Blood everywhere. That's when he called us. The manager, I mean."

No kidding.

"Shotguns are loud," said Norm. "Didn't anyone hear the blast?"

Wainwright nodded. "Couple of the clerks said they heard something, but there's a storage room full of sacks of feed and stuff between the showroom and alley, and the doors were closed. They said things bang around out in the alley all the time. Deliveries and garbage trucks and such. They didn't think much about it." He fixed me with a cold stare and leaned in a bit. "But we're looking for a possible eyewitness."

"I think we might have a few witnesses of our own," said Norm, turning toward me to ask where I had been Tuesday evening

"Dog Dayz. The seven o'clock classes were just starting when I walked into the building. Tom and Goldie and I left together, you know, in separate cars but at the same time, just after eight, and went home." I whispered to Norm, and when he nodded, I said, "I can explain the fingerprints." I told Wainwright about holding the gun while Evan changed his shoes the day I learned that Summer was missing. "Coyotes. Evan said the gun was there to drive off coyotes."

Wainwright snorted. "Looks like somebody got one." He used his phone to establish that Dog Dayz is a fifteen-minute drive at best from Blackford's Farm and Garden. Once he had done that, he asked for names of witnesses and I rattled off a dozen. Then he let me go.

Norm offered to talk it out over lunch on his dime, but I was in no mood to eat and so full of adrenaline I was twitchy. "I think I'll go get Jay and go for a very long walk."

And that's exactly what I did. Jay and I spent three hours hiking the trails at Chain O'Lakes State Park. The water and forest and easy companionship of my dog worked their magic on me, like a spiritual massage. We sat on a fallen sycamore trunk and watched a pair of beavers drag a sapling down the bank and around a bend in a creek. A kingfisher flashed into view along the eastern edge of one of the smaller lakes, and an ear flick alerted me to a doe standing alone and still in a dappled clearing.

As we returned to the van those three hours after we began, I realized I had almost forgotten that two men were dead at the hands of other human beings. I hadn't liked Mick Fallon, had even feared him, but I hadn't wished him dead. And Ray Turnbull, con artist or not, had always been polite to me. Besides, the dogs liked him. Who, I wondered, would want both men dead? Were there two murderers running around the same circles, or had the same person killed both Ray Turnbull and Mick Fallon? I drowned out some of the noise in my head by singing along to the oldies station, and had solved nothing by the time we got home forty-five minutes later.

The fragrance of tomato sauce and basil, fennel and herbs I couldn't name, engulfed me the instant I opened my door. Tom hugged and kissed me and asked about our hike while Jay ate his dinner. I would have felt guilty feeding him kibble with that tantalizing fragrance in the air if he hadn't inhaled his food with such delight.

I went to wash up, and when I got back to the kitchen Tom was setting a steaming carry-out pan of eggplant Parmesan on the table. "Mmmm," I said, dipping a tiny bit of warm, crusty bread into the sauce and teasing my appetite with it. I opened the fridge and grabbed a beer, and with my other hand picked up an eggplant. "I thought you were making dinner with this purple guy. So what's that on the table?" He had called earlier and said he was dropping another couple of boxes at my house and thought he would sit there and grade papers while dinner baked. "Run out of time?"

"Ran out of heat." We sat down and he served the eggplant while he explained. "How old is that oven, anyway?"

"It was old when I moved in." Fortunately, I only ever used the burners. I couldn't remember the last time I slid a pan into the oven for any purpose other than storage.

"Well, tomorrow we're going to buy a new one. My housewarming present for moving myself in."

"I can't let you do that." I wiped my mouth and tried to sort through my thoughts.

"Sure you can." He smiled at me, and when he spoke again it was as if he had anticipated my reaction. "How's this. It will be my appliance because I'm the one who likes to cook. You may use it whenever you like. If you ever kick me out, I'll get it out of your way."

If I hadn't had a mouthful of eggplant, tomato sauce, and cheese, I'd have jumped his bones right there.

SIXTY-THREE

I CAN SPEND ALL day waiting in a bug-infested wetland for the perfect photo opportunity, or shooting photos of dogs or cats or horses in action, but twenty minutes shopping for anything other than pet toys, running shoes, or camera accessories makes me want to curl up like a cat on a cushion. Shopping for an appliance I will use occasionally to boil water? Just thinking of the upcoming ordeal made me itch, but Tom insisted I tag along since the thing would be installed in my kitchen. And he wanted to go early so he would have the afternoon to take the dogs for a swim at Collin Lahmeyer's place.

Pixel is almost trustworthy enough to be loose in the house when I'm gone, but with Winnie there, I decided to shut the kitten into my bedroom. She would have access to everything she needed other than trouble. I left Leo with her for company and tossed a couple of felt rodents into the room for good measure. Tom was shutting Winnie into her wire exercise pen in the living room when I emerged from the bedroom.

"Don't you think she should be in her crate?"

He clipped the final slide bolt into place to close the pen. "She'll have more room in here."

"But she might get out."

"She never has," he said, giving the corner a tug to show me the panels were securely connected. "Anyway, we won't be gone all that long."

How long does it take for an eleven-week-old puppy to get into trouble? I bit my tongue.

"Have you ever left her in the pen before? I mean, when you weren't home?"

He grinned and kissed my cheek and said, "You worry too much. She'll be fine."

I wasn't so sure, but decided to wait and see.

The appliance store had some kind of mega super biggest-of-the-year power sale going on, and an army of salespeople hovered just inside the door. A perky brunette won the sprint to intercept us. "I'm Evelyn," she said. "How may I help?" The low cut of her polyester top said she was in her twenties, but her face argued for mid-forties.

She guided us right by the nearest row of stoves and into one with price tags that would have gotten me a very nice new telephoto lens. Then she began her pitch for the latest in sensory this and electronic that, all aimed at me. I wasn't sure whether to find her assumption sexist or hilarious. Both, I decided.

"Let's see something a bit less precious, shall we," said Tom.

"Certainly," Evelyn said, bustling around the end of the lineup and into the row we had passed by earlier. "Now here's a nice unit," she told me, and started to rattle off all the fancy features.

"We don't need all the bells and whistles," Tom said. "Just a nice basic stove with a self-cleaning oven."

Evelyn shot me a quick glance of what looked a lot like sympathy, and I just couldn't help myself after that.

"Oh, really? We can have self-cleaning?"

Tom looked at me like I'd lost my mind, but when Evelyn explained that a self-cleaning oven would reduce my exposure to toxic cleaners, he started to laugh. The poor woman started to say something else, but closed her mouth and took a step backward.

"Evelyn, I'm the cook at our house, and I'll be the one cleaning the oven." Tom smiled at her, but she looked skeptical. Tom asked a few questions about two competing models, and picked one.

As Evelyn held her phone and waited for delivery information, I smiled at her and said, "I hate to cook." She seemed to have some trouble processing us.

We passed Blackford's Farm and Garden on the way home, and I wondered again about who might have killed Ray Turnbull and Mick Fallon. And where in the world was Summer? "Tom," I said, but stopped because I couldn't seem to shape my thought into words.

"Janet." He glanced at me and grinned.

"Those two guys, the goons from Cleveland…"

"Yes?"

"We've been assuming they came after Evan, you know, to collect the money he owes their boss. But what if once they got here, what if Summer and Ray…" I still couldn't fit the pieces into a coherent whole, and the half-formed question just hung there for a few moments.

"What if Summer or Ray—or both of them—had some history with the guy? Is that where you're going?"

"I think so." I thought about the photo of Summer running away from the encounter between Evan and the two men. "What if they met him in Reno, you know, tried to con him, but didn't really know who he was, what they were getting into? Maybe that's why they left there in such a hurry."

"But why move closer to his home base?"

We pulled into my driveway and Tom turned the engine off.

"Maybe they didn't know he was from Cleveland. Or maybe they thought, heck, it's what, three or four hours from this area to Cleveland, and there's nothing around here to make him likely to visit." I popped my door open, but stopped to add, "They didn't expect Evan to go borrow money from the same guy."

We were just approaching the door from the garage into the house when something hit it from the other side with a solid *thunk*. Tom and I looked at each other, and closed the overhead door and opened the other. I was not surprised to see a dog on the other side. I had figured the crash into the door was Jay or Drake skidding to a stop. The surprise was which dog it was, and the way she looked.

Winnie was a moving collage. Bits of multicolored paper were stuck to her head, her body, her legs. She tumbled over the doorsill and ran two loops around the garage before skidding past Tom and back into the house. She disappeared into the kitchen and the sound of her little paws on vinyl stopped, telling me she was on the living room carpet. We hurried past the laundry room and into the kitchen, where we were met by Jay and Drake. They, too, had bits of paper stuck to their heads, but only a few. Drake held his ears pulled back and was wagging his tail in low, short, fast motions that looked a lot like an apology. Jay squinted his eyes and bared his teeth in a submissive grin. Behind them, the kitchen table was shoved out from its usual home against the wall. The salt and pepper shakers lay under it, and the teddy bear honey dispenser lay in the far corner. It seemed to be deformed.

I pulled a bit of raggedy paper off Jay's cheek. It felt sticky. I ran my finger over it and touched my tongue. Honey. I scowled at the paper bit and realized what it was at exactly the moment I heard "Ohmygod!" from the other room.

Winnie's pen lay where it had been knocked over, the wire panels collapsed but for the puppy toys caught between them. Tom was trying to catch Winnie, but she was too fast and too exhilarated, and small enough to get behind the couch to escape between gleeful circuits of the room. Nothing else looked out of place in the living room, but when my eyes took in my work area, my lungs seized.

SIXTY-FOUR

A MOUND OF CONFETTI filled the space in front of the dining table on which I work. At first, I couldn't make sense of it, but then I saw the plastic milk crate that I used to file and organize printed photos I planned to mail to clients. It had been pulled away from its spot between the table and the credenza, tipped onto its side, and relieved of its contents, which were now torn to bits and scattered across the floor and stuck to the dogs.

I let my body sag into the wall as I took it all in. Jay leaned against my leg, and I looked at him and Drake and said, "Go lie down." They both backed away and disappeared into the kitchen. Just then Winnie dashed out from behind the couch, leaped onto her pile of photo confetti, and lay down and panted with obvious satisfaction. Tom stepped forward and picked her up. Then he turned to me.

"I'm sorry. You were ri—"

I raised my hands, palms toward him, and closed my eyes. "Don't." Tornadoes are common in Indiana in spring, and I felt one spinning inside me as I took in the mess, the lost work, the cost of the prints, the time it would take to replace them and to let my customers know about the delay. All that now lay in tatters on the floor. And there was also the potential danger to the puppy who wasn't ready to be unsupervised, and to the older dogs she took on her juvenile joy ride.

Tom tried again. "I'll clean up the dogs and then I'll get the re—"

"Why didn't you crate her like I asked? You know x-pens aren't—"

"I thought she'd be fine. I used to leave Drake in his ex—"

"—secure," I said, a bit more loudly. "And stop interrup—"

"If you didn't leave your crap all over the pla—"

"Crap?" I stopped picking up bits of photos and whirled toward him. "Crap? That 'crap' is hours of work and hundreds of dollars in printing costs." My cheeks felt so hot I thought they might blow the top of my head off. "And it isn't 'the place,' it's *my* place."

I realized suddenly that Jay and Drake had both come back into the room. They were between us, looking from me to Tom and back, ears down and back, worried looks on their faces.

"This isn't going to work. You haven't even—" I was going to say *moved in yet* and who knows what else I'd have regretted later, but he interrupted again.

"Come on, I'll help clean up and Winnie will pay for the damage." I knew he was trying to lighten the mood, but my mood didn't want lightening. When I didn't respond, he let out something resembling a laugh and said, "I think you're overreacting."

"Just go."

"Janet, I—"

I glared at him and he stopped, a stricken look on his face. My inner good girl, the one socialized to accommodate everyone else's needs, pinched me and whispered, "You can't tell him he can't move in now. He's sold his house for you. Where will he go? He'll have to live in his car with his dogs." But at that moment I didn't care. I wanted him to be sorry. I wanted all my doubts to go away, and I wanted all the work I had put into those now-useless photos to be worth something. I wanted him to say he was wrong and I was right. I said nothing.

"I'll call you," he said, and left with Drake and Winnie.

I turned my back and knelt to pick up some of the paper. The first piece I touched had to be peeled from the carpet, and I wondered whether I'd be able to get honey out of the fibers without professional help. Feeling certain my brother-in-law would know what to do, I called and he talked me through sponging it up with dish soap and water. Then he reminded me of all my wedding duties coming up on the weekend, and checked that I had made the dreaded hair appointment. I didn't mention that Tom might not be at the festivities.

I thought about trading Wednesday-night training for a quiet evening at home, but a hot shower and a grilled cheese sandwich revived me. *Besides*, whispered Janet Devil, *you never know when you'll need an alibi.* Jay had napped while I showered and ate, and he was ready to go again by the time we loaded ourselves into the van. I could swear he knows when a training night rolls around.

Tom's van was already in the Dog Dayz lot when I got there, and I considered going back home. I had spent the afternoon flip-flopping between how much I loved him and how sure I was that living together would be the death of us as a couple. We were going to have to have a long, serious talk very, very soon, but I didn't want to start it that night. I was still too angry about the shredded photos, although my funny bone was starting to react to the memory of happy little Winnie sitting in the middle of her pile of confetti. She must have had a lovely time ripping all the paper to bits. The whole thing would be a great story in a few weeks, I knew, but not just yet.

The parking area near the training building was mostly full, but I found a space about halfway between the back entrance and the exercise area. I went over Jay one more time to be sure I hadn't

255

missed any bits of paper in his thick fur, and led him away from the building along the line of dogmobiles. Most were mini-vans and SUVs adorned with stickers professing to ❤ this breed or that dog sport. Toward the back of the lineup a gray sedan was backed in. At first I thought someone had forgotten to turn their lights off, but then I saw movement in the car.

Gray sedan. My heart sped up as I thought about the Cleveland goons in their gray sedan. Could this be Mick Fallon's partner Albert Zola? I stopped and stared, then looked around. *Get a grip, woman.* How many gray sedan false alarms had I fallen for in the past few days? *But people have died.* I was alone. I'd arrived a bit later than normal, and everyone seemed to be inside. "Come on, Jay," I said, backing up a couple of steps and watching the car before I turned and high-tailed it toward the building entrance. When I got there I encouraged Jay to relieve himself on a rock near the door. Marietta discouraged the practice, but I gave myself a pass this time and went inside. I slid into a shadow and watched out the back door for a moment, but nothing happened. I made a mental note to leave with other people, and hoped that Hutchinson might be there with Giselle.

SIXTY-FIVE

SEVERAL PEOPLE WAVED AS I made my way through the training building, and I overheard a snatch of conversation about the murder behind Blackford's Farm and Garden. That had to be a topic of conversation, since probably a third of the Dog Dayz crowd bought their dog and cat and other animal foods there. Giselle met me with a hug and whispered, "I meant to call you last night but I had class and got, um, busy afterward. I'm glad it wasn't too bad at the police station." She stepped back and looked at me. "It wasn't too bad, was it?" I assured her it wasn't too bad and asked whether Hutch was around.

"Not tonight. He had to go buy his mom a birthday present." She studied my face. "Do you need me to call him?"

"No, no, it's fine." She looked doubtful, but I smiled and repeated myself until we were both convinced.

I tried to ignore Tom as he worked with Winnie in one of the rings, but I couldn't help admire, as always, his easy way of getting the best from his dog. He had staked out a space along the wall across from the rings, near the front door, for his two crates. He had brought the big folding canvas one for Drake, but didn't trust Winnie to fabric and zipper at her young age, so she had a medium-size plastic airline crate with a heavy wire door for training nights. *Oh, sure,* now *you use a crate, when there are plenty of puppy monitors around.* He liked to keep puppy sessions short, and he wrapped this one up and put her in her crate, made sure the latch was secure—not that I was watching—and let Drake out.

Next to Drake's crate was a slightly smaller one with the name "Lilly" embroidered into the mesh front. Four more crates continued the lineup. Two of them were empty, one housed a sleeping Golden Retriever, another a Corgi who sat and watched. One of the empties was super-sized, and I saw by the nametag that it was for Eiger, Jim Smith's Saint Bernard. Flanking the row of bigger crates was a tiny one I recognized as Giselle's. I noticed that the nameplate had been changed. No more pink "Precious" on the little guy's travel home. "Spike" was official.

I found a chair on the other side of the room, as far from Tom's stuff as possible, and put my jacket and tote bag on it. "Okay, Bubby," I said to Jay, "let's do a little work, shall we?" His whole rear end wagged an affirmative and we stepped into the center ring, where group heeling practice was already underway. I waved to Jean, who was on the other side of the ring with lovely Lilly. Giselle and Spike were in the "slow lane" toward the center, and Sylvia Eckhorn and her Cocker Spaniel, Tippy, were farther down on my side of the ring. Jay and I slipped into the line at the first opening, just before Marietta Santini hollered "about turn" in her drill-sergeant voice.

A few minutes later Marietta lined us up for recalls, and Jean led Lilly back to her crate and zipped her in. A young woman I'd never seen before was sitting in one of the folding chairs along the front wall a few feet from Tom's crates. She was wore dark leggings, a dark sweater, a dark beret, and a dark scowl. She hadn't been there when

I arrived, and I figured she must be someone's angsty teenager dragged along to Mom's dog-training class. Jean stopped and spoke to Winnie, petting her through the bars of her crate, and then headed toward the back of the building. I decided I could use a bathroom break, too, when Jean returned.

As I pivoted back into line I noticed another new face. A young man, also dressed in dark clothing, sat outside the front-most ring where Tom was working Drake. He was in the chair closest to the outside wall, right next to another set of crates. Two were clearly empty, their front door-flaps unzipped and folded back across their roofs. The other one was occupied, but I couldn't see the dog and didn't recognize the crate.

Giselle came up beside me. "Oh, man, I have such a headache. I'm going to get some aspirin from my car." Without waiting for an answer she went to her crate, deposited Spike, and walked toward the back door, massaging her temples as she went.

I moved up behind the person ahead of us in line and looked over my shoulder toward the front of the room. Something didn't feel right. One sulky teenager in black watching a training session made sense. I'd seen them here before. But two? *You're just overwrought.* That thought raised the twin specters of two men dead at violent hands, and a slow shudder ran up my spine as I forced myself to focus on the training task at hand.

And so it was that I had my back to the front entrance when I heard *pop-pop-pop*, and the screaming started.

SIXTY-SIX

VOICES ROSE, SHRILL AND loud. Everyone spun toward the sound. Several people dressed in black had burst into the building. They were chanting something, but at first all I could make out was "cruel." Two of them held hand-lettered signs that read "Domestication = Slavery" and "Liberate All Animals." As the group fanned out across the room, I was able to count them. Five. I knew I had been right about the two watchers in black. The figure in the lead seemed familiar somehow, but people—my people—were screaming, and dogs were barking and yelping, some lunging at the intruders, others pulling away from them.

Jay stepped in front of me, teeth bared. I made out more voices, some of which I knew. Sylvia Eckhorn yelled, "Oh my God!" There was another loud *pop*, and then *pop-pop-pop*. Sylvia's sweatshirt exploded in red. *Are they shooting?* Sylvia screamed and Tippy leaped to the end of her leash, yelping. I took a step toward Sylvia and saw her look down and touch a finger to the glistening crimson spatter across her chest. She rubbed her finger and thumb together and a veil of fury unfurled across her face. She must have read my fear when our

260

eyes connected, because she yelled, "Paint balls!" She pressed her open palm against her breastbone and added, "Jeez, that hurts," and turned her attention to calming her dog.

One of the black-clad figures ran toward Marietta and swung what looked like a plastic squeeze bottle in circles in front of her. The center of Marietta's sweatshirt blossomed in bright blue squiggles. She looked down and ran her fingers across the mess. Then someone else screeched, "They're spraying something on us!" and Marietta shouted, "Paint! It's paint!" People and dogs were running every which way, some leashed to one another, others on their own. My view of the ring where Tom has been working with Drake was blocked. So was my view of Winnie's crate and the others near it.

I reached for Jay's collar and started to guide him toward the back door, a hazy plan forming to lock him in the van and come back to help. As I turned, I heard a *pop*, close and loud. Something hit my head at the hairline and warm liquid ran down my forehead and cheek. I swiped wildly at my eye and watched something thick and red drop onto the back of Jay's neck.

At first there was no pain, but I knew that the adrenaline rush could mask it. Everything had happened in a matter of seconds. Maybe the pain just hadn't hit yet.

Voices were frantic around me. People were yelling their dogs' names, yelling slogans, yelling yelling yelling. And then someone yelled above the cacophony, "They're letting the dogs loose! They're letting them out the door!" *Oh, God! Winnie!* Not until that instant did I realize how much I loved that puppy already.

The pain where I'd been hit kicked in just as a hand reached for Jay's leash. He pulled away, eyes wide and ears back as if startled. I tried to look toward the front of the building, toward Tom, but a body shoved up against me and a woman's voice hissed, "Give him to me! Set him free!" I tripped, and my knee hit the floor and sent a

261

bolt of pain howling through my leg in both directions. I closed my eyes against the liquid still dripping from my hairline and tried to wipe my eye against my sleeve. I could smell it now, like fish soaked in dish soap. Jay's leash slipped from my hand, and as I grabbed for it, the blurred image of my attacker came into view. She was leaning toward my dog, reaching for him. I swung at her and connected. The impact against her cheekbone sent a scream of pain racing from my wrist to my elbow. Another scream erupted, and her voice—a voice I now recognized—yelled "Get him off me! Get him off me!" I swiped my eyes clear with my clean sleeve and saw that Jay had a firm, unfriendly grip on Councilman Martin's sweetheart.

"Jay, leave it," I said. He hesitated, rolling his eyes to look at me, but he let go.

She pulled her sleeve up and I could see that he had not broken the skin, although she'd probably have a good bruise. She was going to have a shiner, too, judging by her cheekbone where I'd clocked her.

"I'll sue you!" Chelsea was still screeching. "I'll have your vicious dog impounded!" She took a step backward. Her foot slid forward in a puddle of her own paint and her arms went into windmill mode in an effort to keep her balance.

"Let me help," I said, and pushed my palms against her chest just enough to finish the job the slippery spot started. She went down with a loud *oof.* "Roll over," I said, staring at her. When she didn't move, I said, "I'm not talking to the dog. Roll onto your stomach." She stared at me, then shifted her gaze to my hand, and I realized it was clenched into a fist. I squeezed it tighter and she slowly rolled over. I signaled Jay to straddle her, front feet on one side and back on the other. "Down," I said, and he dropped his body onto her midsection. "Stay!" To her I added, "If you try to get up, he'll go for the back of your neck."

I ran toward the chaos at the front of the room in time to see two of the invaders run out the door. The sulky young man I had seen sitting near Winnie's crate earlier was backed up against a wall, whimpering under the unflinching stare of Mel Able's protection-trained Dutch Shepherd, Hans. The dog didn't appear to have touched the guy, but there was no question he would if Mel gave the word.

So that was two of the terrorists out the door, Chelsea caught under Jay, and this guy. I was sure there had been five. Where was the fifth? I kept moving toward Winnie's crate, dodging people and dogs. Tom was nowhere to be seen, and a crowd had gathered in front of the row of crates where Winnie and Lilly and Spike and the others should be. My feet seemed to be caught in swamp-goo but I finally pushed my way to the front of the crowd just as Jim Smith shoved the fifth invader into Eiger's giant crate and latched it. "You can wait there for the police," Jim said, snapping a padlock onto the door for good measure. Eiger snuffled at the side of his crate and growled.

The rest of the crates were empty.

SIXTY-SEVEN

I SPUN AROUND AND scanned the room. No sign of Winnie or Lilly or Spike. No sign of Tom. Jean had gotten to her crate just ahead of me, and I saw her run out the front door. I raced back toward Jay and Chelsea. I needed Jay to find little lost Winnie. I figured the police could locate Chelsea easily enough if she escaped, but I pointed her out to Jim Smith and he hurried toward her, a man on a mission. "Jay, come!" I called. I was grabbing for the end of his leash when Giselle came through the back door, took in the crowd near Spike's crate, and started to run.

"Giselle, he's not there. He's loose. I'm on my way out to look. Win—" I felt as if a choke chain were yanked across my throat, but I found my voice and said, "Winnie's missing too, and Lilly. You need to go out and call Spike!"

"Ohmygod, ohmygod." she said, each repetition pitched an octave higher. She pulled her cell phone out as she ran beside me to the front of the building. "Did anyone call the po— Hutch! Something terrible's happened!"

We heard at least two sirens in the distance, coming closer, filling the night. Someone had already called. I left Giselle and ran through the parking lot, hoping the loose dogs would head for familiar parts of the property—the exercise area, the agility field, the trees and shrubs that edged the parking area. *Please don't let them run to the road. Not in the dark. Not ever.*

I saw Tom walking the tree line, a dark shadow in front of him that had to be Drake, and I ran to him. Tom had a flashlight, and he was calling in a voice honed by many years of training dogs to remain upbeat in the worst of times. "Winnie, come! Puppy puppy puppy!"

"Should I get Jay's tracking harness?"

Tom turned toward me and the distress written into the muscles of his face stirred a strange cocktail of pain and fury and love in my heart. "We'll find her," I said. "Jay and I will check the agility course while you do this."

Then I'll go back inside and Chelsea and her friends better hope the police already have them in protective custody.

"Spike!" Giselle's voice came from behind me. "Precious Spike! Come! Cookies!"

There were other voices, too, and then Marietta's. "Folks, too many people out here in the dark will scare some of the dogs. If your dog is not missing, please stay in or near the building and let the owners call their dogs!"

Paranoia must have had me in its grip, because when I started for my van, I thought I saw someone standing by the passenger door. Heavy-set, dressed in dark clothing. I broke stride and squinted into the shadow, but by the time I opened the back of my van, whatever it was had disappeared, and Jay didn't show any interest in anything other than getting his tracking harness and longline on. I had him sit and looked into his eyes to be sure he was listening. "Find Winnie. Find the puppy." I had no idea where to start him looking for her scent, but I had a hunch she might follow the big dogs, and they would, I was pretty sure, head for the outdoor agility field. It was where they had a lot of fun.

Marietta had turned the lights on around the field, so visibility was decent. Jorge had gotten the equipment out of winter storage a couple of weeks earlier, and had brought out the portable bleachers as well. I let Jay's longline play out to about thirty feet and just followed and watched. Working a dog on a track is pure mystery. We have no idea what they experience, what they smell, how they find one scent among all the others. But we'd been tracking regularly for more than two years, and I had some sense of when Jay was following a solid track. His body language suggested he was still looking for Winnie's scent. I crossed my fingers and whispered a prayer to the universe.

Jay took off at a run and nearly yanked me off my feet. I held the line tight and followed, trying to slow him down to a safer speed. Safer for me. My peripheral vision picked up motion on both sides. Tom and Drake were coming up on my right. Tom must have seen Jay lean into his harness, a sure sign he was on a scent. I just hoped it was Winnie's. I glanced left. Someone was there, outside the agility field, almost beyond the reach of the lights, moving in and out of the shadow. I tried to get a better look, but Jay sped up again and I had to look where I was going. He seemed to be aiming for the A-frame at the far end of the field. It would be a good place for a frightened puppy to hole up.

Giselle's voice was still behind me. "Spike, come!" Her tone was turning desperate when suddenly it changed. "Spike! Oh, Spike!" A white speedball shot out from under the A-frame and ran straight past me. I turned in time to see Giselle scoop him into her arms and bury her face in his fur.

Jay whined and started to pull again, and I turned to follow. Tom and Drake were beside me now. "Maybe she's under there too?" Tom inflected the words as a question, and I knew that was the sound of hope.

But Jay stopped for no more than two seconds to sniff under the obstacle, and then turned toward the bleachers. I tried to shorten the length of line between me and him, knowing he could easily get tangled if he climbed the risers, but he was moving too fast. The line burned through my fingers and I let go. Then I heard a sharp yip. A puppy yip.

"It's her!" Tom had no sooner said the words than Drake yanked the leash out of his hands and rushed forward with Jay. Tom and I sprinted to catch up, but they were way ahead of us and light-years faster. They had almost rounded the bleachers when Winnie appeared, her leash pulled taut behind her as if she were out for a walk. For a moment, I wondered if she was caught on the structure, and then I saw that she had been in good hands. Or paws. Lilly stepped into view, her lovely muzzle clamped tight to the puppy's leash.

SIXTY-EIGHT

THURSDAY MORNING GOLDIE CAME over, newspaper in one hand and fresh-baked muffins in the other, for an eyewitness account of the evening before. She looked around the kitchen and raised an eyebrow at me.

"What?"

"Where's Tom?"

"Home, I suppose," I said, trying to hide my face in the refrigerator. "His home." *For a little longer, at least.*

"I'd have thought you'd both need a good hug after all that." She tapped a headline with her finger, but all I could see was "o Let the Dogs Out?"

"We hugged when we found Winnie," I said. Goldie hadn't known Winnie was one of the loose dogs, and the puppy's misadventure and rescue by Lilly the Aussie distracted her from pressing me about Tom's absence. And she was right, I had needed a hug when I got home just before midnight. I had crawled into bed and hugged Jay and Leo until I fell asleep sometime in the wee hours.

Pixel had even put up with some hugging before she went off to bat her ping-pong ball around its circular track.

"Were all the dogs found? And safe?"

Just as I confirmed that they were, my phone rang. It was Sylvia Eckhorn. After we rehashed the events of the previous evening, she said, "I asked my husband about livestock insurance, and when I mentioned the Winslows, it turns out he actually knows them. He's their agent. Isn't that weird?"

"Maybe not that weird. How many insurance companies around here handle livestock insurance?"

"Not that," she said. "I mean, he doesn't insure their sheep *per se*. Just their property and vehicles." I didn't know what to say to that, and Sylvia picked up the slack. "If the sheep were covered for 'special use,' like a herding trial off the property, it was with someone else. But that's not the interesting part."

"No?"

"No! The interesting part is that Summer modified the policy to exclude the loss of livestock or crops. She told Ron they couldn't afford the premiums and would just have to take their chances."

"So that means she and Evan weren't trying to defraud the insurance company." *So who had removed the sheep from the event, and why, and how did they end up back at the Winslows' farm?*

"Not Ron's company, at least," said Sylvia. "But get this. She called and cancelled the policy that Thursday, you know, two days before the sheep went missing."

I thanked her and was trying to pick the threads apart as I hung up. Could Summer have cancelled the insurance without telling Evan? Could Evan have staged the theft, thinking the sheep were still insured? Even if they collected on the lost animals, the payment would cover only a quarter of his debt. And how was Ray involved? Or was he? Maybe his death had nothing to do with the missing sheep. My head was spinning when Goldie picked up our earlier conversation where we had left it.

"Thank God the dogs are all safe. Now let's hope the prosecutor follows through with charges." She leaned into the newspaper to read, then let out a hoot. "Oh my! I bet Councilman Martin will be holding a press conference today. Damage control."

"What?" I picked up a muffin and took a bite. "They mention him?"

"Apparently he sent an aide into the police station to collect 'a friend' for him last night, but a reporter recognized the guy and followed him out to Martin's car."

"The Councilman is lucky there was anything to collect," I said. "A lot of people were ready to lynch our friend Chelsea last night." As soon as I said it, Ray Turnbull swung into my mind and I lost my appetite. Goldie didn't seem to notice.

"It says here that the councilman claimed 'Chelsea Donovan is a family friend.'"

"Wonder what his wife would say about that."

"Hang on! Here we go. 'Dorothy Martin, the Councilman's estranged wife, claimed not to know anyone named Donovan.'"

"I guess they caught her off guard." I got up and poured the coffee. "Or Dorothy is puttin' the screws to the Councilman. Does it say anything about who *they* were, or the charges?"

"Let's see." Goldie was quiet for a moment before starting to read again. "Members of an unnamed organization that advocates to end, and I quote, 'the slavery of pet ownership.' They were arrested and charged with trespass, vandalism, assault, and animal cruelty and endangerment." She whistled and Jay jumped up and shoved his head up under the newspaper. Goldie bent and kissed him. "This is about those bad people, my love. Listen to this." He cocked his head and waited. "'An unnamed source added that officials are also considering filing federal conspiracy and terrorism charges.'"

Goldie laid the newspaper on the table, broke a muffin in half, and said, "Do you have any honey?"

"No. There's some raspberry jam in the fridge."

She smeared the jam on her muffin and then sat back and watched me until I blurted the whole story of Winnie's rampage and my argument with Tom, ending with, "It's just not going to work." To my surprise, she didn't press me and didn't offer any advice. She just ate her muffin and said, "There's another short article in there about the murder behind Blackford's. They quote Detective Hutchinson."

"What does it say?"

"Not much. Just that they've interviewed several people, and are looking for a possible witness."

I thought about that, and as I realized what it must mean, my heart sank. Joe, the homeless man. He had been drifting around the general area for a while. Was he living behind Blackford's? What did it mean that they were looking for him? Was he hiding? Had someone threatened him, or worse?

Goldie dipped into the jam jar again. "What happened to your little honey bear?"

"Winnie."

It's scary how often Goldie knows what I'm thinking without being told, and that was another of those times. "Blending families can be difficult," she said. "Different approaches to managing the young 'uns and all." She picked up the dishes and said, "Get dressed. I've decided to buy a new dress for your mom's wedding, and you're going to help me find one."

I told Goldie about Joe, and we drove to Blackford's with a quick stop at Firefly for a sandwich, coffee, and two bottles of water to go. A delivery truck had the alley blocked, so we parked and walked. The alley ran between the back of the building and a strip of scrubby vegetation that edged a drainage ditch.

"He lives back here?"

"He moves around," I said, and then pointed to a refrigerator-size packing crate tucked into an alcove behind the dumpster and recycling bin. A blanket hung over the open end, and a mildewed green shower curtain was tacked over the blanket, its length flung back onto the box.

"Joe?" The only sign of life was a pair of sparrows hopping along in front of the box. "Joe, it's Janet. I brought you a cup of coffee."

Goldie walked around to the store's front entrance to buy dog food while I strolled up and down the alley, peering into the brush along the ditch and checking the lot at the far end of the building. The delivery truck left and still I waited, hoping Joe might reappear.

"No luck?"

Goldie's voice made me squeeze the top off the to-go cup and slosh not-so-hot coffee over my hand. "No." I tucked the sandwich box under my arm and re-settled the lid. "He either isn't here, or he wants his privacy just now." I had raised my voice, hoping Joe would hear and feel safe, whether he came out or not. "I'll just leave the sandwich and coffee inside the door to his house for when he gets home."

SIXTY-NINE

SHOPPING FOR GOLDIE'S DRESS turned out to be more fun than I've had clothes shopping since I tromped around the Southtown Mall with my junior-high pals. Goldie picked out a long, tiered Gypsy-print skirt and vibrant pink peasant blouse in the second store we tried. Best of all, I didn't have to try anything on, and I found a funky pair of dangly earrings on the clearance table for four bucks.

We stopped by Blackford's Farm and Garden again on the way home, hoping to find Joe as close to safe and sound as he ever was. We parked alongside the building and walked down the alley. As we neared Joe's alcove, I called his name. There was no response, but I could tell he had been there since our last visit. The blanket that made his door was folded back over the top of the carton, and the sandwich bag and coffee I had left just inside were gone.

We stopped in the store and looked for Ralph Blackford, but he wasn't there. One of the clerks—Alan, according to the nametag pinned to his madras shirt—was stocking shelves, and I figured he had probably made one or two trips to the alley with empty boxes. I asked if he had seen Joe out there, and had to explain who I meant. Alan hadn't seen him lately.

By the time we got home, I felt ready to sort things out with Tom, if he was willing. I took Jay out back for a tennis game, played feather-on-a-stick with the cats, and checked the time. Tom had office hours scheduled until two-thirty, and I planned to catch him there. We could walk along the river that runs by the campus and have a talk on neutral ground.

Tom's office door was closed when I got there at two-twenty, so I wandered down the hall to read the bulletin board. Flyers and brochures for archeology field schools and intensive language courses and graduate programs festooned the three-by-five-foot surface and made me want to grab my camera and buy a ticket to some exotic place. When the door was still closed forty minutes later, I raised my hand to knock, but decided that any meeting that went twenty minutes past the end of office hours must be important. I backtracked to the office. A young man I didn't know, probably a work-study helper, was slipping bright yellow flyers into faculty mailboxes.

"Do you happen to know if Dr. Saunders is with a student?"

He answered without looking at me. "He left about an hour ago."

"But he has office hours on Thursday."

"Not today."

"Was he okay?"

"Far as I know."

All sorts of panicky thoughts pranced around my mind. I'd never known Tom to cancel a class or office hours. Was he sick? Was something wrong with Winnie? Had she been hurt in the previous night's events? What about Drake? Then I thought about the things I had said after Winnie the Ripper's adventures in paper art, and a ball of lead dropped into my stomach. Had Tom decided not to move in with me? Wasn't that what I wanted, what I had told him, more or less? *Okay, more.* When I got to my van, I tilted the seat back as far as it would go and laid my arm across my eyes and stayed there, just trying to breathe, for a few minutes. Then I called Tom's cell. No answer, not even his voice mail.

I had promised my mother I would stop by Shadetree Retirement Home, and I forced myself to follow through. Jade Templeton, the manager, saw me walking toward the solarium and called, "Janet! I believe your mother went back to her room with your brother." I thanked her, wondering what Bill was doing there in the middle of the day, and she added, "We're all so excited about Saturday's nuptials!"

It was brother-in-law Norm, not Bill, in my mother's room with her. Mom was giddy and glowing, and he was almost as excited as she was.

"Oh, Janet!" Mom said, grabbing me in a smothering hug. Love had been good for her, I thought, and realized with a pang that it had been good for me, too, over the previous year. I had to find Tom as soon as possible.

Mom finally released me and scurried to her bureau. She picked up a plastic bag and handed it to me with a giggle. "For that handsome boy of yours." Calling Tom a boy struck me odd, but I opened the bag and pulled out a black bow tie with silver dots all over it. That seemed even odder until I saw it was attached to a matching dog collar. Mom said, "It's Jay's tux for the wedding!"

Norm grinned at me, and I smiled and looked at Mom. "You want Jay at the wedding?"

"Of course! And I got one for Drake, too!" She picked up another bag and held it out. "Give it to Tom for me." She lowered her voice and said, "I think the puppy is a little young. I hope Tom's feelings won't be hurt."

I've already seen to that, I thought.

Tony Marconi, the happy bridegroom, appeared in the doorway, and greetings quickly turned to last-minute logistics. Norm confirmed that I planned to be there in the morning to help decorate the solarium and that yes, I had an appointment to "do something about" my hair. I claimed to have a photo shoot and left Norm with the lovebirds. As I hurried down the hall, he called after me. "Family dinner tomorrow evening at our house. See you at six!"

Tom still didn't answer his phone, so I left a message. When he still hadn't called back by four-thirty, I had cycled through several stages of phone grief. First was shock that he hadn't called back all afternoon. Then anger, its target evenly distributed between the two of us. Bargaining came next—if he calls, I'll do my best to have a rational discussion about my fears and our future. *Really.* If I remembered correctly, the final stage should have been acceptance, but one afternoon just wasn't enough time for that. Besides, I was worried. I called again, but got a recording saying his voice mail box was full. It just wasn't like Tom not to return my calls, or check his voice mail, and he must know I was trying to apologize. At least I hoped he knew that.

Another thought came unbidden as I puttered around the house. What if something had happened to him? What if he was sick? That would explain why he cancelled his office hours. But what if it was serious? My own dad had died of a heart attack in the middle of a Montana trout stream two decades earlier. He was only fifty-six. The thought that something might have happened to Tom almost gave me a cardiac event of my own, and I grabbed my jacket and keys and ran to the door. Jay was right there, eager to go, but I told him no, not this trip, and took off.

Several cars were parked in driveways and on the street. Until that moment, I hadn't realized how many gray sedans are running around. I could see five of them in my own block, and that vision conjured another. What if Mick Fallon's buddy, the fat goon, had done something to Tom? *Why would he?* It was my inner voice of reason. *To get at you,* said my other voice, the panicky one. *To get the photos they think you have.* I slammed the van into reverse, and may have laid rubber in front of my driveway when I peeled out. By that time, my imagination was in full gallop. *What if those wackos from the night before went after Tom?* I tried to convince myself that they had no reason to target him specifically, and even if they did, they wouldn't know where to find him.

Tom didn't answer the doorbell, and the blinds were down on the garage window so I couldn't tell whether his van was in there. Drake stood wagging at me through the glass panel by the front door. I rang again, waited, and then went around to the back of the house and peered in through the sliding door. All was quiet in the family room. I went back to the front, and stood on the porch for a moment. Finally, I pulled out my keys and let myself in.

"Tom?" I walked through the house, my heart in my mouth, but he wasn't there. Winnie whined and banged around in her crate, and I figured she needed to go out. I took my time with the dogs, hoping Tom would catch us, but no luck. I put Winnie back in her crate with a third of a carrot, gave the rest to Drake, wrote a note, and left it on the counter.

His voice mail was accepting messages again, meaning he had checked in, but he still hadn't called by the time I fell asleep. It was after two a.m.

SEVENTY

Late nights make for sleepy mornings, and I was already running late before I woke up Friday morning. My shower could wait, I decided, until the decorating was done. I fed Jay and the cats, cleaned up after them, pulled on jeans and a sweater, and called Norm to let him know I was on my way.

"No sweat," he said. "I figured you'd be late. We have it under control."

We? Bill had said he couldn't be there to decorate, and I hoped Norm wasn't allowing Mom to help. Her bossy side, the one I'd been accused of inheriting, tended to kick in whenever she tried to work with other people.

I stopped at the Firefly for coffee and a breakfast sandwich and continued south on Anthony. Traffic was light and my sandwich was still hot when I unwrapped it in the Shadetree parking lot. Norm's VW wasn't in the lot, and I realized he must have parked near the back entrance to simplify unloading. I washed my sandwich down with the last of my coffee and pulled my cell phone out of my pocket. One message. I retrieved it, hoping to hear Tom's cheery morning voice, but it was the printer. "Julie passed me your message, Janet. Bummer. Bet that puppy is in the doghouse." Laughter. "Anyway, I'll start reprinting those orders. Looks like a light weekend, so I should have them for you Monday or Tuesday. Oh, this is Eric at … Never mind, you know. Okay, have a good one." At least my livelihood was likely to survive the weekend, if not my love life. I started to call Tom, but ended the call before it went through. The three messages I'd already left were plenty.

The festooning was, as Norm had said, under control, and the transformation of the solarium would have been magical had I been in a more romantic mood. Tiny white lights highlighted a garlanded arbor flanked by an eclectic mix of my mother's favorite flowers—African violets, zinnias, orchids, birds-of-paradise, daisies, and more—all live and growing in cobalt-blue pots.

Norm was arranging folding chairs in a semi-circle in front of the arbor, leaving a path down the center. He rushed to hug me. "Janet, I'm so excited, you'd think it was my own wedding! I wouldn't let Mom in here, told her it was bad luck, which it might be in her case, but Tony popped in a while ago and … oh, dear, I am blathering, aren't I?"

"Blather away, Norm." My shoulders relaxed and a weight dropped off me as Norm's mood caught and lifted me.

"How many more do we need?"

The voice came from behind me, and I turned. "Hi, Tom." My legs went a little shaky as I watched him unfold four more chairs.

"Morning!" Tom kept his voice pitched toward friendly, but he made no move toward our usual hug-and-kiss greeting.

I could feel Norm watching us, and then he said, "Okay then. Janet, could you do the tablecloths? We'll set the cake up there," he pointed at a table near the wall opposite the arbor, "and the rest of the food there, and although Mom and Tony said no gifts, of course there will be gifts. We'll put them on that last table. Maybe move it farther away from the food."

"It's okay, Norm," I said, turning toward him and keeping my voice low. "Don't make such an effort. We'll be fine." *I hope.*

But we weren't fine the rest of the morning. We didn't exactly ignore each other, but we spoke in short, task-oriented sentences until I finally looked at my phone and announced, "Oh, my, I have to get going. I'll just barely make my hair appointment." I didn't add that if I left right then, I would have three hours to drive the two or so miles to the hair salon.

"Thank God." Norm lifted a lock of my hair as if assessing the mess, then burst out laughing. I hugged him and thanked him for all he had done to make Mom's wedding day special. When I let go, Tom was right behind me.

"I'll walk you out."

Neither of us said anything else until we reached the front door. He stepped outside with me, pulled an envelope from his jacket, and said, "I'm sorry about Winnie's little adventure. If this doesn't cover it, let me know and I'll make up the balance."

"This is way too much," I said, peering at the check in the envelope and offering it back. "Let me get the invoice and—"

"Nah, take it. If it's too much, you can take us out for a fancy dinner." He smiled, and as I looked into his warm brown eyes I felt tears rise in my own. Tom wrapped his arms around me and said, "You worry too much." We stood like that for a moment, and then he whispered, "Now go get your hair done before Norm has a breakdown."

"But we need to talk."

He took my hands in his and said, "We do. But let's get through tonight and tomorrow first."

It wasn't until later that I thought those words might be a warning.

SEVENTY-ONE

GOLDIE CAUGHT ME LEAVING the house for my hair appointment and sent me back in. "Put on a nice top and some makeup so they take you seriously. For heaven's sake."

"This from a woman who hasn't cut her hair since nineteen sixty-seven?"

When I walked into *Chez Charles*, though, I was glad she had made me dress for the occasion, although I wondered briefly whether I might not need a space suit. The place, all chrome and white plastic, looked like it might take off, and a few of the patrons could have been aliens, judging by their multi-hued sticky-out hair. I half expected Tommy Lee Jones and Will Smith to show up as *Men in Black*.

Chas—Charles of *Chez Charles*—sat me down and stood behind me, assessing my reflection in the mirror with his lips pouched into an O that made me think of Pixel. My three requirements were that the cut be pretty much wash-and-wear, that it not require a lot of goop to hold it in place, and that it not be too short. Beyond that, I decided to take Norm's advice to heart and just relax and let Chas work his magic. I had him turn me away from the mirror so I couldn't be tempted to stop him.

When he finally spun me back to my reflection forty minutes later, I thought the mirror had been removed and I was staring at one of the aliens. But if I was, Chas had a twin who was also staring back at us, and he and the Chas behind me were gushing, "I *love* it!"

What was left of my hair stuck out in all directions and multiple lengths. I clamped my teeth together and slowly reached up to touch it. The clumps were stiff and sticky to the touch, and barely moved when my fingers pressed against them.

"Oh my God," I said when I could get my jaws apart far enough.

"I *knew* you'd love it!"

"I don't love it," I said, my voice coming back and getting louder with every word. "I've seen better looking roadkill!"

"Now, Jan, just—"

"It's Janet, and just nothing." Patrons and stylists were turning my way, and I looked at the woman on my left and said, "Does this look like something anyone would do intentionally?" She shook her head. I pulled the smock off with a *zzzzzppp* of Velcro letting go, and pushed myself out of the chair.

"But it looks so rad."

"It looks like revenge!" My voice broke as my anger gave way to horror. "I would have been better off going to a dog groomer." I grabbed my tote bag and glared at Chas. "If you think I'm paying for this, you're nuttier than I look." I tried to pat some of the spikes down with my palm, but no luck. "This crap better wash out."

I stormed out the door and down the sidewalk, blinded by a stew of emotions, and missed the curb. My left ankle turned and I swear I heard something tear just before my hands and knees hit the asphalt with a joint-jarring thud. The rough black surface took several layers of skin from my palms, and my right knee seemed to balloon on contact. I rolled onto my behind and just sat there a moment, wondering why falling down hurts so much more than it did twenty years ago.

"Are you okay?" It was a young woman in a suit, heels, and a normal haircut, and she was leaning toward me. "Do you need help? Are you hurt?" She was staring at me, and I could tell that her concern wasn't entirely due to my tumble.

"Just my pride," I said, knowing it was a stretch. "I'm just furious about this ridiculous haircut." She nodded. I thanked her for helping me up, picked up my bag, and jumped into my van, afraid someone I knew might see me. I fished around in my tote bag until I came up with a baby wipe and Jay's pin brush. The wipe stung, but showed that the scrapes were superficial. Then I grabbed the brush. If anything could fight its way through the mess that had been my curly hair, those metal pins could.

But they couldn't. The shellac Chas had dumped into my hair trapped the brush and I had to fight to get it back. I swore as I pulled a clump of hair out of my scalp and stared at the mirror. My mascara had run, giving me an electrocuted Goth look. *Perfect.*

Goldie was gathering a bouquet of tulips from the border between her front yard and mine when I pulled into the driveway, so slinking into my house unseen was out of the question, and when I stepped out of the van, she froze in place as if she had met Medusa. I took a step and almost fell as a bolt of pain shot through my left ankle and leapt to my right knee as I overcorrected.

"What happened to you?" Goldie had dropped the flowers and run to support me. "Were you assaulted? Should I call the police?"

Pain, anger, and bad-hair blues had brought me to the brink of tears, but the idea of calling the police on Chas started me giggling. I leaned back against the car, wrapped Goldie up in a one-armed hug, and laughed until I was crying.

"Janet, calm down."

"I'm fine," I said, swiping my sleeve over one eye, then the other. "Not fine, actually, but not hysterical."

"If you say so."

I tried to walk, but my ankle wasn't having it, and Goldie pulled my slacks up for a look. The joint was twice its normal size and turning an ominous shade of ruddy mauve. "Aw, crap," I said.

"I'll help you to my car and take you to the emergency room."

"No, I'll just ice it. The wedding . . . the dinner tonight." I unconsciously started to run my fingers through my hair, but they went in as far as the first knuckles and hit concrete. I yanked my hand out and said, "And anyway, I can't be seen in public like this!" I wanted to bawl.

"Phooey." She moved in under my arm to support me again and said, "It might be broken, and who cares about your hair."

When Goldie got back to her car with her purse, keys, and two plastic bags full of ice chips for my ankle and knee, I said, "I called my doctor. The nurse told me to go to the emergency room, not the office." I pulled the visor down and stared at the mirror, trying to pull some of the ridiculousness from my hair. If anything, I made it worse. That was confirmed by the emergency room volunteer's expression when he brought a wheelchair to the car. I wondered what he thought had happened to me.

Goldie parked the car and found me just as the check-in clerk called me to her counter. I'd met her before, but she didn't seem to remember. She was focused on her computer screen. "Are you in our system?"

When my name and social security number brought up my record, the corners of her shiny red lips twitched and then blossomed into a big smile. "I remember you," she said.

"Hello, LaFawn."

"How's your butt?" She giggled. She had checked me in after an unfortunate incident the previous fall. Now she looked at me and said, "Girl, that does look like an emergency, but we don't do hair here."

"I'd forgotten how funny you are, LaFawn." But she had me laughing by then, and I wondered whether they could just shave my head after they checked my ankle.

SEVENTY-TWO

My ankle wasn't broken, and Goldie's ice had brought the swelling down to a manageable puffiness by the time we left for dinner. She had also managed to wash the "product" out of my hair and the cut itself turned out to be a little shorter than I'd wanted, but shapely. I assured Goldie that I was fine to drive and we took my car.

Norm hugged me and then studied my hair and said, "Now see! I told you Chas would shape your hair up!" Goldie made a zipping motion across her lips and I bit my tongue. I couldn't completely hide my limp, though, and Norm sat me down in Bill's recliner with pillows on the footrest to raise my feet. Tom arranged ice packs on my ankle and knee and asked, "How in the world did this happen?"

I glanced at Norm and back to Tom. "Tell you later."

"You boys have done so much to the house." Mom had lived in that house since we were kids, but she hadn't been back since we moved her to Shadetree and Bill and Norm moved in. I couldn't tell whether she was impressed or appalled by the changes they had made—a wall gone between the dining and living rooms, flooring changed, kitchen cabinets reconfigured. "I can't wait to see what you do with the gardens."

Bill didn't seem to get it, but Norm did. Her garden was my mother's masterpiece, nurtured over the years with love and back-break and sweat. Norm took her hand and squeezed. "Why would we change the gardens, Mom? They're perfect! We'll be bringing you over for frequent consults once the weather warms up."

Mom was radiant and her beau, Tony Marconi, looked proud as a peacock despite his cane. Tony's daughter, Louise, reflected her father's happiness, and I was glad to see that she seemed fully recovered from the sudden death of her husband a few months earlier. Jade Templeton, the manager at Shadetree, had become a good friend and had championed this romance between Tony and my mother, and she was beaming. It was a lovely group, and I was glad the dinner was not in an impersonal restaurant. It was also a relief to have a few hours of conversation with no mention of murder or larceny, stalkers or fraud.

We were almost home when Goldie finally asked, "What's up with you and Tom?" I didn't answer and she dropped it, but I knew she would circle back eventually. She changed subjects when we turned onto our street. "Well, someone's having a party here, too."

There must have been forty vehicles parked along both sides of the street, and some of the drivers hadn't been too fussy about who else they inconvenienced, especially whoever owned the Lincoln that was blocking half of my driveway. I did a mental scan of my refrigerator contents and asked, "You have any eggs?"

Goldie laughed and said, "Don't even think about it."

"I like thinking about it."

"Let me move my car over and you can park in my driveway."

"It's okay, there's a place there." I drove to the end of the block, made a U-turn, and pulled into the one available space smack in front of Councilman Phil Martin's living room window. His house was dark, but it was only eight o'clock on a Friday night. As if she were reading my thoughts, Goldie said, "Maybe he has a date," and we both started to laugh.

"Yeah, maybe. I wonder how things are going between Chelsea and 'Daddy' since her run-in with the law. And the press."

Goldie offered to help me in, but my ankle was feeling pretty good, and my knee was tender only to the touch, so I declined. "Why don't you bring Bonnie over? The dogs can have a romp and we can have a nightcap."

I changed into sweats and Crocs and took Jay out back. Goldie and Bonnie joined us, and the two dogs played chase around the yard for a few minutes. It was a clear, crisp evening with barely a trace of wind. A scatter of stars danced across a moonless sky and the first hint of honeysuckle hovered over the backyard. Finally, though, the cool air turned cold and we called the dogs and went inside.

"Bonnie seems to have settled in nicely."

"She's such a dear," Goldie said, the love in her voice palpable.

We talked a bit about the police investigation, but neither of us knew anything new. Around nine-thirty, Jay raised his head to listen and Bonnie jumped to her feet, raced to the front window, and started to bark. We heard voices and car doors and engines starting, and I knew the party must be over.

"Bonnie, quiet! Be quiet!"

Bark bark bark.

My first reaction was *good luck with that—she's a Sheltie,* but then I remembered watching Ray handle her. I said in a normal voice, "Bonnie, that'll do." She let out one more woof, then trotted back to the kitchen, stopped at Goldie's knee for an ear-scratch, and lay down beside Jay.

"That was magical."

"I saw Ray work with her."

Quiet returned outside, and our conversation turned to the trouble between Tom and me. Goldie listened silently as I spilled my fear and desires, doubts and dreams, all over the table. We sat in more silence for a few minutes, and finally she said, "A solution will appear."

"What do you mean?"

She shrugged. "I don't know. I just feel that a solution, a compromise, will present itself." She smiled at me. "I know that's a bit too airy-fairy hippie-dippie for you, Janet, but you'll see. All will be we—"

Bonnie cut her off with an explosion of barking, and this time Jay joined her. They raced to the living room, jumped onto the couch and barked out the window, both heads cranked toward Phil Martin's house.

"Bonnie, that'll do!" Goldie said. Bonnie turned to look at her, but jumped off the couch and ran to the back door, barking like there was no tomorrow.

Jay was very agitated, his paws on the back of the couch, his voice varying from low and booming to high-pitched and frantic. I moved to the window and looked out. Martin's car had materialized in his driveway, but the street seemed to be deserted. Bonnie scurried back to the couch and the two of them barked and looked at us and barked and looked out the window and barked some more.

"Maybe there's a dog out there, or something?" Goldie asked, leaning against me to see out.

"Maybe," I said, but I didn't think so. "I'm going to look from the backyard."

I could barely get the door open for the dogs trying to shove past me. They shot off the patio and straight to the fence, the very definition of raising hell. I started to run after them, but the step off the patio set my ankle on fire and I had to slow down. The dogs were running back and forth along a twenty-foot section of fence, barking and stopping to jump against the chain-link as if frantic to get past it. Martin's yard and the rooms at the back of his house were dark, and at first I couldn't see anything. Goldie's voice made me jump, it was so close, but she didn't seem to notice. "The sliding door isn't closed."

"How can you tell?"

She pointed and said "Look."

A dark curtain floated out the door, fluttered in the rising wind, and disappeared. And then we heard, just barely over the frantic barking, a crash, and a scream.

SEVENTY-THREE

THE SCREAM FROM PHIL Martin's house was followed by yelling, but I couldn't make out the words. Jay and Bonnie raced up and down the fence between Martin's yard and mine, and how they managed not to crash into one another was a mystery. Goldie and I turned toward the gate, and I was deciding whether to take the dogs with us when Bonnie made the decision for herself, clearing the four-foot fence with room to spare.

"Oh!" Goldie's eyes went wide at the sight of her dog flying over that fence. She turned and ran for the gate. I gimped along behind her.

Bonnie raced across Martin's backyard and disappeared through the open door. Jay was lining up to follow her over the fence when I called him. He ran along the side of my house toward the gate and shoved it out of his way as soon as I released the latch. Goldie's long hair had come unpinned and was like a silver banner as she whirled past the gatepost and began to run. I ignored the pain in my ankle as well as I could, but it still slowed me down and Jay and Goldie were out of sight around the back of Phil Martin's house by the time I rounded the corner.

A popping sound came from inside the house and I yelled, "Goldie! Gun! Don't go in there! Jay!"

Too late. The dogs had disappeared past the flapping curtain and into the house.

"Bonnie!" Goldie was almost to the open slider and still running. "Wait! Look!"

She stopped and turned toward me as I picked up the garden rake Martin had left leaning against the back of his house. "Good idea," she said, looking around for a weapon of her own.

The house was dark but alive with sound. Bonnie alternated between high-pitched yips and the sorts of snarls you hear in a tug-o-war game. Deeper, more business-like growls told me Jay had joined the fray. I found a switch and light flooded the kitchen and guided me toward the front of the house. My ankle was on fire, threatening to quit, and I used the kitchen table as a crutch as I crossed the room.

Human voices mingled with the barking and snarling. Something hit the floor and slid, and I hoped it was the gun. A man yelled, "Get off maauugghhh!" followed by an impressive series of expletives and then, "My arm" and a howl of pain. I thought I knew the voice. Despite the desperation and change in pitch, I was pretty sure it was the goon, Albert Zola. But what had he to do with Councilman Martin?

The living room was aswirl with dogs, men, and long shadows. One of the men stood a little to the side and appeared to be swaying as he reached for something. He let out a long moan, spun a quarter turn, and fell to the floor. That had to be Martin, and I wondered whether he was injured or just overwhelmed.

The dogs had targeted the other man, and his curses and howls increased in volume. I was sure now that the voice belonged to Mick Fallon's partner, Albert Zola. Bonnie continued to bark, with sporadic breaks to dive at the man's legs.

"Hit him!" It was Goldie. "Don't let him hurt the dogs!"

The goon was whirling one way, then the other. In the dim light, he and Jay appeared to be engaged in some bizarre tug game, but Jay's snarling didn't sound remotely like play.

"Goldie, do you see a light switch?"

I heard a wall switch click, but nothing happened. I stepped in closer to the fracas, hoping to see well enough to conk Zola. Jay's body slammed into my leg and when I landed on my left foot, I thought the pain that rocketed through my ankle and up my leg might knock me flat.

Light flooded the room. Goldie had found the chain for a floor lamp.

"Get them off me!" Desperation twisted Zola's voice and pitched it so high it was almost unintelligible. Jay had a firm grip on the man's wrist and seemed to be trying to dislocate his arm. Bonnie snapped at his calf, his butt, his ankle, raising a bark-storm between strikes.

I held the rake up, tine-end toward the man's chest, handle gripped like a javelin. "Stop fighting and I'll call them off." One side of the man's face seemed to be a mass of scabs, as if he'd exfoliated with a vegetable grater, but it was so contorted with pain and fear that I wasn't sure what else was wrong.

"Okay! Okay!"

"I'm calling an ambulance," said Goldie. "Martin is hurt."

Zola flailed at Jay's head with his free hand.

"I said stand still," I aimed the end of the rake at his face. "If you try to hit my dog again, I'll shove this rake into your face."

"Okay, just get it off me!" He held his free hand up in surrender. There was nothing funny about the moment, with my neighbor lying injured on the floor, but when I remembered the scene later, I wished someone had videotaped the last few seconds. Jay had lost his grip on the man's wrist but was still yanking on his shirt and jacket sleeves and had pulled the shoulder seams halfway to Zola's elbow. Bonnie had him by the front of his pants, and judging by the look on his face, she had more than fabric between her teeth.

"Are you going to stand still?"

"Yeah! Yeah!"

"Jay, drop it."

Goldie was on the floor beside Martin. She called, "Bonnie, that'll do."

Bonnie released Zola's fly and ran to Goldie. Jay rolled his eyes at me, still holding the sleeves. I forced my voice to be low and calm. "It's okay now. Drop it." He let go but kept his eyes on the man.

Sirens broke through the sudden silence, distant but getting louder. I glanced at Goldie, but she was busy pressing a chair-arm cover against Martin's shoulder. "Did you call for help?" I asked.

"No, but we need to. He's been shot."

I turned my attention back to the man in front of me and took my hand off the back end of the rake handle to get my cell phone. The attacker saw his chance. He raised his arms, fingers spread, and lunged toward me.

SEVENTY-FOUR

ONCE AGAIN, MY YEARS of observing animals paid off. I sensed more than saw the beginning of movement when the thug from Cleveland made his move. I regained my grip on the rake handle just as he started to lunge toward me and thrust the flat edge of the tines into his face. The metal bar hit his nose with a stomach-turning crunch and snapped his head back. Blood spilled past his howling mouth and onto his shirt. When he spoke, the words were hard to make out. All I got was, "… you later," and fear traced a path down my spine.

The sirens were loud now, and flashing red lights filled the room. Zola staggered backward a few steps before he turned and ran out the way we had come in. Jay started to chase him, but stopped when I told him to lie down. Two police cruisers parked in front of the house and I moved to the front door to let the officers in. Bill Washington, Martin's neighbor on the other side, met them on the lawn and had a few words. I didn't know any of the police officers, and once they were inside and partly up to speed, I retreated to the kitchen and called Hutchinson.

After I gave him the basics, I said, "He's hurt, Hutch. I don't know how badly, but I probably broke his nose, and I think he has some dog bites on his arm and legs and possibly his privates."

"What?"

"Bonnie had him by the fly."

When Hutch stopped laughing, he said, "You shouldn't have gone in there, Janet," but then he relented and said, "but I have to admit, I feel a bit sorry for any bad guy who takes on you and your friends, furry or otherwise." He said he was on his way and would alert law enforcement and area medical facilities to be on the look-out for a heavy-set guy with a scabby face, a broken nose, and dog bites.

An ambulance arrived a few minutes later for Martin. He was conscious, but barely, from what I could tell. They were pulling away when I sat down beside Goldie to ask if she knew which hospital they would take him to. Jay sat beside me and leaned into me, and I wrapped an arm around his shoulders.

"Parkview." She was sitting cross-legged on the floor, hugging Bonnie to her chest and rocking back and forth.

"I think you might want to wash up," I said, and she followed my gaze to her blood-smeared hands.

"Yes, I guess I should," she said. "It was Martin's own gun, the fool. He said he pulled it from that drawer to 'defend himself.'" She gestured toward an end table and shook her head. "The guy took it away from him and shot him."

"How bad?"

She shrugged. "I'm no nurse. I know enough, though, to know he was lucky it wasn't six inches lower." She placed her hand over her heart.

One of the police officers squatted in front of Goldie and said, "Ma'am, do you need medical attention?" When Goldie said no, she wasn't hurt, the officer turned to me. "I noticed you were limping. Are you injured?"

"No. Well, yes, but not from this fiasco. I sprained my ankle earlier. It just hurts a bit."

Officer Judith Mason nodded, and then earned a huge gold star in my book when she asked whether either dog needed veterinary attention. She told Goldie she could clean up if she wanted, but asked us not to leave until they sorted things out.

We just sat for a few minutes, each lost in our own thoughts. Goldie finally broke the silence. "Janet, that was the guy, right? The one from Dom's Deli? The buddy of the guy who was killed at Blackford's?"

"That's him."

"Why in the world would he be after Councilman Martin?"

"I've been thinking about that," I said, "and I have a terrible feeling he got the wrong house."

Goldie stared at me for a moment, and then said, "Your car."

I nodded. My car was parked in front of Martin's house because I hadn't been able to get into my own driveway when we got home earlier. What if the guy had been looking for me, or for the pictures they seemed to think I had? What if he had still been looking for Summer and thought I knew where she was?

"Janet, what if he comes back?"

"My thought exactly," said a masculine voice behind me. Hutchinson stepped into view, squatted in front of us, and stroked Jay's cheek. "But first things first. Are you all okay?" When he was convinced that we were, he said, "Okay, ladies. I would prefer that you pack up your animals and stay somewhere else until we catch this guy. I can't make you do that, but … Janet, I think you should go to Tom's and if he has room, take Goldie and her crew with you."

The last thing I wanted to do was explain my romantic troubles to Hutchinson. "Hutch, my mom's wedding is tomorrow. I can't, I mean, I need things here, at home."

"I'm not leaving my home either," said Goldie.

Hutchinson let out an "I-knew-it" sigh. "Okay. I'm posting a car to watch both your houses. Leave your outside lights on, and as many inside lights as you can sleep through."

Sleep? He thinks we'll sleep after all this?

We answered questions and handed over phone numbers, and Hutch had Officer Mason escort us home. She checked my locks, had me turn on every light in and outside the house, and moved on to Goldie's house. When she was gone, I lay down on the couch with my feet pressed into Jay's belly and a cat on each side. I pulled my favorite fleece throw over us and settled in, expecting to replay everything that had happened all night long. The next thing I knew, my phone was vibrating in my pocket and the sun was up.

SEVENTY-FIVE

EVEN THE CRITTERS SLEPT in Saturday morning until Norm woke us with a phone call at eight-fourteen. He wanted to know what time I would be at Shadetree to help Mom get ready for the wedding. "It's so cute," he said. "She's quite the blushing bride!"

"I know. I'm really happy for them." *Maybe there's still hope for me.* Not that I aspired to blushing bride status, but the love and happiness were on my bucket list, if I could figure out how to have them and my autonomy, too.

After I assured Norm that I would be there in plenty of time, I hobbled to the window and looked out. A police car was still parked there, but the street was quiet otherwise. I fed the animals and woke Mr. Coffee up. My ankle loosened up a bit as I walked. It was still swollen, although not as much, but the bruise had blossomed in disturbing shades of purple. I had been planning to wear a pair of two-inch heels that hadn't been out in public in about three years, but decided I'd better stick with flats. In the meantime, I wanted to see whether Joe had returned to his home behind Blackford's Farm and Garden and stop by the hospital to check on Phil Martin. I didn't like the guy, but guilt was eating at me. After all, Zola had probably been looking for me when he was misled by my van in front of Martin's house.

Blackford's was open by the time I got there, but I parked near the back alley, not the door. I had picked up two breakfast sandwiches, a large coffee, and two bottles of water on my way. Even if Joe was still hiding, I felt pretty sure he would pick up the food and drinks if I left them where he would see them.

The blanket and shower curtain were down over the opening to Joe's box home, indicating that he might be there. "Joe?" I waited, then tried again. "Joe, it's Janet. I just wanted to be sure you're okay." Nothing. "Okay, well, I was supposed to meet a friend for breakfast, but she didn't show up. I had already ordered her food, and, well, I didn't want to waste it, so I'll just set it here, inside your door."

I squeezed between the recycle bin and the wall to get to the alcove, careful not to rub against them, and moved the coverings over Joe's doorway just enough to set the paper bag inside. I wanted to look inside in case he was in there sick or injured, but couldn't bring myself to invade his privacy that way. I stood and waited another moment, scanning the alley and listening to a cardinal singing in a nearby tree. Finally I turned around to return to my car and saw Joe entering the alley from the parking lot. I walked toward him and smiled.

"Hi, Joe."

He wore a blue plaid flannel shirt over a red sweater, brown chinos, and high tops. He wasn't much of a fashion statement, but I was always surprised at how clean and tidy he kept himself under the circumstances. He had a bottle of pop and a Butterfinger in his hands. His hair looked damp, and I guessed that he had made the purchase at the gas station across the road and used their bathroom to clean up.

Joe had pulled two battered but functional folding chairs out from behind his box for the two of us and he was just digging into his second sandwich when he froze mid-bite. He stared at something behind me, eyes wide. I glanced around and quickly back at Joe. "It's okay," I said. "He's a friend of mine."

"Cop?"

"Yes, a detective. You can trust him."

Joe didn't look too sure about that, but he resumed chewing.

"Janet, what are you doing here?"

I interpreted the question to mean "Why are you sticking your nose into police matters again?" but I just smiled and said, "Having breakfast with my friend Joe. What are you doing here?"

The back door of Blackford's opened and Ralph Blackford stepped out, a trash bag in his hand. He looked startled to see us, but seemed to grasp what was happening and stayed where he was.

Hutch held a hand toward Joe and introduced himself. "Joe, we're looking into a murder committed back here on Tuesday evening. If you have a little time, I'd like to ask you some questions."

"I had to do it!" Joe started to stand, and my heart fell to the pavement.

Hutchinson's voice stayed calm and he held his palms toward Joe in a placating gesture. "Whoa, whoa. Let's slow down." He squatted beside my chair. I knew the gesture was meant to make him less threatening to Joe, and I was still trying to put that together with Joe's apparent confession when Hutch spoke again. "What was it you had to do, Joe?"

"Wait a second." It was Blackford. "Should Joe have an attorney?"

Hutchinson smiled at Joe. "You're not a suspect. I'd just like to know if you saw anything that would help us." Joe nodded, and Hutch went on. "What was it you had to do, Joe?"

I held my breath, expecting Joe to confess to Mick Fallon's murder, although I had no idea why he would have had Evan Winslow's shotgun.

"Hit him!" He practically shouted it. "I had to hit him!"

"What did you hit him with?"

I noticed that Hutchinson wasn't taking notes as he usually did. He was looking directly at Joe, something a lot of people don't do with the homeless.

"Two-by-four," said Joe. "I keep it there," he pointed, "under the dumpster. Just in case."

"Joe, who did you hit?"

"Those bad men, the one that got shot and the other one." He popped the last of his sandwich into his mouth and chewed hard, staring at Hutchinson. He swallowed and drank some coffee, and spoke again. "One of them is dead."

"Yes." Hutch nodded.

"I didn't do that. Not really."

Not really? I couldn't imagine what he meant by that, but Hutchinson just nodded again.

"Okay. Why did you hit him?"

"Both of them." Joe picked up his Butterfinger and broke it into four pieces. He laid one on his knee and offered the other pieces to Hutch, Ralph, and me. I begged off, blaming my dentist, and Ralph said he had just eaten, but Hutch took a piece and nibbled the end. Joe studied him for a bit and finally said, "Maybe just one. The one with the gun. They were trying to kidnap that lady."

"That's terrible," said Hutch, and Joe nodded but didn't speak. "So you hit him to protect her?"

"Had to." Joe squirmed in his chair, and when he spoke again, his voice was very soft. "I didn't mean to ..."

Hutch waited a beat, and then tried again. "What happened when you hit him?"

"They didn't know I was there. I saw them follow that lady to her truck, and she saw them and pulled the gun from the rack, you know, one of those gun racks some trucks have? She was pretty. She had pretty hair."

Summer. "Did she have long red hair, Joe?"

"Black hair, red hair. And she turned around but he shoved her into the side of the truck and her hair almost fell off and he grabbed the gun and the other one said now they had her and and and—"

Her hair almost fell off? Black hair, red hair? What did that mean? And then it clicked. Summer had worn a dark wig in the picture from Reno. I thought of the woman I had seen going into Phil Martin's house, the dark-haired one I had thought moved like Summer. I was sure now that it *was* Summer I had seen.

If Summer was in this alley with a truck, then Evan knew she wasn't missing. I thought back to the day we found Rosie the sheep's grave at the farm. Giselle had thought someone was in the yarn shop, although no one answered her knock. It must have been Summer. I was practically bursting to talk this out with Hutch, but this wasn't the time or place. Joe needed to finish his story.

"Okay, and then what happened?" asked Hutch, gently putting the brakes on Joe's delivery.

"I crawled through there," he gestured to the space between the recycle bin and the building, "and hit him with my two-by-four." Joe swung an imaginary bat. "Whomp! I hit him hard in the back of the legs and he sort of slipped and stumbled and I think he dropped the shotgun and bam! there was an explosion, you know, a blast, and and and—"

"And he was accidentally shot?"

Joe shook his head. "The gun shot them."

"Them?" Hutch and I spoke at the same time.

"Yes, but only the one with the gun died. The other was just marked." Joe looked thoughtful and turned to me and lowered his voice to a stage whisper. "Some people might say it was an accident, but it wasn't."

Just when I felt hopeful for Joe, my heart took another nosedive, but I whispered back, "What do you mean, Joe?" and held my breath.

"Angels watch," he said. "They see what we do and they give us what we deserve. An angel saw what those men tried to do, and caught that gun."

SEVENTY-SIX

JOE'S THEORY ABOUT ANGELS was still on my mind as I walked into Parkview Hospital and asked for Phil Martin's room. Based on the number of people already there, you might have thought the guy was well-liked, but the angry voices wafting out the door suggested otherwise. I peeked around the doorframe and tried to sort out the scene.

Martin was propped up in bed, his face pallid and moist. Tom nodded at me from the far side of the room, and Hutchinson stood near the foot of the bed. A well-coiffed, well-preserved woman maybe ten years my senior owned the loudest of the voices. I had seen her enter the room as I got off the elevator, and now I recognized her from photos and TV news. Martin's wife. She had her hand clamped around Chelsea's upper arm and if I hadn't side-stepped, she would have shoved the younger woman straight into me. "Stay away from him," she hissed. "You've done enough damage." Then she fixed her angry gray eyes on me and said, "Who are you?"

Part of me wanted to ask her the same question for etiquette's sake, but I decided she deserved a break. I offered my hand and said, "Janet MacPhail. I live next door to Councilman Martin."

"Former Councilman," she said, and then her expression shifted from anger to something I couldn't define, something suggestive of mutual interest. "I'm Anna Martin. You're the woman with the dogs."

"One dog," I said. "But yes, that's probably me."

"Thank you for saving my husband's life."

"Oh, no, that wasn't me," I said. "That was another neighbor, Goldie Sunshine. She stopped the bleeding."

She looked confused. "So two women came to his rescue?"

I smiled at her. "And two dogs, actually. Mine and Goldie's."

She gave me a little nod and turned on her husband.

"How did you know about this?" I mouthed the question at Tom, watching Anna Martin and her husband from the corner of my eye. Judging by his wife's posture, I wasn't sure the Councilman was out of danger quite yet.

"Goldie called me," said Tom, moving toward me and, by default, the door. "Maybe we should leave."

"No, don't go." It was Phil Martin.

Hutchinson cleared his throat and said, "I just have a few questions, Councilman, but I can come back."

Martin dismissed that idea with a wave.

"Okay, sir. Do you have any idea why you were attacked?"

Martin shook his head, and his wife jumped in. "They were looking for that woman, the one who was blackmailing you." Martin seemed to shrink under her glare, and he flinched when she spat, "The red head."

Martin's eyes went wide and what little color was left abandoned his face. "What—"

"She came to me. To me! For God's sake, Philip. She wanted money to get away. She told me about your little scheme."

Hutch looked at me and I shrugged.

"Did she show you—"

Anna sounded like she wanted to spit on Martin. "No, dear, she didn't show me the photos. She didn't have to."

"What did you, I mean, did you give her—"

"Money? Not on your life."

"But wait," I said. "Why did she want to leave?"

Anna gave me a one-shoulder shrug. "Phil wasn't her first fool. I guess she finally picked one she couldn't bully with her dirty pictures. Not like this one." She pointed her chin at Martin and paused as if considering whether to tell us more. "She said there were two men looking for her, employees," she sneered the word, "of a thug of some sort from Toledo or Cincinnati—"

"Cleveland," said Hutchinson.

"Whatever. She said her own stupid husband got himself in trouble with some unsavory people and they came looking for him. Her bad luck he played poker with a gentleman she conned in Las Vegas."

"Reno," said Hutchinson

Anna shot him a look. Then she turned back to her husband and said, "You've had your fun, Phil. Now grow up. You're resigning from the Council for health reasons, but first you're going to withdraw that ridiculous pet limit bill your little friend seduced you into putting forward. You're getting rid of that house and you're coming home. And if you see that little tramp again, you'll wish the shooter had aimed better." She started to turn, but added, "And you'd better get that little chippy's bail money back." She stopped on her way to the door and took my arm. "I'd like to take you and your friend—Goldie, is it?—to lunch one day soon."

307

When she was gone, I turned toward Martin. He looked like he might need a nice big drip bag of morphine.

"I hear you're going to be fine," I said.

He nodded and cleared his throat. "I'm sorry for ... well, I'm sorry. Thank you. I wish I could thank your dogs. They ..." He sniffed and shook his head.

"You can thank them," I said. "Do what your wife asked. Withdraw the bill. It's a bad law." He nodded but didn't say anything. I was about to apologize for my role in the attack, which I still thought was a case of mistaking Martin's house for mine, but he started to speak again. "I've made a lot of mistakes. I don't know what got into me. Those young women."

Hutch and I exchanged a look, but kept quiet.

"I'm an old fool." He gave a sad laugh. "Or as Anna says, a stupid dirty old man. They were just so pretty. They made me feel young—" Martin tried to shift himself in the bed, but caught his breath and grimaced. When he could speak again, he said, "Bella. Beautiful Bella. Bella the bitch."

Bella Verano. That was one of Summer's aliases.

Martin's tone shifted to a snarl. "And her old man."

"Evan?" I blurted.

"Who's Evan?" Martin asked. "I'm talking about her husband. Fancies himself a cowboy. Rex something." Or Ray Turnbull, I thought, before Martin cut me off again. "He's the muscle, but she's the dangerous one. She's the brains."

I wanted to stay and hear more, but I had too many errands to run in too little time, so I excused myself as Hutchinson asked Martin what his wife had meant by "little scheme." I almost turned back when I heard Martin say, "Detective, let me tell you about the crime I almost committed."

SEVENTY-SEVEN

IF MY MOTHER HAD ordered a perfect spring day for her wedding, it could have been only slightly more lovely than the one we had. It could have been warmer, but the sky was a pristine robin's-egg blue so clear it made my heart ache, and the most tentative of breezes swayed the daffodils and tulips and redbuds that were all suddenly in full bloom. Goldie met me and Jay in the driveway. Her colorful skirt and rose-pink peasant blouse set off her silver hair, worn now in a loose upsweep. She carried a book of poems.

"You clean up pretty good," she said. "Turquoise is the perfect color for you. And your hair looks great." She bent to pet Jay. "And you look absolutely dashing in your sparkly bow tie, young man!"

It felt odd to be going to a wedding without my camera gear, but I wanted to be fully in the moment rather than behind a viewfinder. My colleague Susan Traiger had volunteered to take the photos and send them to me as a wedding gift to Mom and Tony. I checked in with her and Jade Templeton when we arrived. Norm was making last-minute adjustments to the chairs and arbor. "Are you okay, Norm? You looked flushed."

He hugged me and laughed. "Did you see the cake?" He steered me to the table. "Isn't it perfect?" It was. Doreen had created the perfect cake for my mother—simple and stunning, a moderate-sized two-tiered affair with delicate multi-hued flowers around the edges. "I was a nervous wreck driving it here," said Norm, drawing me to him with one arm. "I would have died if it had been spoiled." He let go of me and slipped his arm through Goldie's. "I'm going to steal you away to be sure everything you need is all set."

Bill was talking to the two cooks he had hired to prepare the finger foods, but broke away to hug me. "You look great, Sis! You should dress up more often." I thought maybe Bill should help with more weddings, it put him in such a good mood.

"I'll second that." The voice came from behind me and I turned. My heart did a little pirouette when Tom smiled at me. I had never seen him in a tux before, and rarely in a suit, and although I still preferred him in jeans and chambray, the formal duds looked good. Our eyes met and held, and something warm and fearless spilled in waves through me. Tom made an almost imperceptible nod and we moved into one another's arms. He whispered, "You promised you weren't going to cry at this wedding, remember?" We held another moment and I closed my eyes, breathing in his scent and resisting the urge to rip off his clothes.

When we let go, Tom gave me an "I know what you're thinking" wink and I smiled and changed tracks. "Did Martin have anything interesting to say after I left the hospital?"

"Summer and Ray had run a con on Martin when he was in Reno several years ago, just before they were scared into hiding. They never followed through, but Summer still had the photos, and when Martin showed up on her local radar, she went after him."

"And she got him to help her set up an insurance scam?"

"That was the plan. She went home that Friday night, supposedly to stay there and take care of the animals on the farm."

"That explains why Evan didn't question her absence that night," I said.

"Right. She came back with a rented stock trailer and Hugo, the Bouvier, and used him to open the gate and drive the sheep."

I thought back to Summer's near-hysteria the morning the sheep went missing. "She missed her calling as an actress, that's for sure."

Tom agreed and continued. "So Summer called the police and reported the sheep missing, and Martin was supposed to push the paperwork through. Summer threatened to take her photos of their little encounter to the press if he didn't." Tom chuckled. "I almost felt sorry for the guy. Anyway, the sheep were insured for more than their market value, so she would have collected about eight grand." He paused. "That wouldn't have helped Evan much, but I suppose it was a start."

I thought about the note Summer had left Evan. "I don't think it had anything to do with Evan's debt," I said. "I think she was planning to leave, had been planning it for a while."

Tom nodded.

"Let's talk more later, okay? It's all rather depressing, and I don't want anything to spoil these few hours." I excused myself to help my mother, and Tom said he would get the dogs and meet me behind the arbor just before the ceremony.

My job, it seemed, was mostly done when I got to Mom's room. She wore a simple pale sea-green dress and one of her resident friends, a retired hairdresser, had arranged her hair in a soft and simple style. I unboxed her bouquet, a simple mix of lavender, pink roses, and baby's breath. I delivered her to a beaming Tony Marconi and stepped into the solarium.

By the time I got back to the solarium, most of the forty chairs were occupied by family and a few friends plus Shadetree residents and staff. I found Tom and the dogs waiting behind the arbor as promised. Jay and Drake knew something special was afoot, and they pranced and grinned as if to say, "If our people are happy, we're happy!" Tom put an arm around my shoulder and I leaned into him for a moment.

The ceremony was simple and elegant, and it was all I could do to stick to my no-crying promise. Two of Mom's Shadetree friends provided the music, all popular songs from the fifties and sixties arranged for flute and guitar. The bride and groom came in holding hands, and I couldn't remember ever seeing a happier pair. Tom and Drake stood beside Tony, and Jay and I stood with my mother.

Goldie had been certified as a secular celebrant since Indiana legalized secular weddings in twenty-fourteen and she made the ceremony magical. Mom and Tony had written straightforward vows, and Goldie spoke briefly, her theme being "it's never too late for love." *I hope not.* When it came time for the rings—a lovely matched pair of handmade gold bands—I expected Mom to hand her bouquet to me. Instead, she said, "Jay," and he stepped around me, took the bouquet, and sat down to wait as if they'd rehearsed. When Goldie pronounced them "spouse and spouse," a cheer rose from the guests and we all turned toward them. Norm and Bill were holding hands in the front row, and seemed to have their roles reversed— Norm was beaming while my brother wiped his eyes.

As Mom and Tony made their way through their friends, stopping to hug and shake hands, my peripheral vision caught movement in the hall just outside the arched doorway. Something large and moving fast. But when I turned to see, there was nothing.

Jade Templeton appeared in front of me and grabbed me in a rib-cracking hug. "Who would have thought?" When she finally stopped rocking me and stepped back, her mascara was smudged into the smile lines around her eyes. "Your mama has come a long way in the past year. I'm so happy we've been part of her journey."

I started to thank her for standing by the lovers when Tony's former son-in-law tried to ruin it all a few months earlier, but Tom appeared beside me with the dogs. He gave Jade a little hug and turned to me. "It's cool enough outside. I'm going to put the boys in the car. It's too crowded in here and you know they'll wind up mooching."

"No no no!" said Jade. "Put them in my office. Percy's in there. They'll be fine." I should have known she had brought her Poodle with her.

I didn't need to tag along, and my throbbing ankle begged me not to, but I wanted to see if whatever I thought I'd seen in the hallway was still there. It wasn't. Still, I had an unsettled feeling, and it ballooned when Jay dropped his nose to the carpet and growled. I stopped and looked one way, then the other, but nothing seemed out of place. Tom turned toward me from the office door and said, "What's up?"

I shook my head and smiled. "Nothing." I closed the door behind us and pulled Tom to me for a long kiss, the kind I could get lost in, the kind that turns minutes to lifetimes. I barely even noticed the three dogs trying to squeeze between us. When we came up for air, I started to speak but Tom laid a finger on my lips and said, "Not now," and I nodded.

The party was in full swing when we got back, and Norm rushed over. "It's perfect, isn't it?" We agreed. "I'm thinking we'll cut the cake in about ten minutes, before people start to fade. What do you think?"

"Sounds good," I said, scanning the room full of laughing, dancing, chattering people, "but it looks like most of them will be good for a bit longer. Let them enjoy themselves."

Norm hurried off to help infirm hands carry plates of finger food to tables and whatever other host-like things needed doing, and Tom went to get us some punch. I thought I heard Jay bark, which he rarely did, and looked past the doorway and hall to Jade's office door. All seemed quiet. I turned back toward the gathered guests, delighted that everything had gone so well. Mom and Tony were in the center of the main crowd, framed by the arbor thirty feet across the room. I limped toward them.

And so it was that for the second time in four days I had my back to the source when the screaming started.

SEVENTY-EIGHT

THE SCREAM CAME FIRST, frail and wavering. Then a single *pop*, sharp and loud, from behind me. I may have imagined it later in retelling, but I could swear I heard something whizz past my head just before the top of the arbor exploded, setting off a shower of flowers and plastic and tiny white lights.

"He has a gun!" someone yelled.

"Janet!"

I didn't recognize the first voice, but the second was Tom's. As I wheeled around I saw two punch cups fly into the air as he tossed them upward and ran toward me. I stretched my hands toward him, palms out, and shouted, "No! Get down!" but he kept coming. I bent and turned toward the source of the shot, expecting to see the crowd running away.

But they weren't. They were converging on a heavy-set man in the same rumpled brown suit he'd worn the night before. *Zola.* Everything seemed to slow down, and I processed the scene in what could only have been a second or two. A spattering of dark brown stains straddled one shoulder of the man's suit and ran down the

315

front of his jacket, and I realized it must be dried blood. What was it Joe had said? The second man was "marked." Now it made sense. He'd been hit by the spray of buckshot when Mick Fallon was killed. And I was sure I'd broken his nose with the rake.

Even as I turned and ducked, the attacker moved toward me, but he seemed to be pressing his legs together with each step. I pictured Bonnie gripping his crotch and made a mental note to give her a special treat if I got out of this alive. *We all need to get out of this alive.* Yet Tom was running toward me, toward the line of fire.

And people were closing on Zola. I looked into his eyes and realized he may have left a good part of his mind in the alley where Mick Fallon died. I watched the gun come up, the muzzle looking for me. A heavy briar cane came down with an audible *whomp!* on the man's wrist. It was wielded by Tony, my new stepfather. Zola screeched but held onto the gun and brought it back up. It was pointing at me. Something metallic flashed under the lights and came down like a cage over Zola's head, rubber feet pointing my way. A walker.

Tom caught me in his arms without slowing down and pulled me toward the kitchen.

"Wait!" I resisted, and pointed. "Look!"

A man I had often seen snoozing in the atrium raised his arms in victory behind the gunman, grabbed the walker, and slid it back and forth, knocking the frame into the gunman's head and neck with each jerking slide. Zola raised his hands and there was another loud *bang!* and a ceiling tile shattered and rained down. Tony's cane whacked the man's forearm again, and the curved handle of another cane jabbed into his belly. The gun fell to the floor, and Bill grabbed it and dropped it into the punch.

Tom was holding me so tight I could barely breathe, and I realized I too had my hands clamped onto his forearm where it crossed my chest. "Are you hurt?"

"No." And as I watched the scene unfold, I started to laugh. He loosened his grip and we moved toward the melee.

The goon was turning side to side, dodging blows as he tried to pull the walker off his head. He almost had it when a tiny little woman I thought of as the bird lady flung a crocheted shawl over his head, blinding him. Someone drove an oxygen cylinder on wheels into his shin, and a muffled howl rose from under the shawl.

I heard barking over the shouts, and suddenly it got louder. I looked toward Jade's office. The door was open. Jay and Drake raced into the room, Jade Templeton's Poodle, Percy, right behind. The big dogs focused on the strange figure now staggering in circles. Tom called Drake and the dog changed directions, racing toward the voice he loved. Percy looked around and made a beeline for Jade. I called Jay, but it was too late. He had already launched himself at Zola. His paws hit the man square in the chest, and Jay bounced off, spinning as he hit the ground and racing to obey my call. I hugged him to me.

The goon had somehow stayed upright, but it was clear from the staggering and screaming and flailing that it wouldn't take much to finish him. A swath of pale green silk passed between me and Zola. *Mom.*

She reached up and pulled the shawl off the man's head. "Just who do you think you are, crashing my wedding?" She grabbed the legs of the walker and gave them a shove, driving the crossbar into what remained of Zola's nose. He let out a long, blood-chilling howl and staggered backward, arms windmilling as he tried to stay upright.

"Oh no, oh no, oh no!" It was Norm, and he was running toward Zola from the side, trying to avert disaster.

It was too late. The gunman toppled backward onto the folding table. It wasn't made for that kind of weight, and the end he hit collapsed with a loud *crack!* The other end stayed up, its top surface sloped toward Zola. Norm leaped over the man's legs and made a brave effort to intercept the cake as it slid.

He missed.

SEVENTY-NINE

Tom and I finally left Shadetree three hours later. He had driven the newlyweds to their honeymoon hotel while I consoled Norm and helped clean up some of the mess. The ambulance had whisked Zola away under guard long before, but the police took some time asking questions and taking names. The residents seemed to enjoy the process—the ones who stayed awake, at least. Hutchinson had been off-duty but got the call, and since he'd been with Giselle, she insisted on coming along. When she saw the remains of the cake, she had said, "Oh, there has to be wedding cake!" and half an hour later she was back with a reasonable replacement from a nearby Scott's grocery. Norm had put his best face on the cake disaster.

Tom had to swing by his house to get Winnie, and I was lying on the couch with Jay and the cats, my ankle elevated and wrapped in ice, when my cell phone vibrated.

It was Hutch. "I thought you should know. Summer's been arrested."

"What? But they never actually made the insurance claim, right? So what—"

"No, not that," he said. "There are several outstanding warrants for more serious charges in Nevada. That's why we put out the alert. She'll be heading west as soon as the paperwork goes through."

"Where is she?"

"They took her off the train to Chicago this morning. Elkhart police are holding her pending extradition."

"This morning?"

"I was off duty. I just found out."

I felt a strange mix of emotions about Summer—anger, sadness, loss, disgust. She had never done anything to me, but she had hurt a lot of people, and had done so with cunning and intent. She wasn't directly responsible, but people had died because of her actions.

"Have you called Evan?"

"No. I drove out there. It didn't seem like the sort of thing you tell a guy on the phone."

"How's he going to manage?"

"Seems he was expecting something like this," said Hutch. "He said the neighbor, the fellow you met—"

"Meyers."

"Right. He's offered to buy Evan's place and the sheep. Seems he has a daughter who's interested in taking over the shop."

"Did he say anything about Nell, his dog?" If no one wanted her, I decided, she could come to my house.

"Well, Evan told her it was just the two of them now, so I guess he's keeping her."

I thanked Hutch and hung up when Tom came through the door with Drake and a folding metal crate. "Winnie's staying in here while we're gone," he said. I buttoned my lip.

Life-threatening experiences make me ravenous, and since the only thing I had eaten since morning was half a slice of cake, Tom suggested a nearby Indian restaurant. "But first," I said, "I want to stop by Blackford's. I think Joe should know the goon won't be back."

But Joe wasn't in the alley, and worse, his box home was gone. So were his beat-up folding chairs. There was no sign that he'd ever been there, and my heart sank. Had he been frightened away? Had Ralph Blackford run him off? The store was closed, but a car I thought to be Ralph's was still in the parking lot and the lights were on inside, so I knocked on the front door.

Ralph smiled when he saw us. "Come in! Come in!"

"Sorry to bother you, I was just worried about…"

A door at the back of the store opened and Joe stepped out of the storage area and waved.

"Oh, I thought—" I said, smiling at Joe. "I was afraid—"

"Joe's going to be helping me out," said Ralph. "I've been worried about security, so Joe's going to be staying in the store to keep an eye on things at night and on Sunday mornings."

Joe nodded. "I get a room, too, with a bed."

Ralph cleared his throat and looked down, shuffling his feet. "We needed to get my son's old bed and his dorm fridge and hotplate out of the house anyway, and there's an office back there just sitting empty."

Joe added, "I'll get paid every Friday, too." It may have been the first time I'd seen him really smile.

I was still glowing over Joe's good fortune when we filled our plates and settled in to eat and catch up. I told Tom about Summer, but added, "I have a very good feeling about people tonight, in spite of everything."

He smiled and said, "I missed the rest of the story when I drove Tony and your mom to the hotel. What else did that guy—what's his name, anyway?—what else did he say?"

"His name is Albert Zola. He and Fallon worked for some guy in Cleveland named Cucinelli who has his fingers in all sorts of illegal and semi-legal stuff." I scooped some *chana masala* into a bit of *naan* and savored its gingery bite, then went on. "He sent Zola and Fallon looking for Evan, and they found the farm just as Evan and Summer were leaving for the herding event, so they followed them. They didn't recognize Summer because they knew her with dark hair and sexy clothes, and they weren't expecting to find her in Indiana. It was a complete fluke that they spotted Ray."

"So, Ray and Summer had conned Cucinelli?"

"Yep. Just like Martin and who knows how many other guys. She'd gotten Cucinelli into a hotel room in Reno where Ray had set up cameras and tried to extort a bundle out of him. Hutch was too embarrassed to tell me everything, but from what I gathered, Cucinelli liked to play dress-up games. But he didn't extort well, and when they figured out that he wasn't really a shoe salesman, they ran."

"But not together."

"Hutch thinks they may have been planning to split up and rendezvous somewhere. Cucinelli's people were looking for a man and woman together, so that makes sense. But when Summer spotted Evan, she latched on." I thought about how long it had taken me to feel safe after I dumped my ex, and wondered whether Evan would ever trust another woman.

Tom said, "What kind of man makes his living by blackmailing people who have sex with his wife?"

"I guess they deserved each other."

"Do the police think she killed Ray?" asked Tom "After watching her hoist sheep onto their feet, I still say she's strong enough—"

"No! Zola confessed. He was kind of out of it, just rattling on. He said he and Fallon didn't mean to kill Ray. I suspect he meant not right then. Anyway, he said they just wanted to know where Summer was. I don't know if that's true, but anyway, they conked him on the head and dragged him into the storage room, and when he came to, they started breaking his fingers. And he died." I thought about it for a moment. "The autopsy will probably show a heart attack. Once he was dead, they decided to hang him to scare Summer. They knew she was around, and didn't think they'd have any trouble finding her."

"They must have seen her during the weekend event."

"Probably," I said, "but again, they were looking for a thinner dark-haired woman. So my hunch is they just didn't recognize her until they saw her with Evan's truck that evening at Blackford's. She was wearing a dark wig so people around here wouldn't recognize her, and that obviously backfired."

"Now that Zola's telling all about his boss, Evan is probably off the hook for the money."

We were drinking our *chai* when I changed the subject. "Tom, I've been thinking."

"I have, too." He looked very serious, and I felt a flutter of fear, but forged ahead.

"You know I've been afraid to give up my independence, but, well, I think we should give it a try, as we've planned. I'll adjust. I hope you'll still move in with me."

"I've already made other arrangements," he said, staring at his chai. "But we can still see each other."

More ominous words have seldom been spoken.

EIGHTY

We can still see each other. The words cycled through my mind, and the churning in my stomach made me sorry I'd eaten so much. Tom folded his napkin and set it on the table. "Come on, I'll show you the house I may buy."

I was so numb that for the first ten minutes I didn't notice where we were going. Eventually, though, familiar landmarks began to filter into my awareness, and when Tom turned onto my street, I managed to say, "I thought you were going to show me your new house?"

He just smiled and drove past my driveway and turned into the one next door. We were in front of Phil Martin's house. Tom turned off the engine and said, "Well, what do you think?"

"About what?"

He took my hand and squeezed it. "After Martin's wife told him to get rid of the house, I thought he might entertain an offer, so I went back to his room after everyone left the hospital."

"Really?"

"It's not a done deal yet. I wanted to see what you think, and see the house. But it seems like a plan, don't you think?"

He was right. If the pet limit passed, we'd still be okay. We'd have our privacy and wouldn't be driving back and forth all the time. We could be together, and apart, as much as we both liked.

"Martin is willing to sell at a loss and get out quickly, since his wife is on the warpath." Tom got out and came around to open my door. He offered his arm, and I stepped forward and took it. "I have the key. Let me give you the tour."

As we walked toward the door I was still limping, but I felt stronger with every step.

THE END

© PORTRAIT INNOVATIONS

ABOUT THE AUTHOR

Sheila Webster Boneham writes fiction and nonfiction, much of it focused on animals, nature, and travel. Her first Animals in Focus mystery, *Drop Dead on Recall*, won the 2013 Maxwell Award for Best Fiction Book from the Dog Writers Association of American (DWAA) and was named a Top Ten Dog Book of 2012 by NBC Petside. Six of Sheila's nonfiction books have been named best in their categories in the DWAA and the Cat Writers Association (CWA) annual competitions, and her book *Rescue Matters! How to Find, Foster, and Rehome Companion Animals* (Alpine, 2009) has been called a "must read" for anyone involved with animal rescue. Sheila has a PhD in folklore and MFA in creative writing, and frequently teaches writing classes and workshops. She enjoys talking to groups of all kinds about writing and animals. You can reach her through her website at www.sheilaboneham.com or her Facebook page at www.facebook.com/sheilawrites.